MARSH'S VALLEY

C.J. PETIT

C.J. PETIT

TABLE OF CONTENTS

PROLOGUE

Missoula, Montana
March 11, 1884

John looked at his brother Frank as his other three brothers looked on, then took a breath, exhaled and wished there was a better way to get it done. The plan just seemed a bit too complicated, but the rewards would be worth it – if it worked.

"Okay, Frank, just go down to Denver and find a good one. She's got to be a real looker with no family to miss her, and a kind of innocent look, too. I don't want no damned whore. We're not going to have someone who will feel free to run at the first chance. We need someone desperate and once you get her married will have to stay put. You need to get her under control, and whatever else you do, you can't get her pregnant. We don't know how long this is going to take and we can't have her looking like she swallowed a damned watermelon."

Frank was frustrated as he replied, "What's good about marryin' her if I can't get a good poke now and then?"

John snarled, "If she gets here and I find out she's pregnant, you can guess what'll happen to you and to her. Just get down to Denver and bring her back."

―――――

May 27, 1884

Rachel sat on the edge of her bed in her nightdress feeling like a fool. It was the middle of the day and Frank had told her to stay in her bedroom and in her nightdress until he returned at two o'clock that afternoon.

Her relationship with her husband of less than three months had been bizarre by all standards. They had never consummated the marriage, despite his obvious desire to do so. He had beaten her with his belt often to make her understand who was in charge, even though she never had done anything remotely worthy of discipline.

And now, he obviously wanted to finally bed her in the middle of the afternoon?

She sighed and began tapping her bare feet against the floor, feeling more ridiculous by the minute.

She heard the door open and close again, then bootsteps slowly crossing the main room. She sighed again, thinking this may be the least romantic consummation in the history of marriages as she slid further onto the bed, laid down, then pulled her nightdress up exposing herself from the waist down while she stared at the ceiling and closed her eyes, letting the humiliation wash over her. *Why had Frank left such exact, yet inexplicable instructions for the act?* If it hadn't been for the constant threats and other intimidation, she would have at least been able to ask. As bad as it was before, this marriage was already turning into the biggest mistake of her life.

The door opened, she heard his gun belt fall to the floor, then she heard clothing being dropped alongside. Why Frank insisted on being silent was one more strange aspect of this disgusting day.

She felt him sit on the bed, then could hear his rapid breathing before she picked up the scent of his breath as he leaned over to kiss her. As his lips pressed against hers and his hands began to fondle her, there was a loud crash as the front door slammed open. Rachel was startled into opening her eyes which created an even bigger shock for her stunned mind when she saw the equally startled face of Bob McCallister as he was quickly swiveling his eyes to look at the bedroom door.

Her husband stormed into the bedroom and shouted, "You whore! McCallister, you're a dead man!"

He was pulling his pistol as a panicking Bob McCallister jumped up from the bed wearing only his pale skin and put his palms out in front of him to stop the expected bullet.

"Wait! Frank! It's not my fault! Your wife invited me to come here and take her! Please don't shoot me! I beg of you!"

Frank growled as he cocked his Colt, "I ain't got any reason to let you live, McCallister."

"Wait! Wait! Surely, we don't have to get drastic here. I…I can make things right without resorting to bloodshed," he stammered as every part of him shook while his wide eyes were locked onto that cannon-like muzzle.

Frank glared at McCallister and then back to the bed where Rachel had already pulled her nightdress down to cover herself and sat on the bed with her head resting on her bent knees in utter shame, even though she was sure that Frank had arranged this whole charade. She just didn't understand why; at least not yet.

Frank slowly and dramatically released his pistol's hammer and said gruffly, "Get your damned clothes on and meet me in the kitchen."

Then he turned to Rachel and snarled, "And you, bitch, just stay right there. I'll deal with you after your lover is out of the house."

Rachel's forehead was still pressed against her bent knees as she heard Bob McCallister dressing hurriedly, finally fully understanding everything and chastising herself for not having seen this whole ploy from the start. She was nothing but a pawn in a blackmail scheme. She felt like a whore, but wondered why they hadn't just picked up a prostitute instead of going through the sham marriage. There were always women available who would do anything for money; including being part of a blackmail scam.

She also understood; or thought she did, the reason for her fake husband's failure to consummate the marriage. Suddenly, that very real possibility loomed large in her mind and made her even more worried. Her mind then passed by what she now considered the likelihood of being raped by that man to what would happen now that she was unnecessary. *Would he kill her or would they just turn her into the whore that she now believed herself to be?*

She couldn't come up with an answer to his intentions by the time she heard Bob McCallister leave. She hadn't been able to hear clearly what was being said in the kitchen, but after she heard the back door open and close again, the much more dreadful sound of Frank's loud footsteps echoed from the hallway.

She didn't even look up as he entered the bedroom because she knew that he wasn't going to simply beat her this time. She heard him remove his heavy belt, which was his favored weapon, and Rachel almost prayed to hear the whistling sound as the belt whipped through the air before striking her.

But that previously terrifying sound didn't come, instead she felt Frank's hands grab her, pull her to her feet and without giving her a chance to react, simply ripped her nightdress from her body and threw it to the floor.

Her eyes were frozen wide open as she tried to cover herself with her hands, but knew it was useless to fight as he was so much bigger and he was legally her husband.

Frank slapped her across the face and snarled, "I've waited for this for too damned long and now I don't care if you get pregnant or not. Now, I'm gonna get what I want."

He then threw her to the bed and watched her greedily as he quickly shed his gunbelt and dropped his britches. He was still wearing his boots and shirt when he consummated the phony marriage with a violent attack.

When he was finished just five minutes later, he simply pulled up his britches, then slid his belt from around his waist and administered the beating that she had expected.

As he slid the belt back where it belonged, he pointed his finger at her and said in a threatening voice, "You'd better not plan on goin' anywhere, Rachel. My brothers will chase you down and kill you if I don't do it first. You're gonna be a good wife and keep me happy or you ain't gonna see another sunrise."

Rachel closed her eyes and nodded before she heard him walk away. Once the front door closed again, she stood, then slowly walked to the small dresser, pulled out a drawer and began to dress.

She had to fight back her mind's insistent demand to run away because she knew that Frank and his brothers would expect her to run right away and that would mean her death.

She needed to calm down, and hopefuly when their vigilance was lower, she could make her escape. Where she could go was secondary to getting out of this place where she knew she would die when Frank tired of her; if not sooner.

———

Four hours later, Rachel was in the kitchen making dinner for Frank while he met with his four brothers in the office off the main room. She had been warned by Frank to stay in the kitchen whenever his four brothers arrived for a meeting, and Rachel had always abided by his threat because she knew it was far from just a warning.

She was carving a steak from a slab of beef as she wondered if this was a good time as the brothers were all in the office, but soon discarded that idea because it was still broad daylight and they'd find her in less than an hour. She surely couldn't go to see the sheriff either, because he was in the office with his brother, Frank. The sheriff was her brother-in-law.

Rachel set down the knife and wiped her hands on a nearby towel before leaving the kitchen and walking as quietly as she could to the main room before she reached the doorway to the office and put her ear near the door to listen to their conversation. She knew she was taking a terrible risk, but she had to know what they were planning on doing to her. Her recently disgarded escape attempt might be necessary after all.

———

"So, that's the deed," Al Shipman said, almost giggling as he did.

The oldest brother, John, waved the folded sheets of paper, grinned and replied, "Yup. Now, we've just got to arrange for a buyer. Frank, your name is on the deed, so tomorrow, take it

9

over to the land office at the county and get it registered. Then, go to the bank and see Harvey Freestone and tell him it's up for sale. If he asks, and he shouldn't, tell him you won it in a high stakes poker game down at Dierman's."

"What about McCallister, Frank? Is he gone yet?" asked Lou, the youngest brother.

"I told him he could stay another three days so him and his missus could get packed up and leave Missoula. He says he's going to Cheyenne. I said I was letting him stay that long because I was being a good Christian," Frank answered with a snicker.

Sheriff John Shipman scanned the faces of his brothers, a contented smile on his face.

He said, "I told you boys that this was gonna work. McCallister was too much of a churchgoer to let it get out. Men like that will pay anything to keep their reputations."

They each nodded, and Billy said, "I gotta admit, I figured we'd be able to squeeze a few hundred dollars out of him, but I didn't think he'd give up his ranch."

Frank chuckled and said, "The funniest part is that he didn't even get what he was paying for. Now that it's done, John, I think I'm gonna go and get busy making up for all those nights I had to sleep alone. You're all welcome to have a good time yourselves, but not until tomorrow."

The brothers all had a good belly laugh, except for Al, who said loudly, "You can all laugh all you want, but I'm not gonna be happy until that cash is in my pocket."

Frank turned and replied, "Al, you always were Mister Naysayer. You never had a fun day in your whole life."

The four other Shipman brothers laughed again; this time at Al's expense.

Rachel was stunned by two things she heard. They had gotten possession of McCallister's ranch and Frank was offering her to his brothers. Her stomach was in turmoil as she imagined them tromping into her bedroom one after the other. Frank was a monster, and the thought of five of them using her almost daily and as cruelly as Frank had earlier was horrifying.

She was so numbed by the discovery that she stayed next to the door and hadn't noticed that the conversation and laughter had ended. She still hadn't come out of her disconnected state until she heard footsteps on the other side of the door.

She grabbed her skirts, turned and walked hurriedly across the main room, then turned down the hallway to the kitchen.

But her delayed rush away from the office door was too late. Lou had opened the door quickly, stuck his head out and had seen her skirts entering the hallway accompanied by her rapid footsteps.

He turned back into the office and said, "Frank, you got a problem. Your wife was spyin' on us."

Frank snarled, "That bitch! I'll deal with her in a few minutes. You all better go."

John replied sternly, "You'd better deal with her, Frank. She's the only loose end now."

Frank nodded as his four brothers all moseyed out into the main room, grabbed their hats and then left the house; Lou slamming the door on the way out.

Rachel heard loud bang from the front door, but wasn't sure if they had seen her. She tried to act calm as she pumped water into the coffeepot, but she was wound tighter than the mantle clock on Monday morning.

Frank sat at his desk, seething at his wife's eavesdropping and let his anger build. He finally stood and as he began to walk out of the office, he slid the heavy leather belt from his waist, folded it over and cracked it against the desk as he passed.

Rachel heard the crack, stopped pumping, and began to shake. *Here he comes!* Her question of whether she had been detected was answered by that sound, and this time, she knew that it would probably be even be worse than the one she had received that afternoon.

She put her back against the sink and watched fearfully at the hallway entrance to the kitchen as she heard Frank's heavy bootsteps thud closer. She suddenly turned her head to the counter and saw the gleaming ten-inch blade of her best kitchen knife. Without even thinking, her right hand flashed to the knife, grabbing the heavy wooden handle, then brought it around quickly to the front, and pointed it menacingly at the hallway.

Frank's eyes were afire as he cleared the hallway, then saw Racel standing defiantly in front of him with a shining sharp blade in her hand.

He pointed at her, his wicked belt hanging from his hand and shouted, "Put that down, Rachel, or I'll really go hard on you this time!"

Rachel's rage overcame her fear as she yelled back, "No! You're not going to beat me again! You did that whole charade with Bob McCallister, so you and your brothers could blackmail him! You are a filthy bastard, and you're not going to touch me!"

Frank saw the hate and rage in her eyes but it didn't inspire the least bit of fear in him as he slowly walked toward her. She was just a damned weak woman that he outweighed by more than a hundred pounds.

"I'm gonna make you pay for them words even more than for your spyin'! You ain't gonna be able to walk after I'm done with you! Hell! You ain't even gonna be breathin' 'cause this is gonna be the last beating I ever give you!" he snarled as he raised his right arm, letting the belt rest momentarily on his shoulder blade, as he built the power in his right arm for a crippling blow.

Rachel watched as the heavy belt she had felt so many times before move to its ready position and as she saw the malevolence in his eyes grow as his muscles tightened, she took one fast step forward, and with the knife handle gripped tightly, threw her right shoulder back and with all the power she could muster, plunged the knife into her husband's stomach, the tip penetrating quickly, passing through the fat and muscle of his abdomen, slicing open his small intestines and then slashing open his abdominal aorta.

Frank was so shocked by his wife's attack that he never had time to scream or even utter a sound as the blood poured into his abdominal cavity and out of the knife slit. He just looked at her with wide eyes and an open mouth, as he fell to his knees, the belt dropped to the wooden floor, then he tipped over and rolled onto his left side, the knife still protruding from his gut.

Rachel had stepped back as soon as the knife was buried into her husband, and let the handle go. She was in a total state of shock at what she had done. She stood in place as her heart raced and Frank's blood pooled around her feet. *She had just murdered her husband!*

It took almost five minutes for Rachel to comprehend what she had done Again, she fought back the panicking need to run. This wasn't the time yet; she needed to think calmly and plan a genuine escape. So, she closed her eyes, took a deep breath and then took a good minute to just calm her mind.

Once she felt ready, she opened her eyes and scanned the room to decide what was necessary for her to stay alive.

The first thing she did was to step away from the congealing mass of blood. She walked just past the large, deep red puddle, took off her shoes, walked around Frank and pumped water over the shoes to rinse off the blood before leaving them in the sink to dry.

Rachel then walked hurriedly to the bedroom, pulled out a large cloth bag and began stuffing her clothes inside. Once all of her things were in the bag, she returned to the kitchen, where she opened the old baking powder tin where she kept her household money. She removed the $7.15, stuffed it into her skirt's pocket, and then walked to the pantry, took an empty burlap potato bag and began selectively adding food. She then returned to kitchen and took a knife, a fork, a spoon, and a tin cup. She added a box of matches before taking the two bags down the hallway back into the main room and into her husband's office.

Rachel walked behind the desk and opened the top drawer, removed his Webley Bulldog pistol, and then pulled open a different drawer and took the box of .44 cartridges. She had never even handled a gun before, but she had seen them used and hoped it would be enough. Then she walked into Frank's bedroom and opened one of his drawers, removed three pairs of his heavy woolen socks and returned to the kitchen.

It was still daylight, so she couldn't leave yet and risk being seen by one of his brothers, especially John, the sheriff. Instead, she prepared herself something to eat even as her husband lay dead in the middle of the floor. She knew it would be the last time she would eat a hot meal for a while.

Five hours later, when the town was quiet, Rachel Anne Shipman donned her heavy coat and her woolen hat, even though it was late spring, opened the back door to the house and disappeared into the night.

CHAPTER 1

Marsh guided his gelding, Sam, down Front Street in Missoula heading for Worden & Company to pick up some supplies. He was trailing one of his mules, Albert, who was wearing the pack saddle today. He tried to balance the use of his four mules as supply carriers so they didn't complain so much. His mules always complained; maybe because he made them do more work than he did.

He pulled Sam to the front of the establishment, stepped down and entered the well-stocked dry goods store, catching the eye of Doris Endicott, who was at the counter. Doris was a middle-aged widow and counted herself fortunate to have been given the job at the store, although she was still in the market for a husband. She had several potential suitors, but was holding out for one with a better offer. She knew she'd never land a man like Marsh Anderson, but she still dreamed and made a point of being very friendly when he came to the store.

"Good morning, Marsh," she said with a smile.

Marsh smiled back and replied, "Good morning, Doris. I need to pick up a big order."

"Did you want to leave it with me, or are you going to get it yourself today?" she asked.

"I have one list for you, but I'll pick up most of it," he answered.

With that, he approached the counter and gave her one list and then headed for the first aisle to begin his own, longer one.

When he finally had his part of the order piled up on the counter and along the floor for the bigger items, he stepped to the counter and asked, "Are you ready, Doris?"

"I've got everything here and already totaled," she replied

Then she paused and asked quietly, "Did you hear about all the excitement?"

Marsh laughed and replied, "Now, Doris, you know I don't hear anything up where I am. What happened?"

Doris glanced in both directions, then leaned forward and whispered, "Rachel Shipman murdered her husband last night. Stabbed him with a big butcher's knife right in the belly."

The news was startling, but even more so because he didn't know any of the five Shipman brothers were married.

"Who is Rachel Shipman?" he asked.

"Oh, that's right. You probably don't know, do you? Well, Frank Shipman went down to Denver a couple months ago and came back with a wife. Honestly, I thought she was much too young and pretty for the likes of Frank, or any of those other brothers for that matter. I thought she was really nice, too, whenever she came into the store."

Marsh grinned, then said, "And this nice, pretty, but obviously stupid or blind young woman killed Frank? I'm not blaming her for that, anyway. It was probably a lot better decision than marrying him in the first place."

Doris did her conspiratorial scan again before replying in even a lower voice, "I wasn't as surprised as you seem to be, Marsh. You must not have heard that Frank caught her in bed with someone, so Rachel must have killed him because Frank caught her in the act."

"Now that's almost as strange, Doris. A pretty, young woman marries Frank Shipman, then almost immediately has an affair and kills him in a jealous rage?"

Doris smiled and said, "You just don't understand how furious women can be."

"If they don't know who her fellow adulterer was, and Frank's dead; then how do they know about the affair that supposedly triggered the murder?" he asked.

Doris replied, "I don't know how they found out, but his brother Billy told me this morning."

Marsh shook his head and asked, "I still don't understand how they could know about the affair and not know who the man was? Were they protecting him for some reason?"

Doris finally threw up her hands in exasperation.

"You ask too many questions, Marsh. I swear you should be a Pinkerton detective or something."

Marsh smiled, then asked, "I know. I just hate mysteries. It's a fault. So, is his wife in jail now?"

Doris shook her head rapidly before answering, "No, not at all. She ran off on foot in the middle of the night after killing him. Sheriff Shipman deputized his three brothers, Zeke Chambers and Steve Bristow to hunt her down and they left this morning.

I'll bet they catch her soon, too. They'll hang her for sure, unless she tries to shoot it out with them."

Marsh's head was buzzing with all of the bizarre revelations. *This woman was an armed outlaw who was going to engage in a gunfight with a posse of six men? And why in God's name did Sheriff Shipman need five more men on the posse?*

"If he needed more men, which is odd in itself, why didn't he just take one of his two deputies?" Marsh asked.

"He didn't say. I guess he wanted them to stay in the office, so they could handle things while he was gone."

Marsh shook his head. That made no sense, either. The sheriff could have taken one of them and left the second to watch the desk. Two armed lawmen should be more than enough to find and arrest a woman out in the open country on foot. With the way Missoula was laid out, the only direction she could have gone would be north; unless she walked across the railroad bridge, which would be dangerous at night, to say the least.

Marsh sighed and said, "Let's get this order packed up. I'm going back to my place where things are nice and quiet and all I have to worry about are bears and cougars."

Doris laughed, gave him his total, which he paid, then he began packing his empty panniers. As each one was filled, he lugged it out to Albert, hung it on his pack saddle and returned for the next. Doris was watching Marsh so intently that Mrs. Aldrich had to clear her throat four times to get her attention. Doris sighed, then turned to wait on a very irritated Helen Aldrich. Doris thought it was a sinful waste to let that man live by himself without a good woman to keep him warm.

Ten minutes later, Marsh was riding Sam and trailing a complaining Albert as he headed out of Missoula. He'd follow the northbound road for eight miles, until he turned northwest, following his own wagon tracks as he headed for his valley.

Marsh Anderson had lived twelve miles northwest of Missoula for four years now. He had never explained to anyone why he had left Denver and found such a secluded place to live; believing that it was his business and no one else's.

When he had departed Colorado, he knew what he was looking for, and even after leaving the train at the end of track, continued westward after buying a horse and a pack mule. He had passed through Helena, and then Missoula, not finding what he wanted, until he was ten miles out of Missoula when three men popped out from behind a rock formation a quarter of a mile east of the roadway. He had immediately turned and raced west cross country looking for cover to mount a defense, pulling his Winchester '76 as he scanned the terrain for something to provide protection.

The robbers were gaining ground on him and firing their rifles hoping for a lucky shot, but not getting one. Marsh hadn't found anything to hide behind, but with them closing, he finally just quickly dismounted and dropped to a prone position and opened fire.

The highwaymen had expected him to cut the trail rope to his mule and make his escape, but when he didn't behave as anticipated, and suddenly began returning fire, their thoughts of a quick grab were lost. Then, when one of them took a hit off the side of his left knee, they realized they were now much more vulnerable than he was and wheeled their mounts back to the east and raced toward the road.

After they had disappeared from sight, Marsh had mounted his gelding and continued west toward the mountains rather than risk being jumped again. He planned on just camping for a night or two, but that changed when he found his valley.

It wasn't a big valley, just about a mile across and four miles deep, but it was so perfect that he knew he had found what he was searching for. It was going to be his refuge and his new home.

It was a hard place to find unless one knew of its existence. The surrounding mountains shielded it from the heavy winds and snow; it was rich in lumber with lush grass and plenty of water, including a wide creek that ran its length which also created a good-sized lake at the far end of the valley before it rose into the foothills.

He'd bought the entire valley at a very good price from the Northern Pacific Railway, who had been given land grants and was selling them to raise capital to lay their tracks. After the Panic of 1873, the railroad, like almost all of them, was desperate for cash. While the lands in western Minnesota and Dakota Territory were fetching good prices because they were flat and fertile, land this far out was of little value to the company. So, Marsh was able to buy the entire valley for a very good price. In addition to the valley, he owned the three miles of land from the mouth of the valley to the roadway. There were ranches bigger than his seven sections, but his was odd in that it was one section by seven. He only had to buy four sections as the other three were owned by the federal government, but no one would be able to access them without crossing his land. It was the back four sections, the ones that encompassed the valley itself that his personal paradise.

His first trip into Missoula after he bought the land was to buy a wagon, three more mules, and a lot of supplies and building tools. That had taken three trips to haul it all out to his valley. Once he had the tools and materials, he did what he did best – he built.

Back in Denver, before had had come to Missoula, he was in the construction business. In fact, he had been the owner of the company, and still was. His father had started the firm and developed a solid reputation and long list of clients. His two older brothers were more interested in the business side of the operation, while Marsh had shown more aptitude in the hands-on part of construction. He had worked with the crews since he was just ten, building a reputation as a hard worker and a valued member of any of the construction disciplines as he grew older and much bigger.

His oldest brother, Sean, was inspecting the progress at worksite for a new bottle making plant when a kiln exploded just eight feet away, killing him and eight other men in June of 1870.

He was fourteen when Sean had died, and sixteen when his other brother, Nathanial, was crushed by a runaway coach as he crossed Hamilton Street in Denver; and that left only Marsh. His father, James, not wishing to lose his last son, had been firm in his decision that Marsh no longer go out on jobs and that he settle down to the life of a businessman. He had respected his father's wishes, studied the business aspect of the company and did well which had pleased his father immensely.

Marsh was running the company by the time he was twenty-one and his father's health was failing due to a bad heart, which took his life two weeks before Marsh celebrated his twenty-third birthday.

It was that same year that Marsh had met Clara LaPierre. She was twenty-two, and a sight to behold. She was petite, but still managed to overwhelm Marsh, whose previous dalliances with women were just that and nothing more.

They had married two weeks later, but she had died just six months later when she had committed suicide, leaving a cryptic note about not being able to live with her shame and telling him how much she loved him.

Three days later, he accidentally discovered the reason for her decision to end her life, and the combination of her death and the driving force behind it, had a dramatic change on his own outlook on life.

Marsh disappeared for a week, then when he returned to work, he lived at the office or on the work sites, constantly working. He kept that up until March of '80, when he left the business in the capable hands of his good friend, Vince Cirillo. After taking a thousand dollars from his bank account, he left Denver on the train heading north to Cheyenne and then west, leaving the railroad in western Wyoming and taking the roads north into Montana Territory. He didn't know exactly what he was looking for, but felt a driving need to find the peace it could provide.

When he had discovered and bought the valley, he had quickly built a cabin using some of the abundant growth of pines in the forests before the weather turned bad. It had suited him well that first winter, but then after the weather warmed, he started making trips into Missoula to Urlin's lumber yard and Reinhard's hardware, and began to construct a proper house. It had taken him two years, but it was done now. It wasn't a large house, but it was solidly built and suited Marsh.

He could have used one of the two construction firms in Missoula, but he needed the work more than he needed the house and barn.

He had built a lot of the furniture in the house, but still required a lot of trips to furnish it properly with furniture from Sweeney's in Missoula; which had the unusual distinction of being both a furniture store and mortuary. He did have to move the cookstove in piecemeal, but when the house was complete, it was very comfortable even in the sub-zero winters. Building the house and then the large barn had acted as a catharsis for Marsh, and after he finished the house, he began making more frequent trips into Missoula which reawakened his natural affability and he became more familiar with the town's residents.

Since the arrival of the Northern Pacific last year, more businesses had been established, and it was on the verge of becoming a city. It now had four hotels, three churches, a hospital, three general stores, five saloons, and even a jeweler.

His valley was still remote, though, and although many knew of its location, he rarely had visitors. The trail he followed to his valley was almost as plain as the road itself because of his frequent trips from Missoula with a heavily laden wagon, which had initially given him some concern because of his vulnerability of living alone. He had corrected that somewhat by adding an unusual construct to the original cabin when had built an observation tower some twenty feet higher than the peak of the roof. It wasn't the most esthetic thing he'd ever built, but it served its purpose.

———

Now, as he was riding Sam back home and was just a mile from the turnoff to his valley, he spotted a large dust cloud approaching from the north, pulled out his Winchester and cocked the hammer, knowing that there was a cartridge in the breech. Judging by the size of the cloud, it was probably at least four men and assumed it was the posse that Doris had told him about, but it never paid to take chances.

He didn't stop riding even as he finally identified the riders. It was, in fact, Sheriff Shipman and his excessively large posse. By the time they were close, he could see that they weren't happy, probably because they had failed to find their prey, which he found humorous. Six big, nasty men on horseback with rifles and pistols couldn't find a woman on foot.

He released the Winchester's hammer and slid it back into its scabbard, trying not to appear to look too snarky about their incompetence as they approached.

Marsh pulled off the road slightly to let them pass, but they didn't. Instead, Sheriff Shipman pulled the group to a halt next to Marsh, allowing the large cloud of dust to engulf everyone.

"Morning, Anderson. Did you leave your place this morning?"

"I left at seven or so and rode into town, picked up my supplies and I'm heading home. I'm kind of surprised I didn't see you on my way into town. You out looking for somebody?"

"Yeah. We're hunting my sister-in-law, Rachel. You haven't seen her, have you?"

"Nope. I didn't even know you had a sister-in-law until I just heard about it in town an hour ago. How come you're hunting one woman with six men, anyway?" Marsh asked.

"That's my business, Anderson. Mind if we check your place?" the sheriff asked.

"Not a problem. You can follow me," he replied as he returned to the road.

After riding that last mile, he made the turn onto his trail, and could tell that the posse was getting annoyed with his slow pace. He was leading a pack mule, so it wasn't as if he was intentionally taking his time; well, maybe just a little bit. He never cared for any of the Shipman brothers, thinking they were all useless thugs, including the sheriff, who at least managed to hide behind a more polished veneer. The other two men, Zeke

Chambers and Steve Bristow, he knew only passingly as ranch hands out at the Double M ranch and were of the same ilk as the Shipmans.

"How much further?" an exasperated Sheriff John Shipman asked.

"Not far, another couple of miles. We should be there in about twenty minutes or so."

"Mind if we go ahead and look around?" he asked.

Marsh replied, "You can go ahead, but I'd ask that you stay out of my house until I get there. It's locked anyway. You can check inside my cabin and barn, though."

"You've got a house and a barn?" asked Lou Harrison.

"Yes, and I'd appreciate some measure of courtesy while you're conducting your search."

"We'll be careful," the sheriff answered over his shoulder as he waved his posse to a canter, leaving Marsh behind.

Marsh watched them ride off and tapped Sam's sides with his heels sending him into a fast trot.

He arrived at his valley just minutes behind the posse, and found them still mounted and searching the grounds around his buildings. He was already more than just annoyed watching the six men whipping their horses in circles and then riding off to look at another spot.

Marsh reached his house, stepped down and began to walk toward Sheriff Shipman, who had finally corralled his posse and directed them all to dismount.

"Sheriff, you want to go in my house now? I'd rather only you come inside. so I don't have to do too much sweeping out after you all leave."

Shipman snickered and replied, "Sure," then turned to his posse and shouted, "You boys break up and search the cabin and the barn while I go and search inside the house."

He led the sheriff onto the porch and made a show of unlocking the door before swinging it wide and stepped inside.

Sheriff Shipman began looking around and evaluating the house in addition to making his search. The entire search didn't take long, but should have taken half the time that it did as Marsh noticed the sheriff looked in places that were much too small for even a toy doll; much less an adult woman. He also spent a lot of time in his weapons room; almost taking inventory. That tugged on his unhappy string, too, but at least he understood his fascination with his guns.

Marsh walked behind the sheriff as he left the house through the back door.

"You got a nice place out here, Anderson. What do you do for a living?" he asked.

"I'm still building things, and after that I'll be bringing in some horses."

The sheriff nodded, then spotted his three brothers who were still in the barn and trotted off to join them, while Marsh headed toward the cabin where the other two, unrelated deputies were still searching. He was concerned because they were taking such a long time to inspect a one-room cabin.

He had just about reached the cabin when he heard one of them say to the other, "I woulda loved to see McCallister's face when Frank pulled that gun."

It was followed by a mixture of laughter and snickering from both men. A curious Marsh held off entering the cabin and instead walked around to the back to inspect his vegetable garden to make sure they hadn't churned up the young plants with their horses.

The garden was fine, so he then walked back to the cabin, and stepped up onto the porch announcing his arrival. By the time he got to the still open door, the one who had been talking, Zeke Chambers, had popped up from his bed where he had been lounging, then he and Steve Bristow hustled out the door. Marsh looked inside at the mess they made and shook his head. *Slobs!*

He left the cabin cleanup to later and followed the two men back to their horses. The Shipman brothers were all mounted and waiting as the two non-Shipmans jogged to their horses and stepped up into their stirrups.

"You boys find anything?" the sheriff shouted.

Zeke Chambers replied, "Nope, we even climbed his tower near the cabin and looked down the valley."

The sheriff had seen the odd structure long before reaching the house, turned back to Marsh and asked, "What the hell did you build that tower for?"

"Lots of reasons. I can see way down into the valley for game, and I can watch as far as Missoula in one direction and ten miles north in the other."

The sheriff just shrugged, swiveled their horses back toward Marsh's trail, then they all simply rode away without so much as a 'thank you' or 'sorry for the inconvenience'; not that Marsh expected any such niceties from that bunch.

Marsh stood on the porch, watching them disappear and shook his head. None of them possessed those qualities that he believed made a man a man. They were all nothing more than hoodlums. John Shipman had been elected county sheriff the year before Marsh arrived, and he guessed it was because he could speak well and act like a nice guy. With all the seedier elements in the county voting for him, he'd only need about a third of the decent folks to get elected and once in, he'd be hard to get out of office.

Marsh then stepped down from the porch and began to move his supplies inside. Most were food items, except for some replacement clothes, some cleaning supplies, and some more ammunition for his guns. When he left Denver, all he had was his Colt Peacemaker and a Winchester '73, but had been adding weapons ever since, as he found guns necessary for different purposes. He had two shotguns, one loaded with birdshot and the other with #4 buckshot, another Winchester '73 and two of the '76 models, one of which he usually carried with him. The big gun was his Sharps Big 50 that he had found in Missoula.

It was a favored weapon of the easterners who traveled out to Wyoming and Montana to hunt buffalo, bighorn sheep and elk. Marsh found early on that he needed one when he encountered a large brown bear and the Winchester '73 he was carrying wasn't enough to even kill it. He had pumped three .44s at just fifty yards into that big animal, and all it had done was to make him angry before he finally ran off. He knew the '76 could probably kill him with one or two shots, but he wanted something with enough power to definitely take down a big bear with one shot.

He found the Sharps in Staus Gunsmith & Machinist's. It was even new, as they had ordered it the year before, expecting a slew of hunters, but none had materialized. He bought all three boxes of ammunition for the beast, had them order four more, and still had five full boxes available.

He'd used the other cartridges mostly for target practice, but had shot two bears with the rifle, including the one that had the three .44 slugs already in his body. He had skinned both bears using their fur hides as rugs. The bear grease had its purposes as well, but the meat was exceptional. He usually left the bears alone, as long as they didn't bother his mules or Sam, but last month, he'd spotted some prints that he knew belonged to a big brown bear just by their size and the claw marks. They were so large, he began taking his Sharps with him whenever he went deeper into his valley, but never spotted the giant bear.

He did all his hunting at the other end of the valley, and after harvesting what he needed, he'd leave the remains of the carcasses for the bears or the cougars. He caught some nice trout in the wide creek, too. In addition to his house, barn and cabin, Marsh had built a large smokehouse for preserving the meat that he had taken. It was quite a menu that he had stored in his cold room: deer, antelope, turkey, bear, and trout, in addition to the standard beef and pork, which he bought in Missoula.

After he had everything put away, including Sam and Albert, who joined the three mules in the barn, he needed to go and clean up the mess the posse had made in his cabin, taking more than a half an hour to get everything put back together.

He rarely used the cabin, but kept it clean and ready to use just because it was his nature. The cabin itself wasn't very large, as it was intended to be a temporary home. In fact, his original intention was to tear it down and reuse the logs as firewood, but he decided to leave it, and even added the tower after his first year in his valley.

Leaving the tidied-up cabin, he climbed the tower and when he reached the parapet, stepped onto the plank flooring and looked toward Missoula, and could see the tiny specks of the posse in the distance as they continued their search. He snickered again and couldn't help but be amused by their incompetence. *How had a woman on foot eluded a six-man posse?* He'd never met the woman, and despite her alleged murder of Frank Shipman, he hoped she had successfully escaped and maybe caught the train out of the area.

He clambered back down the ladder, walked across to his house, entering through the kitchen door, built a fire in the wood cookstove, and began to set up for his lunch. He could have ordered a coal cookstove, but he had decided to buy a wood burner because he liked the smell better and could cut his own wood. His heat stoves were coal-fired, and he had quite a large supply in case he got snowed in; which had happened several times.

As he sat at the table twenty minutes later with his coffee and food, he found himself wondering about the woman's situation. The whole story reeked of mystery. None of it made much sense; especially the size of the posse that was out looking for her. He may not have known the whole situation, but there were so many things about this whole sequence of events that stunk like rotten eggs.

Doris had described her as a young, pretty woman with a pleasant disposition, yet she marries a complete nothing like Frank Shipman, comes to Missoula, then has an affair, and is caught in the act by Frank, who she murders before running away on foot, and is then hunted by a six-man posse who can't find her.

He wished he could have met the woman just to get her side of the story, but there was something else, too. Zeke Chambers had said in the cabin that the man involved in the supposed adulterous affair was Bob McCallister.

Bob McCallister was an important citizen in Missoula. He owned a nice-sized spread about five miles north of town, the Double M; had four full-time hands and ran about six hundred head of cattle. He was a prominent member of the Methodist church and was well-respected. He was married, but didn't have any children. Bob was about average height, average weight and just about everything else about the man was average.

But Marsh had also heard the other side of Bob McCallister's reputation from some of the rougher crowd on Front Street down near the Hell Gate River. It seemed that Bob would sometimes take a train to Helena and not return for two or three days. The rumor was that he frequented the houses of ill repute there, so he could maintain his image in Missoula.

If he was the other side of Mrs. Shipman's affair, then maybe he'd shine some light on the mystery after some judicious questioning. He could start by asking about buying a bull and some cows to get a ranch started and see if he could drift into the topic of murder.

Curiosity was Marsh's greatest handicap, and had gotten him into trouble more than a few times as he grew up; occasionally with severe repercussions.

He decided to cut cross country after lunch and visit the Double M and strike up a conversation with Bob McCallister. His ranch was closer than Missoula, only about eight miles cutting cross country; but first, he'd have to eat.

———

At the Double M, Bob McCallister was packing. He hadn't told his wife, Lillie, about giving away the ranch, nor did he intend to. He had taken forty-five hundred dollars from the bank account after giving the deed to Frank Shipman, leaving her less than three hundred dollars; and just minutes ago, he had emptied the safe in his office of another two thousand. Payday for the ranch hands was in three days, but that would be Lillie's problem.

Lillie was out in the barn milking the two cows, so he knew he'd only have about thirty minutes to make his escape. The whole episode with Rachel Shipman was a foolish thing to do. He'd taken great pains to avoid any hint of a scandal about him in Missoula, but when he'd gotten that note from Rachel Shipman asking him to steal silently into her bedroom and she'd be waiting, willing and ready to receive him, he just couldn't help himself. He'd seen her a few times in public when Frank Shipman had invited him to stop by, which had surprised him at first, but once he saw Rachel, he knew he'd have to come back. She was nothing less than a fantasy come true.

He had always fancied himself a ladies' man, and wasn't that surprised by the note. He had hurried over at the appointed time and then disaster struck when his worst nightmare quickly replaced his dream fantasy.

He stopped packing and closed his eyes, recalling the sight of Rachel lying on the bed with her nightdress pulled up exposing herself to him; then the kiss and the feel of her under his hand. He still shuddered when he thought about it. It was almost worth the price that he paid, if only they had let him finish what he had started. He had no doubt now that it was a setup, but he still couldn't stay knowing that his place in the community would be gone and it was time to move on. Beside, even more than being seen as a phony philanderer; his friends and neighbors would know him to be a fool.

Frank had asked for money, but he knew if he gave him money, he'd come back for more; but if he gave them the ranch, he'd be free to disappear with his cash. He had been tired of Lillie for years anyway. Over the past three years, he had been contemplating all sorts of ways to get away from her, and while this may not have been the cheapest way out, it was the way he was taking. Besides, the funny part was it wasn't even his ranch to begin with, it was Lillie's. Her father had started the ranch and he had married into it ten years ago.

He finished packing his two travel bags and walked quickly out the front door. Before he had packed, he had Zeke Chambers harness the buggy and bring it around for him, so all he did was cross the porch, step into the front yard and toss his bags into the buggy before climbing in and driving off.

The rolling wheels stirred up the dust as he departed, and the cloud was still hanging over the yard when Lillie exited the barn carrying two large pails of milk. Lillie wasn't a very tall woman and the pails were both heavy and difficult for her to manage.

When she spied the buggy being driven off by her husband, she set the pails down and blew a wisp of her sandy hair out of her face, folded her arms across her chest and continued to watch the buggy depart toward Missoula; suspecting that he was leaving for good. He hated to use the buggy, and only did when he took her to church every Sunday. If he was using the buggy now, it was for a different reason.

She stared at the disappearing buggy for another minute, then stooped over and picked up the two pails of fresh milk and continued on to the house, suspecting that Bob wouldn't be coming back. He had been making noises about how tiresome she was becoming for a while now, and she knew he couldn't divorce her because he had no cause. She was well aware of the purpose of his trips to Helena which had become more frequent this past year, so she had almost expected him to run.

He wouldn't raise his hand against her because he was a weak man, so she never worried about him trying to do anything drastic like making himself a widower. Running away was much more in character for Bob. But because he had married into the property, she thought that now it was back in her hands, she would be able to run it the way she thought it should be operated. She didn't suspect for a moment that he would sell her ranch.

After she hauled the two pails into the kitchen, she set them down and decided to make a cup of tea to decide what she would do if Bob failed to return. After she put the water on, she moved the two pails into the cold room and walked to their bedroom to see if he had really gone. It didn't take long to find the empty drawers and the missing travel bags which confirmed her suspicion. She sighed and knew she was effectively a widow; then returned to the kitchen to make her tea and think about what she should do now. What she should have done was to quickly check to see if he had taken their money.

———

Rachel had watched the posse leave from a half a mile deeper in the valley where it was easy to find a hiding place in the trees, bushes, rocks and other natural sanctuaries. Her biggest problem was her blonde hair, but she minimized that with her dark green woolen hat.

Now, she had to make a decision about her next step. She knew she was safe for a while as she had enough food to last a week or so; but sooner or later, she'd have to leave, unless she could convince the owner to let her stay. It would be a considerable gamble to trust Marsh Anderson. She had heard about him from Doris, who had gushed over how handsome and nice he was and had also mentioned that he lived by himself northwest of Missoula somewhere. It hadn't been hard to find the wagon tracks leading to his valley, either. She had arrived in the predawn and had been surprised to find a nice house, barn and a cabin with a bizarre tower. She had to fight the urge to go into the cabin and get some sleep, but kept walking past the structures and had found a good hiding spot about a half mile from the house. It was up in the trees on the northern climb from the valley, but she could still see the house and cabin.

Now she was here, alone in his valley, just watching. She had seen him ride away earlier, but couldn't get a good look at him at this distance. She noticed how big he was, though, and that matched what Doris had said about him.

She was still watching when the posse arrived, followed shortly afterwards by Marsh Anderson. She expected to see the sheriff and maybe a deputy but was stunned to see six of them. When they were near the cabin, she was able to identify each manl spotting the sheriff, John, who was Frank's oldest brother, and then each of the other three brothers, but to have those other two men with him was downright scary. As bad as the Shipman brothers were; Zeke Chambers and Steve Bristow were even worse. She suspected that if the posse found her, she'd never make it back to Missoula. It also meant that Zeke Chambers and Steve Bristow were probably in on the scam to blackmail Bob McCallister They both worked as ranch hands on the Double M, so they would know a lot about the ranch and Bob McCallister.

But now, she had to decide. *Did she trust Marsh Anderson to not turn her in?* She had the pistol, but had never fired it before and was sure that she could never shoot someone. Killing Frank was necessary, and even that had bothered her tremendously. It still did weigh heavily on her conscience, and she wasn't sure if it would ever go away. She could use the gun as a threat, but doubted if it would be an effective threat; besides if she were going to ask for his help, it wasn't a good way to start. She was torn between walking up to him, smiling and asking for help;

pulling the gun and demanding his help, or staying put until things quieted down. She opened her food bag, found a sausage, pulled it out and bit off a large chunk. She needed time to think.

Rachel decided to wait until it was at least sunset just in case the posse returned. She would also make her decision on how to approach Marsh Anderson before then. She made herself as comfortable as she could and tried to get some sleep.

———

Sheriff John Shipman and his three brothers returned to Missoula, while Chambers and Bristow cut cross country to the Double M. The brothers rode to Frank's empty house rather than the jail where his two deputies were because they needed the privacy.

Once inside, John hurled his Stetson across the room in disgust. *How could a woman just disappear?* This was a woman on foot without a clue on how to survive or elude his posse, yet she had. First, they had checked the train depot, but no trains had arrived or departed in the six hours since the killing. She didn't have a horse, so she had to be on foot, and that meant going north.

The trouble was that none of them were true trackers. What Rachel had done was to not wear shoes or boots, but to wear three pairs of Frank's heavy socks, making thick cushions that would leave little evidence of her passing. As she walked in the bright moonlight, she'd look at the trail behind her, satisfied that it was the best she could do. She took the road north following the horse traffic and when she arrived at the turnoff to Marsh's valley, she had stayed thirty feet off to the side of the tracks and followed the trail to his valley.

A good tracker would have seen the disturbed earth and crushed grass, but the six men in the posse were looking for footprints and not any other minor disturbances in the terrain.

"All right, boys, where the hell did she go?" snarled John.

"I think somebody picked her up," suggested Billy.

"Who would that be?" asked John.

"Maybe McCallister. He must've been mighty tempted seeing her like that. I know I would," replied Billy with a grin.

John shook his head in annoyance, then glared at each of his brothers in turn before asking, "Do any of you other geniuses have any ideas?"

Lou replied, "I still think that Anderson is hiding her. He's got the only place north of here that isn't loaded with family, and you know that no big family is gonna hide her."

Al added, "I think so, too, John. He's got a lotta land out there to hide her away."

"So, do we go back there, John?" asked Lou, the youngest Shipman.

John thought about it, then answered, "Tomorrow. When we go back, it'll be nice and quiet, but not all of us. I'll take Billy with me, so we can surprise him. Today, I've got to go over to the courthouse and get the court to stop her from inheriting anything that Frank owns and making me his heir."

"Why do you have to do that?" asked Al.

John blew out his breath in frustration and replied, "Because the deed was signed over to Frank, who is now dead. His wife would be the legal heir to the ranch, but if she's either convicted of his murder or dead, she can't inherit a damned thing. I'd rather she was dead, though. If she's allowed to start blabbing in court, a lot of bad things could happen. We need to find her."

"What if she ain't there?" asked Billy.

"Then we go and find her," snapped John.

———

Bob McCallister left his buggy at the livery and walked the two blocks to the train depot where he purchased a ticket to Helena and then sat and waited for the 2:15 eastbound train. He pulled his pocket watch, found that it was already half past one, so he'd be out of Missoula and out of his predicament in a little over a half hour.

———

Marsh was riding Sam along at a medium trot as he crossed the open country between his valley and the Double M while debating the wisdom of sticking his nose into this whole mess. But his interest had been piqued, and he was hungry for more information. He was still thinking of ways to bring up the subject with Bob McCallister.

It took him less than an hour before he spotted the Double M ranch ahead. He'd never been on the ranch before, but had met Bob McCallister a few times. Marsh had thought he was quite the hypocrite; openly chastising other men for their behavior and sitting proudly in the first pew at the Methodist church while he pursued his Helena activities. Maybe the rumors of what he did in Helena weren't true, but Marsh liked to think that men like Bob McCallister hid all their own faults while gladly pointing out the same faults in other men.

He was almost at the access road and had been watching as Zeke Chambers rode up to the house, dismounted, and stepped onto the porch. He kept Sam trotting toward the house and was surprised that Chambers didn't see him and then even more surprised to watch Chambers just walk through the door without knocking. Even long-time ranch hands had to announce their presence. Only family members didn't have to knock, and he didn't believe that Zeke qualified.

———

Zeke Chambers had been concentrating so hard on what he was going to do that he didn't even notice Marsh's approach. Visitors to the ranch were rare, and he had Lillie McCallister on his mind. After he had harnessed the buggy for Bob McCallister's departure, he had stayed nearby and watched McCallister exit with the travel bags and knew that the rancher was going to skedaddle on his own, leaving his wife behind. That meant that Lillie McCallister was alone in the house and soon wouldn't even belong there. He was sure that Bob hadn't told her that he'd given away the ranch and probably taken all the money, but it didn't matter to him. Lillie was now fair game.

He had stepped up on his horse and ridden out to the pasture, called Steve Bristow over and confided in him that the McCallister had just flown the coop and that he intended to visit the missus. Bristow had laughed and said that he'd give Zeke two hours, then he'd come and join the party. Zeke had waved and ridden back at a fast trot.

When he had ridden out to talk to Steve, he had spotted Lillie as she carried the milk cans into the back of the house and smiled. Lillie wasn't young anymore, but she still carried a good figure at thirty-five and wasn't hard on the eyes.

When he returned, he knew she might see him coming through the back windows, so he rode wide around the house and stepped down in the front of the house, tied off his horse and with a grin on his face, quietly went up the steps to the porch and walked inside.

Lillie was having a cup of tea in the kitchen, still ruminating over her options about the ranch without a husband. She was alone, and it made her nervous. Two of the ranch hands were scary and the other two were gutless.

She had just taken her first sip when she heard the front door open and assumed that Bob had returned, making her thoughts of independence evaporate. She took another sip of tea, waiting for Bob to enter and come up with some excuse for taking all his clothes and the buggy.

She turned, expecting to find a recalcitrant Bob with his weak explanation, but with a plummeting stomach, saw the menacing face of Zeke Chambers as he exited the hallway.

"Hello, Lillie," he said with a twisted smile.

She stood and shouted, "What do you mean coming in here without knocking? I want you to leave my kitchen right now!"

Zeke snickered and replied, "This ain't your kitchen any more, Lillie. Your perverted husband gave the ranch away yesterday and probably ran off with all the money. You got nothin' now, and all you're good for is what I'm gonna use you for."

Lillie growled, "Get out of my house, Chambers, or you'll be out of a job today!"

Zeke didn't respond, but walked menacingly toward Lillie, tossing a chair out of his way before he reached for her and grabbed her right arm.

She screamed, but Chambers didn't care one bit. The other hands were on the other side of the large ranch, and Steve Bristow would keep them there. If she tried to fight him off, it'd be more exciting.

Marsh had heard Lillie's scream as he was preparing to hello the house to ask permission to step down. The front door was still agape as Marsh quickly dismounted, stepped up onto the porch, heard scuffling inside, followed by a loud slap, a crash, then fabric ripping.

Marsh didn't bother pulling his pistol. He needed both hands free for what he expected to find as he walked quickly, but quietly, down the hallway.

Zeke Chambers had subdued Lillie and was undoing his belt when he caught a shape out of the corner of his eye. Before he could do anything in the way of a defensive reaction, his collar was yanked backwards, and he went with it, crashing onto the kitchen floor on his back then sliding into the cook stove. He came to an abrupt stop, smacking the top of his head and losing consciousness, having never seen his assailant.

Marsh turned to Mrs. McCallister, and said, "Are you all right, Mrs. McCallister?"

Lillie was stunned by the attack and then by her miraculous rescue and failed to cover herself or answer Marsh's question.

Marsh then removed his jacket, took one long step, and crouched next to Lillie, placing his jacket over her.

"Ma'am? Are you still here?" he asked when he was close.

Lillie blinked twice and then focused on Marsh, not recognizing him, but finding concern in his blue eyes.

"Who are you?"

"My name's Marsh Anderson. I have a valley about eight miles west of here."

"Oh. You're Marsh Anderson. I've heard about you. Could you help me up, please?"

Marsh assisted Lillie to her feet and then walked her down the hallway.

When they reached her bedroom, she said, "I think I'll be okay now. I'll get dressed and be back in a minute."

"I'll be in the kitchen, ma'am," Marsh said as he turned to check on Zeke Chambers.

When he arrived in the kitchen, he stepped over to Chambers, and saw that he was breathing, which Marsh regretted somewhat. As he stared at Zeke Chambers unconscious form, he wondered why he would so boldly attack Mrs. McCallister in her own home. He would only do that if he knew he could get away with it, which meant that Bob McCallister was taking the coward's way out and abandoning his wife rather than facing possible humiliation. But if that were so, she'd be in charge of the ranch, and Zeke would still face severe consequences for what he was about to do. There must be something else going on.

As he was thinking about it, Lillie McCallister walked quietly behind him with his jacket in her hand.

"Mister Anderson? Here's your jacket. Thank you for saving me and then being so considerate afterwards."

Marsh snapped out of his trance and turned to Lillie and accepted the return of his jacket.

"What do you want me to do with him, ma'am?" he asked.

She scrunched her face in concern and replied, "I'm not sure. Before he attacked me, he said that my husband had given away the ranch and had run away. I'm sure he was right about Bob leaving, because his clothes are all gone. But why would he give away the ranch?"

Marsh glanced over at a moaning and on-the-verge-of-consciousness Zeke Chambers, pulled his pistol, took two steps toward him and whacked him across the head again. If it killed him, so be it. It hadn't, but it stopped the moaning.

Marsh then turned back to Mrs. McCallister as he slid his pistol back into its holster, and took a deep breath.

"This morning, Zeke, Steve Bristow and the Shipman brothers, led by the sheriff, conducted a search of my buildings looking for Mrs. Shipman, who they said murdered her husband, Frank. While they were in my cabin, I overheard that one down there saying he wished he had seen your husband's face when he was caught with Mrs. Shipman. The brothers were also starting rumors that Mrs. Shipman had been having an affair with an unknown man. It sounds like it was your husband, ma'am."

Marsh had expected her to react more intensely than she did when she sighed and said, "I suppose it was only a matter of time before his lust for different women came back to haunt him. I'm just surprised he did it in Missoula."

"So," asked Marsh, "you believe it's true? That he was caught with Mrs. Shipman?"

"I'm sure it is. But did he really give away the ranch like Zeke said?" she asked, hoping that it wasn't true.

44

"It's very possible, ma'am. But I don't think it was an affair. I believe it was a setup to blackmail him because nothing else makes any sense. The only question was the price. They might have even been surprised when he offered them the ranch. With that much cattle and with the railroad close by now, it's worth a lot of money."

Lillie was furious inside, and letting that anger show in her voice, said, "That sounds like something that weak bastard would have done. It would have been easier for him to give away a ranch that he did nothing to earn but to marry me, than it would be to pay cash. I'll bet he took all that too. I have nothing now, do I? He's given away the ranch to protect himself from shame and probably to get away from me, and taken all our money. Can you come with me to his office? I want to see if the safe still has some cash."

"Yes, ma'am," Marsh replied as they began to walk down the hallway.

When they entered the office, Lillie didn't have to even open the safe to see if it was empty. Bob had left it open in his haste to get to the train station.

Lillie's jaws tightened at the sight, then turned to Marsh and asked, "What can I do, Mister Anderson?"

"My concern right now is what happens when Steve Bristow returns. He and Zeke are partners, and I don't want to start shooting people until I know what's going on, and I surely don't want to leave you here with them. I think it would be safer if you packed your things and came with me to my valley. I have my house and a cabin, so you'd be able to stay in the house until we find out what is happening."

Lillie thought about it, but not for very long. The thought of being left alone with Zeke Chambers and that equally repulsive Steve Bristow made her queasy.

"Can you wait while I pack?" she asked.

"You might want to change into something you can wear while riding, too. I'll go and saddle a horse for you. Do you have one of your own?"

"There's a mare that I usually ride in the barn. Bob rides the gelding, if you want to bring him along, you can have him. There are only our two saddles in the barn, too."

"Okay. You go and get packed and changed and I'll get the horses ready."

She turned and trotted back to her room while Marsh jogged the other direction. He quickly crossed the porch and turned left toward the barn, scanning the area for other ranch hands, unsure of what their role, if any, was in this convoluted plot that now included blackmail on top of murder. He was already regretting making the ride, but then, he felt better for having rescued Mrs. McCallister from her horrible situation.

He hadn't seen any of the ranch hands, but didn't slow down as he entered the barn and saw the two horses. Both were in excellent condition, so he began saddling the mare first. It didn't take him long, so he soon started on the gelding. After they were both ready, he fashioned a trail rope for the gelding and then led them from the barn to the front of the house where Sam stood waiting.

After tying off the mare to the rail and attaching the gelding's trail rope to Sam, he stepped back onto the porch and through the open door.

"The horses are ready, Mrs. McCallister," he said in a loud voice.

"I'm almost done," she replied from the middle bedroom.

Marsh waited somewhat impatiently, wondering if he had conked Chambers on the head hard enough, but Lillie popped out of the room carrying two cloth bags just moments later.

"He took both of our travel bags," she spat as she walked into the room.

"Is there anything else you need? I don't have any womanly things like soaps or hairbrushes."

"Oh! Thank you. I'll be right back," Lillie said as she spun on her heels and trotted into the bathroom.

She emerged just seconds later carrying a towel converted into a sack for carrying what she needed for hygiene, opened one of the two bags, slipped the sack-towel inside and reclosed the bag.

Marsh stepped over, picked up both bags and followed Lillie out the door, leaving it open. He quickly walked to the horses, and as Lillie was mounting, Marsh hung both of her bags over the spare gelding's saddle horn, untied Sam, and then stepped up himself.

Without saying anything, they turned and rode at a fast trot away from the ranch house, passing under the Double M sign just a minute later. Marsh would glance back periodically looking for anyone coming in from the pastures or Zeke leaving the house. He spotted one rider up in the pastures, but there was nothing he could do about it.

After they'd gone three miles, Marsh slowed them down.

"Mister Anderson, not that I'm not eternally grateful for your arrival, but why did you come to the ranch in the first place?" she asked.

"When I heard Chambers say what he did about your husband being the one who had been caught with Mrs. Shipman, I was just curious. The whole story surrounding her seemed very odd, so I thought I'd ride over and talk to your husband to get some information."

"So, none of this involves you at all?" she asked incredulously.

"No, ma'am. Other than the visit from that posse this morning and Chambers and Bristow making a mess of my cabin, none of it has anything to do with me. It's just a fault of mine. I hate unsolved mysteries of any sort, and this is the biggest one I've ever come across."

Lillie shook her head, marveling at the twist of fortune that had brought him to her door at exactly the right time and having him have the moral strength to intercede on her behalf.

———

Steve Bristow knew what Zeke was doing back at the ranch house and had given him his time to enjoy himself before he decided to go and take his turn at Lillie McCallister.

He trotted his horse to the back porch's hitching rail, stepped down, and tied him off before hopping quickly onto the porch, striding to the door, pulling it open and entering the kitchen with a smile, until he spotted a groaning Zeke Chambers sitting on the floor with blood-caked hair. He was holding the other side of his head and tried to look up at Steve but wound up falling onto his side when he did.

"What the hell happened to you?" shouted Steve as he bent over Zeke, who regained his sitting position.

"Don't yell! I don't know. I was just about to have her when somebody grabbed me and tossed me across the room. I clunked my head on the stove, and don't remember anything after that."

"What about Lillie?" he asked.

"How the hell should I know? I just woke up," he snarled.

"Want me to go and tell John?" he asked.

"Hell, no. I'd feel like a damned idiot. Besides, it mighta been one of his brothers. Who else knew about McCallister losin' the ranch?"

Steve thought about it and realized that Zeke was right. The only ones who knew about the deed were the Shipmans and the two of them. *But why would one of the brothers get mad about what he was doing to Lillie?* Heck, they all told him to do what he wanted with her if she didn't go off with her husband.

"Maybe it was McCallister. Maybe he came back for something and did it," Steve suggested.

Zeke thought about it and it made more sense, but only a little. Bob didn't seem all that put out about losing the ranch, but he never really cared about Lillie, either. And Bob McCallister didn't have nearly the strength to fling him across the room; but a man's pride can make him do strange things. Maybe he came back and took her with him after all. It was the only thing that made a lick of sense.

"Help me up, will ya?" Zeke finally asked.

Steve assisted him to his feet, but Zeke was mighty woozy, so Steve guided him to the kitchen table and sat him down.

"I've been thinkin', Steve. I think you're right about Bob comin' back. If she ain't here, he mighta come back to get somethin' and caught me, then got all sorts of mad and decided to take her with him. If she ain't here, and he's gone, then that's what I figure happened."

"Well, Zeke I'm gonna clean up your blood. We don't want the new buyer finding blood stains in his kitchen," Steve said with a snicker.

Zeke just mumbled an unintelligible response and sat at the table with his head down.

———

As Steve was cleaning Zeke's blood from the kitchen floor, Marsh and Lillie arrived at his valley. Like most people, Lillie had never seen it before, so she marveled at the house, barn and even the cabin. But she was most surprised at the tower next to the cabin; as was everyone who had seen it.

"You built all this?" she asked with wide eyes.

"Yes, ma'am. But I did have the assistance of my four mules," he replied with a smile.

"Could you call me Lillie, please? I'm not that much older than you are," she said.

"Only if you'll call me Marsh, Lillie," he replied, wondering if she really believed that almost a decade qualified as not much older.

Lillie smiled back and asked, "I'm sure you get asked all the time where you received your name, so do you mind if I ask?"

"Not at all. It's short for Marshall, which was my mother's maiden name."

She looked over at the huge man and said, "I think the name suits you."

"It's the only one I have, so it had better," he said as they reached the barn.

They both dismounted, then walked the horses into the corral behind the barn where they were greeted by the curious mules.

Marsh removed her bags and said, "I'll take these inside for you after I unlock the house. I'll come back and take care of the horses after that."

"Thank you for everything, Marsh," Lillie said.

"You're welcome, Lillie."

After he had let Lillie into the house, gave her a bedroom and dropped off her things, he returned to the corral and began stripping the horses.

———

A half a mile west, on the northern rim of the valley, Rachel Shipman slept. She had barely gotten any sleep the night before when she walked the entire way, and now it had caught up to her. She had fallen asleep right after she had watched the posse leave around ten o'clock, and still hadn't awakened by the time Marsh returned to the house a little after three o'clock that afternoon.

———

At the same time, Sheriff John Shipman was sitting in the chambers of County Judge Lawrence Davis. The judge was a hefty man, and when wearing his judicial robes, resembled an upside down hot air balloon. But today, he was wearing a light gray suit and sat at his desk with his round fingers intertwined over his prodigious belly, listening to the sheriff.

"You say that your brother Frank won the ranch in a poker game at Dierman's saloon?" he asked, his eyebrows raised.

John could see that the judge wasn't buying it, so he decided to go the more believable route, and shrugged his shoulders.

"I didn't want to say anything, Your Honor, but that's the story that we're telling everyone to try and protect Bob McCallister's reputation and Mrs. McCallister's trust in her husband. You see, he was the man that Frank had caught with his murderous wife, Rachel. When Frank caught them, he was ready to shoot them both, which would be within his rights, but Bob McCallister convinced him to hold his fire and then offered him the ranch rather than suffer the humiliation of being known as an adulterer. He signed over the deed that afternoon and my brother never got a chance to register it with the land office. My concern is that Rachel, who killed him, probably out of vengeance for scaring away her lover, would inherit the ranch legally with Frank's passing."

"I thought that might be something like that rather than a poker game. There are rumors, you know. But I'm sure that you're aware that she couldn't inherit if she is found guilty of his murder, but she hasn't been found yet, has she?"

"No, Your Honor, she hasn't. And that's why I believe she may be dead. A single woman alone out in the wild country isn't likely to survive for very long. We've conducted a thorough search of all the ranches in the area and there were no signs of her anywhere."

The judge exhaled sharply, then said, "I can see your problem, Sheriff. Now, I can't give you ownership of the ranc; at least not yet. If she's found and convicted, it will be no problem at all, or if you can find evidence of her death, that would do it as well."

"Thank you, Your Honor. We'll keep looking."

John Shipman left the judge's chambers in a mixed mood. He had established that the transfer of the ranch to Frank had been legal, but not persuaded the judge to issue an order making him the heir. They had to find and kill Rachel. He didn't want to give her get a chance to tell her story on the witness stand. A pretty woman like her would win over more than just a few of those men on the jury, and he didn't want a single beam of light shining on the alleged affair, either. He needed to let everyone believe the story about adultery and planned murder, and the alternative, yet accurate account, was only known by Rachel. She had to be found and buried.

———

Lillie insisted on making dinner as they talked, and Marsh wasn't about to contest the issue.

"So, what happens next?" she asked as she began cutting some smoked pork.

"That's a good question. You're not sure that your husband emptied out the bank account, but it seems likely. Did you want to go to the bank to be sure?"

She set down the knife and thought about it.

"I suppose it doesn't matter. If he took all the money from the safe and disappeared, I'm sure he'd empty out the bank account as well. If the ranch has been given away, you could check on that, couldn't you?"

"I can do that for you, but by the sounds of it, I'd say that it has; but it's also possible that it hasn't been registered in the land office yet. If Frank and his brothers were using Frank's wife as a lure to trap your husband into being caught in the act, then I could see your husband panicking and signing over the ranch to Frank to buy his silence."

Your husband then empties out the bank account and goes home to get the money in the safe before leaving. What will be interesting is what became of the deed. If your husband signed it over to Frank, and he didn't register it yet, it would be a big problem for them, because with Frank dead, they couldn't register it. There would be only three ways out of their dilemma: they find Frank's wife and have her convicted of murder, or they kill her before she goes to trial. The third way out is if they show you the deed with your husband's signature and have you sign it over to one of the other brothers."

"Why would I do that?" she asked while she was cutting.

"They could intimidate you or tell you it will cost you thousands of dollars to have attorneys fight their claim, which is probably true," Marsh answered.

Lillie was thinking about the quandary that her husband had left her in. She couldn't see any way out, and the sudden insecurity that wrapped around her began suffocating her, and she found it hard to breathe.

The knife fell from her hand as her eyes rolled back in her head and she passed out, crumpling to the floor before Marsh could reach her.

He scooped her up easily and carried her to her bedroom, gently laid her on the quilt, and returned to the kitchen where he filled a glass of water before quickly walking back to the bedroom, setting it down on the bedside table and sitting down next to her.

He leaned close and said softly, "Lillie? Are you okay, Lillie?"

Lillie's eyes fluttered open and she saw Marsh just a foot away and felt a warm rush before she asked, "What happened?"

"I don't know. We were talking about checking on the ranch's deed and you just fainted. Luckily, you missed the knife blade that was just a few inches to your right."

Lillie smiled up at Marsh and said, "I'm sorry, Marsh. I made you carry me in here, didn't I?"

"You don't weigh very much, Lillie, so it wasn't a problem. I brought you a glass of water, so why don't you rest. I'll go out and finish cooking dinner and you can come back out when you're ready. Okay?" he asked with a smile.

Lillie nodded and replied, "Thank you, Marsh. You've shown me more consideration in a few hours than my husband showed me in ten years."

Marsh couldn't respond to that, so he sat up straight before standing and leaving the bedroom to get their food preparation restarted.

Lillie sat up and took a few swallows of water. Now that she had a chance to think about her situation, she thought of what she had really lost. Even though it had been her family's ranch, since she was married to Bob, all she did was to cook, clean, provide wifely duties on demand, and go to church with him on Sundays. There was never any passion in their lovemaking; it was all lust on his part, especially when he hadn't been able to go to Helena for a while. He never showed her any love at all. The other women in church would tell her how lucky she was to have a good-looking, prominent man as a husband, and she had always just smiled and agreed; maybe because she never expected any more than most women anticipated.

So, now that she had a chance to think about it; *what did she have now?* She had a nice room in Marsh's house, and she had the attention of Marsh Anderson, who was everything she ever dreamed of while she was a girl; tall, strong and handsome, with light sandy hair, and he even had blue eyes. She felt a chill go up her spine when she thought about him being so close. Yet here he was living alone. She didn't doubt he could have any woman he wanted, but he chose to live alone, and she wondered why. Maybe he didn't like women, but she doubted it. At least she hoped it wasn't true.

She took another long drink of water, stood and walked to the kitchen.

———

Rachel had awakened while the sun was still in the sky and guessed it was almost five o'clock. She rummaged through her food, found a can of beef and then realized she had forgotten to bring a tin opener or even a sharp knife. She knew the table knife she had brought with her couldn't penetrate the tin, so she began to look around and found a fist sized rock with a dull, pointed end. She picked up the rock, aimed the pointed end at the can and smashed the top of the tin with the rock. It punched a hole into the can, but it also exploded the gravy that surrounded the beef creating a meat geyser that showered her with brown liquid.

Rachel cursed herself for doing something so stupid that only a man could be capable of doing, took out one of her two towels and began to wipe the thick brown liquid from her face and arms.

When she was cleaner, she used her spoon to retrieve some of the beef from the mutilated can. Once she had eaten all she could, she tossed the can away under some bushes, took a drink from her canteen and used another splash of water to wash off the remaining gravy from her face.

Then she sighed and began to take off her soiled dress.

After she had changed, she sat on her coat and debated about going down to the house to talk to Marsh Anderson, but she still wasn't sure. He had let the posse look over his place, but he really didn't have any choice in that. She simply didn't know him at all. She had heard Doris over at Worden's almost swoon when she spoke of him, including how polite and kind he was; *but was the opinion of a lonely widow enough to make her risk her life?* She knew that her time was already running short and she had to decide soon.

There were other factors driving the decision; she was hungry, she was already feeling dirty, and couldn't imagine spending too much longer outside. After it was dark, she'd go down to the large creek that ran down the center of the valley, wash and refill her canteen, but just being outside was keeping her on edge. She had heard animals moving about in the dark, and wasn't about to confront any. She had the pistol, but knew that if she pulled that trigger, she'd be announcing her presence. In the end, she decided to stay where she was and rough it one more night at least, and see what tomorrow would bring.

———

After the dinner cleanup was done, Marsh said, "I'll go start a heating stove. I don't think it will be cold enough to need two tonight. After I've gone, go ahead and lock both doors. If you need anything, I'll be in the cabin."

"Are you sure, Marsh? I feel guilty for kicking you out of your house. I really wouldn't mind sleeping in the same house with you."

Marsh smiled and replied, "No, the cabin's fine. I lived there for two years and it's very comfortable. I'll see you in the morning, Lillie."

Lillie tried again, saying, "Marsh, I'd really feel safer if you were nearby. I'm not worried that you'd take advantage of me or anything."

"You'll be perfectly safe, Lillie. Just lock the doors. They don't even know you're here," he said with a reassuring smile.

Marsh didn't waste much time after her second request for him to stay in the house. He just picked up his Stetson, walked to the door, and left. Lillie seemed like a very nice woman and pleasant to the eyes, but he was worried about being this close to any woman in his state of self-imposed celibacy.

He hadn't been with a woman since Clara died, and it wasn't because he didn't have the urge. In fact, it was well past a simple urge and was close to a full-fledged screaming tantrum. Marsh simply didn't want to get involved with a woman just for a night of pleasure. He had been waiting to find one that created the same sensation he had felt when he met Clara and believed it wouldn't be fair to either him or the woman to just satisfy his lust and then send her on her way. Besides, Lillie was married and that made it out of the question anyway.

He took the quick climb up the tower before heading to the cabin and once in the papapet, could see the lights beginning to appear in Missoula to the southeast and not much else. After just five minutes of scanning the dark horizons, he dropped back down to the ground, and went inside his cabin.

CHAPTER 2

Marsh was up shortly after sunrise, then took care of his morning needs, including shaving. Shortly after he left the cabin, he was surprised to see smoke curling out of the cookstove pipe. Lillie must have awakened even earlier than he did, so Marsh closed the cabin door and headed that way. When he reached the back door, he rapped on it twice and waited.

Lillie opened the door and Marsh was about to chastise her for not locking it, when he couldn't help but notice that she was still in her nightdress and it clung to her figure provocatively, as if she had taken a bath and not dried completely. So, he forgot about mentioning the unlocked door, and just entered.

"Good morning, Marsh. Come in, it's your house, after all," she said, smiling as she turned and walked to the cook stove.

Marsh couldn't help but detect a distinct sway as she walked away in her clinging nightdress and wondered what had caused this radical change from the woman he had wrested away from her tenuous situation just yesterday afternoon. She now apparently was trying to lure him into his own bed, but he was still a bit surprised. Maybe it was because she saw him as a white knight that had saved the fair damsel from the dragon.

He walked to the stove and took the coffee pot, filled the two cups that were already on the table and took a seat as Lillie brought the two plates of bacon and eggs. She must have been up even earlier than he had previously thought to get this much done already.

"Did you sleep all right, Marsh?" she asked.

"I always do, Lillie. How about you?"

She smiled and replied, "I haven't slept that well in years. I guess it was because I felt so alive again. I haven't felt this way since I was a teenaged girl."

That answered the question of the nightdress anyway. Marsh thought back to yesterday's conversations about her husband and she had mentioned that he hadn't shown her any consideration in ten years. Add in the rumors of Bob's trips to Helena, to her ready acceptance of the gossip of her husband having an affair, and he guessed that Lillie, like many women, after a few years of marriage, was treated as nothing but another piece of furniture. He thought that Lillie McCallister, despite being a married woman, was lonely. He thought that she saw Marsh as a prospective bedmate if not more, and he knew that this was a very dangerous situation. The problem was that she was an innocent woman caught up in a bad situation, and he felt obligated to help.

As they ate, Lillie asked, "Are you going to go into Missoula and check to see if the deed has been changed, Marsh?"

Marsh slipped some eggs into his mouth and shook his head before swallowing.

Then he replied, "It's Sunday, Lillie. I'll check tomorrow."

She laughed and said, "I totally forgot in all the excitement."

"Let's hope the excitement stays down for a while, although I'd really like to talk to Mrs. Shipman about what really happened between her and your husband and why she killed Frank. I hope they don't find her first."

Lillie tilted her head slightly and asked, "Isn't she in jail?"

"Oh, I forgot to tell you that. No, she disappeared after the stabbing by just walking out of town in the night, and that's why the posse showed up yesterday morning. I wouldn't be surprised if they come back, either. If they haven't found her yet, they'll retrace their steps at least once more, and my valley is high on their list because I live alone, and from what I hear, she's a very attractive young lady. They'd naturally assume that a single man like me would hide her away and keep her as a consort rather than turn her in."

"Would you?" she asked with a slight smile.

"I'd hide her, but only if I was convinced she was innocent."

Lillie's eyebrows arched slightly as she asked, "You don't think she killed him?"

"Oh, no, I'm sure she did, but I'd be surprised if she murdered him. I think she probably had to kill him in self-defense. I think she'd be in real trouble after their blackmail scheme was done, and maybe that's why they brought in an outsider that no one knew. She'd be easier to make disappear. I just want to know, not speculate."

Lillie replied, "Well, wherever she is, I don't give her much chance of getting away. A lone woman out in this territory on foot? I wouldn't be surprised if she's not already dead."

Marsh shrugged and replied, "It's possible, but she showed a lot of gumption and smarts to be able to get out of that situation without panicking. She must have one hell of an interesting story to tell and I'll bet that big posse wasn't about to let her return to Missoula and tell it, either."

Lillie then said, "Can we talk about something else, please?"

Marsh took a long sip of coffee and answered, "Sure. What would you like to talk about?"

She leaned forward, put one elbow on the table, set her chin on her left palm, and said, "Can you tell me how you got here?"

Marsh went with his standard short answer and replied, "I can, but it's really quite boring. I worked in construction in Denver, got tired of the big city and left. I was looking for someplace that I could really love and accidentally discovered this valley. I was able to buy it at a very good price from the Northern Pacific four years ago when they were really hungry for cash after the Panic of '73 and I've been improving it ever since."

"What about your family? Do you have any brothers or sisters?"

"I had two older brothers, but both died in accidents, and my father died of a heart attack just a little while after my second brother died."

"So," she asked softly, "you have no one in this world to share your life with?"

Marsh smiled and replied, "I have my four mules and Sam, my horse. I may even get a dog one of these days."

She laughed and then leaned back, took a drink of coffee and smiled.

"I enjoy talking to you, Marsh," she said softly as she looked moony-eyed at him.

"It's nice having you here, Lillie," Marsh replied, hoping it was non-committal enough, but doubted it when he saw Lillie beam a giant smile at him.

He should have just smiled and kept his mouth shut.

Marsh finished the last of his coffee, then stood and took his plate and flatware to the sink, but when he began washing them, Lillie protested his doing woman's work.

Marsh didn't turn but said, "Women do too much work, Lillie. Work is work. If I can do it, I will do it."

After setting the plates and cups in the drying stand, he turned to Lillie, who was still gazing at him with her big smile, and said, "I'm going to go out and take a gander from my tower. It's a morning ritual to give me a read on what's going on around my valley. With the likelihood of that posse returning, I don't want to be surprised."

"I'd better get dressed, then. Do you think I should hide in case they show up?"

Marsh answered, "No, Lillie. There's no point in hiding. The minute they stepped into the front door, they'd know you were here."

She was startled and asked, "How?"

"You have a gentle, flowery scent that is easily detected. I noticed it when I walked into the kitchen. You don't notice it because it's around you all the time. You just get dressed and if they show up, I'll talk to them."

Lillie smiled again because Marsh had said that he noticed her sweet scent, and said, "Alright, I'll go and get dressed and we'll just have to see what happens."

Marsh nodded and headed out the back door and let his breath out loudly when he reached the porch. This was a dangerous situation on so many levels. *What if the sheriff had arrived while she was still wearing her nightdress?* As it was, it would be difficult to explain her presence even when she was dressed.

As he headed for the cabin tower, he began to think of good explanations for Lillie's presence in his house. He began his climb and settled on just telling a slightly modified version of what had actually happened. He might even get to turn it to his advantage and get some more information from the sheriff.

———

Sheriff John Shipman and his brother Billy were riding west as Lillie dressed.

"When I'm looking in the house, I want you to check out the barn and that cabin. If they're empty, climb that tower he built and take a quick look down that valley. In fact, you stay there until I come and get you. Look for anything that moves on two legs or any bright colors. That dress she was wearing was white and dark blue," John said.

"You don't think she changed, John?" Billy asked.

"Nope, she was wearing the white and blue one when we saw her last and it wasn't in the house."

"She took some more clothes too, John," Billy pointed out.

John snickered and replied, "She ain't gonna get naked in the cold, Billy; but I sure wouldn't mind seeing her, either. She sure filled out that blue and white dress nice."

Billy then asked, "John, if we find her, do you think we could maybe have a go at her before we have to shoot her for escaping?"

John laughed and answered, "Of course, we will. I get her first, though."

Billy grinned and then asked, "What about Anderson? Are we gonna arrest him for harboring a fugitive?"

John shook his head, then replied, "Nope. If she's there, then she probably told him what happened, so we shoot him first. After they're both dead, we clean his place out. Did you see all the guns he had in there? I'll bet he's got money, too."

"Where did he get the money, anyway? He ain't old enough to be rich."

"Who knows? Maybe his pa is rich, and he inherited," John replied and then cut off the conversation.

————

Marsh didn't even have to go halfway up the tower when he spotted the two riders and quickly climbed back down before trotting back to the house.

Once inside, he shouted, "There are two riders on their way, Lillie. I'm pretty sure that one of them is the sheriff."

Lillie popped her head out of her bedroom and asked, "What do you want me to do, Marsh?"

"Go ahead into the kitchen, sit down, and have another cup of coffee. Just let me do all the talking to the sheriff."

Lillie thought it was an odd thing to have her do, but she walked slowly into the kitchen, casting glances back at Marsh as he headed into the main room.

Marsh walked into the main room, turned right, entered his gun room, and after he picked up his Winchester '76, walked back to the kitchen, poured himself a cup of coffee then leaned the Winchester against the wall near the door.

"Are you just going to wait with me?" Lillie asked.

"Wait and enjoy my coffee, Lillie. I doubt if it will come to a shootout, so you shouldn't worry."

"But what will you tell them about me being here? I mean, I'm not worried about being seen with you or anything. I just don't want to be the cause of some trouble."

"The truth...mostly," he replied with a grin before taking a swallow of hot coffee.

Then they just waited for the sheriff to arrive.

————

Sheriff Shipman and Billy Shipman had made the turnoff toward the valley and were following their own tracks from the day before. The trail was turning into a road with all the recent use.

As they rode along at a medium trot, they both had been scanning the area for any signs of Rachel on the off chance that she might have left the house earlier and was trying to run again. They didn't think it was likely, but they kept looking anyway.

Fifteen minutes later, they approached the house and slowed down, spotting the smoke from the cookstove pipe.

"He's in there, John," said Billy unnecessarily.

"I can see that, Billy. I'm not blind, you know. I'll give you a minute to get around the back and watch the back door in case she tries to sneak out of the house."

They reached the house, dismounted, and Billy trotted around to cover the kitchen entrance, pulling and cocking his Colt as John went to the front door.

John waited for almost a minute for Billy to get into position and then made a loud display of his arrival when he stomped onto the porch, then waited for a few seconds before he pounded on the door.

Inside, Marsh had to keep from laughing at the sheriff's overacting, picked up his coffee and walked quickly toward the front door and opened it as soon as he arrived.

"Sheriff, you're just the man I wanted to see. I was just about to come and find you," he said loudly.

"Is it because of Mrs. Shipman? Someone reported seeing the fugitive enter your house," he asked, providing the phony reason for his return in the process.

Marsh almost laughed at his excuse, but said, "Whoever reported that to you might have spotted Mrs. McCallister coming into the house. She's in the kitchen now. That's why I needed to talk to you."

Sheriff John Shipman had been expecting some sort of obfuscation from Anderson, but this was a total shock to him and it hit him like a punch in the nose. He had thought that Bob McCallister had gone and taken his wife with him. If she was still here, it could be a major problem, depending on what her husband had told her.

"Mrs. McCallister? Bob McCallister's wife? She's here? How did that happen?" he almost shouted as he asked.

"Come on in, Sheriff, and I'll tell you what happened to her yesterday."

John Shipman stepped across the threshold, his search for Rachel tossed aside for the moment. He closed the door slowly behind him and listened as Marsh told him the story.

"I went over to the Double M just after lunch yesterday to pick up three horses that he was going to sell to me. I got there and heard this racket from inside and then a woman's scream. I ran inside and found Zeke Chambers straddling Mrs. McCallister and about to rape her. Her dress had been ripped apart, exposing her."

I grabbed Zeke by the scruff of the neck, yanked him away, then he slid across the room and his head smacked into the cook stove. I handed Mrs. McCallister my jacket, so she could restore her modesty, return to her room and get dressed. She told me that Chambers had told her that her husband had given away the ranch and that he was the one that had been caught with Mrs. Shipman. She also said that he had emptied their safe and bank account and left her."

She was terrified about staying there, Sheriff. She had no protection after Chambers revived, so she asked if she could come with me until this whole thing was sorted out. I was just about to go into town and report it to you, so I'm glad to see you. What can we do about this heinous situation?"

Sheriff Shipman was stunned for just a few moments. *What the hell just happened?* John knew about Zeke's intentions, but had blown it off as nothing less than fantasy, thinking that Lillie McCallister would be gone with her husband. He didn't doubt Anderson's story, but this could be an absolute disaster.

"I need to talk to Mrs. McCallister," he said, as much for a delay as anything else.

"Sure, she's in the kitchen. And before you ask, as you have every right to as the sheriff, I stayed in my cabin last night while she slept inside my locked house," Marsh said loudly enough for Lillie to hear so she didn't say anything about leaving the back door unlocked.

The sheriff, having not the least interest in whether or not Anderson had bedded Lillie McCallister last night, showed his palm, and waved it once, saying, "No, I believe you. I'm sure you treated her honorably."

Lillie had listened intently as Marsh had told his version of what had happened. The only real differences in what Marsh had told the sheriff was his purpose for visiting the Double M, and the unlocked door, which was intentional on her part.

John was regaining his composure by the time he reached the kitchen and found a distraught appearing Lillie McCallister sitting at the table with a half-full coffee cup in her two hands.

"Mrs. McCallister, Mister Anderson tells me that you were assaulted in your home yesterday by Zeke Chambers. Did you wish to press charges?" he asked; already prepared to argue the merits of just letting it go.

But Lillie replied, "No. I don't think it would matter, but I never want to see that man again."

Then, after a brief pause, she asked, "Is it true, Sheriff? Did Bob give away the ranch to your brother after he caught Bob committing adultery with his wife?"

John nodded, then said, "I'm afraid so, Mrs. McCallister. I'm sorry, but there's nothing I can do about it."

The sheriff's confirmation of what had only been a probability a moment before had a profound impact on Lillie's view of the situation and on her persona. It had been her father's ranch and she suddenly realized that the Shipmans would get it because of Bob's weakness.

Lillie suddenly morphed into a she-devil, glared at the sheriff and said fiercely, "You most assuredly can do something about it! You can tear up that deed and let me keep the ranch. It doesn't matter anymore. Frank is dead, and his wife is probably dead, too. Everyone seems to know that she and Bob had been caught fornicating by Frank. so the ranch shouldn't belong to anyone but me!"

Marsh felt his stomach sink. *Didn't Lillie realize that she may have well signed her own death warrant?*

The sheriff, recognizing the obvious threat that Lillie now posed, said, "I wish it were that simple, Mrs. McCallister. The whole problem with the ranch is in the courts and may not be resolved for some time."

Marsh was standing behind the sheriff, desperately trying to make eye contact with Lillie to drop the subject, but she not only failed to move away from the topic; she made everything worse.

"I don't think it's that difficult, Sheriff. You just tear up the copy of the deed that Bob signed over to Frank and I can return back to my ranch, fire Zeke Chambers and Steve Rawlins and go on with my life."

Marsh stopped trying to silence her. The damage was done, and now, he was neck deep in the problem because he had witnessed the exchange between them, if nothing else. If she had just acted like the quiet, frightened, ignorant wife, the sheriff would have probably just let it go. Now, he couldn't afford to do that.

The sheriff ended the conversation by saying, "I'm telling you, Mrs. McCallister, it really isn't that simple. Mrs. Shipman is technically entitled to the ranch, and until she is either executed for murder or found dead, the deed remains in evidence for the case against her."

Lillie recognized that logic, and finally just nodded, but still maintained her deep anger.

The sheriff was relieved that she had seemingly acquiesced and then returned to his original purpose for the visit, turned to Marsh and said, "I've checked the house, so we'll go outside and search your barn and cabin."

Marsh nodded and glanced at Lillie, who was still staring at the sheriff, before walking to the back door, opening it and then waited for the sheriff.

Lillie was still upset about the sheriff's refusal to do the simple and obvious, failing to make the simple connection between Frank's blackmail scheme and John's involvement. She had believed that because John Shipman carried a badge, he was a lawman and she assumed he was unaware of the scheme.

———

As the sheriff followed Marsh to the doorway, he noticed the Winchester leaning against the wall.

"What's the rifle for?" he asked as he pointed at the gun.

"I went out this morning early to do some hunting. I climbed my tower to check for game, which is one of the reasons I built it, and saw two does about a half mile down in the valley. I was lucky, too. I was upwind and just walked along and I was going to take the shot when this nice buck stepped out of the trees to the south on the other side of the valley. Now, that's almost a half a mile away, but I thought I'd at least get close enough for the Winchester to put a bullet into him. He was a big boy, with at least fourteen points, so I began walking that way slowly and was just getting ready to pull the trigger when I screwed up. I forgot about those two does and they must have caught sight of me and took off. I could hear them running and that buck turned, spotted me and shot away like he was coming out of a rifle. I didn't even waste the shot."

The sheriff was following the story with interest because he had never taken a big buck, so when Marsh finished, John just shook his head and they walked outside. Billy was off to the side, and still had his pistol drawn as the door opened.

"Put that damned thing away!" John shouted when he saw him.

A chagrined Billy released the hammer and slipped his Colt into his holster, but didn't fasten the hammer loop. Marsh noticed the omission and the fact that Billy had his pistol ready to fire in the first place, which meant that they weren't going to try to capture Mrs. Shipman. If she had been in the house and their intention was to return her to Missoula for trial, he could have just grabbed her when she tried to run; but they were going to shoot her on sight. The mystery was now becoming less mysterious and decidedly more dangerous. The sheriff and his brothers, as well as those two miscreants on the Double M, had two women they needed to kill, and now, he was probably added to the list, too.

"Go ahead and check out my barn and the cabin, but don't trash my cabin like those two jerks you had with you yesterday," Marsh said as he followed behind the sheriff across the porch.

John ignored the comment about Chambers and Bristow; he;d deal with Chambers later anyway. Chambers had created a giant problem now, and the sheriff's mind was already buzzing like a beehive trying to come up with a solution to Lillie. The obvious answer was to kill her, but the issue was how to get her out of Anderson's house quietly. He began thinking about killing Anderson first, but the man's gun fascination had him concerned. The man was probably better with his gun than either he or Billy were, and he seemed leery of Billie, too, so he doubted if Billie could do anything.

With only two of them searching, Marsh was able to keep an eye on them, and they made it easier when they both went into the barn rather than split up. After the quick search of the barn and loft, they headed for the cabin. This time, they did split up, with Billy climbing the tower and the sheriff going into the cabin while Marsh stayed outside and waited. He knew they weren't going to find anything again, so he stayed outside and watched Billy Shipman scale the ladder.

Once he was in the tower, Billy peered east to Missoula first, then turned in a wide, slow circle, impressed with the view. When he initially looked down the valley, he didn't see anything, but then, he spotted motion near the trees on the right about a half mile away.

He cupped his hand over his mouth and shouted, "John! Something's moving out there!"

Marsh thought he knew what it was, then quickly turned and ran toward the house.

The sheriff trotted out from the cabin and looked up at Billy, shouting, "What was it? Did you see her?"

"I ain't sure. But there was something over there!" he yelled back, pointing almost exactly where Rachel was hiding.

"Let's get the horses!" John shouted as he began to run.

Marsh had already trotted back to the house, grabbed his Winchester and then crossed paths with the sheriff who saw him with his rifle and yelled, "Where do you think you're going, Anderson?"

"I think I know what your brother saw, and if I'm right those pistols and your '73s aren't going to stop him," Marsh shouted back as he kept going toward the barn.

He had seen the large, recent prints in his valley and knew that none of the black bears would venture this close to his house after he had killed the other two. Besides, the prints were much larger than any black bear he'd ever seen, or any brown bear for that matter. They had to belong to a grizzly; and a big one at that.

The sheriff wondered what this Anderson character thought he was doing, but Marsh's warning gave him enough pause to let him go. If nothing else, he would lead them to the woman then he and Billy could kill them both.

———

Rachel had awakened hours ago, eaten a sorry excuse for a breakfast and cleaned up after herself. Yesterday after the posse had gone, she had found a small gouge in the face of a granite outcrop that would probably be a cave in a few thousand years, but it had served her well as a refuge.

After she was fully awake, she had left her things in the hole and returned to what she thought was the best observation point about a hundred yards from her hiding spot. She had seen Marsh climb his tower, then hurriedly descent, walk quickly to the house and then she saw the sheriff and someone else arrive and thought it was his brother, Billy. She had been intently watching the sheriff and Billy as they were searching the grounds, and had seen Billy point in her direction and shout that he had seen something move.

She was surprised that he had seen her. She was behind a tree, wearing her heavy black coat and dark green knitted hat, and she surely wasn't moving. She continued to watch, and spotted Marsh Anderson suddenly run into his house, then come back out and spotted his hasty departure on his horse racing toward her with the sheriff and Billy a hundred yards behind. *How had they seen her?*

She turned and began trotting back to her small cave when she heard a deep growl to her left, and felt the hairs on the back of her neck snap to attention.

She turned slowly, saw the bear on all fours staring at her from sixty yards away, then felt the terror rise and bile fill the back of her throat, almost causing her to vomit.

She turned to face the bear as she slowly backed toward the shallow cave with her eyes locked onto the fearful beast, who was watching her with interest. She pulled the Webley Bulldog revolver out of her coat pocket, but knew if she used it, she'd be signing her death warrant when the sheriff heard the report. She held her fire as her wide eyes watched the bear almost waltzing as it shifted back and forth approaching her. She began to move back at a slightly faster pace.

As Rachel was backing slowly toward her hiding spot, the bear mimicked her slow motion, never taking his eyes from her. He wasn't one of the smaller black bears that inhabited the valley; he was a six-hundred-pound grizzly that had recently made the valley his home, and left the tracks that caused Marsh's concern.

Rachel didn't know if it was her scent or the beef can and its gravy that had attracted the beast but the reason for his presence didn't matter. She watched with unblinking eyes as the animal stalked its prey and knew that the giant carnivore may be doing the sheriff's job for him.

Marsh hadn't bothered to saddle Sam, but just leapt onto his back, then trotted quickly out of the barn. In just seconds, he had him up to a canter and was well ahead of the sheriff and Billy as he tore down the valley. Billy had said he had seen it a half mile away, so he hoped that his estimate of distance was reasonably accurate.

Rachel had backed all the way into her cave and had nowhere else to go as she saw the grizzly making a wide turn to be able to see her inside the protective rock; his black eyes never leaving her as she held the Webley tight in her hands.

The bear had smelled both the beef and the human, and was hungry; having failed to catch any trout in the stream that morning. Rachel's scent of fear also added to the bear's interest, but he recognized that she posed a threat with whatever she was holding, so he approached her warily.

Rachel had to squelch the screaming demands she heard in her mind telling her to run away. She knew she'd never come close to outrunning the bear and she couldn't climb, either. She'd never get ten feet up a tree before those giant claws ripped her back down. She didn't realize that brown bears, and grizzlies, which were just bigger brown bears, couldn't climb trees like black bears.

She held the pistol in both hands and pointed it at the bear as it looked at her curiously at first, but then it seemed to have made up its mind and snorted, tilted its mammoth head and roared.

Rachel thought she'd lose control of her bladder as she began to tremble, but still managed to cock the Webley's hammer, which wasn't even necessary, if she'd known it was a double action revolver. She may never have shot a gun before, but even she knew that the pistol wouldn't come close to hurting that monster. She was going to die, and had momentary thoughts of shooting herself when it made its deadly run. But right now, it seemed to be trying to frighten her into submission before the final attack, and it was working, too.

———

Marsh heard the roar even as the sheriff and Billy drew up behind him. They must have heard it, too, because they both immediately pulled up. Marsh slid from the gelding's back, cocked the Winchester and scrambled up the hill, disappearing from the sight of the two other men who both watched in a combination of admiration for his courage, and scorn for his poor decision; believing that Marsh Anderson was running to his death.

Marsh headed straight for the source of the bellow and soon spotted the bear. He knew the grizzly was enormous from seeing his prints, and seeing the monster up close was still a shock, but he didn't have time to waste on awe, he had to kill the beast and was depending on his Winchester and the heavy punch of its .45 caliber rounds.

———

Rachel had her eyes down to slits as the bear rose quickly to its full height, spreading its arms wide and brandishing its enormous claws as it released another terrifying roar. She was preparing to fire her useless shot when she heard a shout from nearby.

"Hey! Big boy! I'm over here!" Marsh yelled as loudly as he could while he aimed his Winchester.

He had no idea that Rachel was in her cave just a hundred feet away. He was concentrating on the bear knowing that he needed not only a straight shot, but it had to be a head shot if he wanted it to kill the beast. He didn't think that even the powerful .45 could kill a grizzly that size anywhere else but the head with just one shot, and he doubted he'd get a second. Even the head shot was iffy if he hit the thick part of the bear's skull. He would have to be almost perfect with his aiming and somehow stay stable. He assumed a kneeling position and tried to calm himself for the shot, which wasn't easy, but using his elbow and knee as a support made it better.

The bear, having just terrified its victim, heard Marsh and immediately dropped to all fours, and swung its head toward the new, more threatening enemy. Again, he bellowed his defiance, then turned and took two long loping strides toward his new foe eighty feet away.

Marsh knew he would come at him quickly, but he had to hold his shot for just another second to make sure the bullet penetrated the thick skull and didn't ricochet away. He kept his sights aimed at the monster's face as he began to trot at him. He was fifty feet away now and still moving.

Then the bear, even as it continue its loping approach, then tilted his mammoth head and roared once more as it neared Marsh whose sights remained locked on the animal's black nose. When Marsh saw the wide-open mouth with its rows of knife-like teeth, he squeezed the trigger.

The Winchester erupted with smoke and a loud blast as the .45 caliber bullet raced the length of the barrel and escaped the muzzle at over a thousand feet per second. The slug of lead arrived at its target almost instantly, breaking off one of the giant teeth before punching through the back of the bear's throat and pulverizing one of its cervical vertebrae. The spent, misshapen bullet then lodged in the animal's spinal cord disrupting the neural flow of information to and from its muscles instantly. The giant animal plowed into the ground at Marsh's feet and knocked Marsh backwards, sending him onto the seat of his pants.

He would have laughed in relief at the sight of himself on his butt, but he had to make sure the bear was dead. He quickly regained his footing, stepped to the still breathing bear and with his Winchester's muzzle just inches away from the massive skull, levered in a new round and fired again, killing the bear.

Rachel had witnessed Marsh's put down of the giant bear, and was so stunned by her sudden reprieve that it took a few seconds for her to realize that she was going to live. She set the cocked Bulldog onto the cave floor and walked slowly out into the open. She expected to see the sheriff coming running up the incline, and suddenly didn't care anymore. She had almost died, and she was tired of fighting the inevitable; whether it was being crushed by the grizzly's teeth or hanged by civilized men, she would die either way.

Marsh was still examining his kill when he heard a rock roll down the incline, jerked his head up quickly and was stunned to see a woman walking his way. *It was Mrs. Shipman!* As much a shock as it may have been seeing the size of the bear, it was a bigger one seeing her walking towards him.

He made an instant decision and suddenly began waving at her to get her attention.

Rachel spotted Marsh's frantic waving and guessed who he was just by his size, then stopped walking, and looked down the slope quickly. *The sheriff wasn't in sight!* When she turned her eyes forward again, she spotted Mister Anderson pointing back up into the trees and then gesturing for her to go back up and hide. She was still in a bit of a haze after her brush with death, but when he began to point at his chest, indicating that the sheriff would be coming, she suddenly nodded and began to scramble up into the trees as fast as she could.

Marsh watched her go and as soon as she was out of sight, he waited another few seconds until he was sure she was well hidden, and then quickly scanned the area for any signs that she was there. He had to jog over to where she had been and quickly began sliding his feet over her footprints until he was satisfied that they were gone, then he began to slide down the hill.

When he reached the bottom, the sheriff and Billy were still a hundred feet away, so he waved them in and shouted, "I got him!"

They both grinned and trotted their horses near.

"What was it? A black bear?" shouted the sheriff as he dismounted.

"Nope. It was a monster of a grizzly. That big boy must weigh about six hundred pounds. It's going to take me a while to get this one down and back to the cabin. You want to see him?"

"Sure!" said the sheriff enthusiastically, the thrill of seeing a giant grizzly totally displacing any thoughts of finding Rachel, and even temporarily setting aside any thoughts of the new danger Lillie McCallister represented.

Marsh was taking a gamble that they wouldn't go any further than the bear. There was no reason for them to do so, but he knew that they'd want to go and see the beast anyway, and for him to not invite them to witness his prowess as a hunter would be unnatural for a man.

When they reached Marsh, the sheriff asked, "Why'd you go after him, anyway? That was a mighty dangerous thing to do."

Marsh replied, "I know, but I'd seen his prints around the barn and knew he'd be trouble pretty soon. I'd been looking out for him the past few weeks, so when your brother said he'd seen something, I knew it had to be him. I wanted him dead before he got into my barn and killed my horses or mules."

His answer seemed to satisfy the sheriff and Billy as they all climbed the incline.

Rachel was another hundred feet up and two hundred feet west of the bear and watched them from behind a tree leaving just a tiny slit of an opening through the other trees between her and them. She was confused why Marsh Anderson had invited them to come up to see the bear and momentarily thought he was going to turn her in; but he was the one who told her to hide while he had a rifle in his hands. He could have captured her easily, especially as she was about to give up anyway. *So, why had he brought them here?*

The sheriff and Billy were stunned by the size of the animal and by the lack of blood as they both bent over examining the dead bear.

"You put two shots in him and there ain't any blood at all!" exclaimed Billy.

Marsh replied, "The first shot was the important one when it was charging. I hoped to get a head shot, because I knew a body shot wouldn't stop him, and was lucky when he opened his mouth to roar and I put the .45 into his mouth, but that only stopped him. I felt like an idiot though, when he slid into my legs and knocked me on my butt. I had to put a second shot through his skull to end it."

"Wow!" shouted the sheriff as he examined the carcass.

Then he said, "You waited until he almost got you, just so you could get the best shot! That took some sand, Anderson."

As they both were crouched over the bear, Marsh gave a quick scan nearby and was horrified to spot two footprints just six feet behind the sheriff's back. He was tempted to run over and scrape them into oblivion, but didn't want to call attention to them, so he avoided looking at them and returned to looking at the bear.

"Say, Anderson. Do you mind if we grab a couple of these claws?" asked the sheriff, looking up from his crouch.

"Go ahead," Marsh replied as he began shifting slowly behind the sheriff with his arms crossed, so they didn't think he was going to try anything.

But they had no interest in Marsh, or even Rachel for that matter. The two men were almost giggling as they drew their knives from their sheaths and began to remove one claw from each of its front paws. As they cut away their trophies, Marsh reached where the footprints were, glanced down to be sure, and slowly began sliding his right boot over the offending marks.

After they each had their long claws, they both stood with big grins across their faces and admired the mammoth trophies, which they had earned for doing nothing more than sitting on their horses. But Marsh could care less about their temporary satisfaction, and now, he just wanted them gone.

"You want any more, Sheriff?" asked Marsh, hoping he declined.

"Nah. Me and Billy will make the other boys jealous with these. I've never seen any this big before."

Marsh nodded and smiled in relief as they both stood and began scrabbling their way down the incline with Marsh following.

When they reached the floor of the valley, they were both admiring their treasures as they walked to their horses.

"You need any help getting the carcass down, Anderson?" asked the sheriff as he mounted.

"Nope. I'll drag him out of there with two of my mules. That's what they're good for."

The sheriff laughed and said, "Ain't that the truth."

Then he and Billy wheeled their horses back to the east and trotted away, both of them waving as they departed. Marsh returned their wave then watched until they reached the barn, and once he thought they were gone, turned and headed back up the hill.

But John and Billy didn't leave the valley. After they had ridden a couple of hundred yards, John turned to Billy and said, "We've gotta stop at the house and I need to go in and convince Mrs. McCallister to come with us. I'll tell her I'm going to give her the deed after all. We can't afford to have her around, Billy."

Billy replied, "I was wonderin' about that. You want me to wait outside?"

"No, you head into the barn and start saddling her horse. I'll tell her you'll be going into Missoula to get the deed and I'll escort her straight to her ranch to protect her from Zeke and Steve. I don't want anybody seeing her with me in Missoula."

"What about Anderson? He'll know she went with us."

"If he comes into town asking, we tell him that she wanted to go back to her ranch after I promised her to get rid of Chambers and Bristow. We'll have to take care of him when we get a chance anyway. Right now, that woman in his house is our biggest problem."

"What about Rachel?" Billy asked.

"I'm beginning to think she's dead. I'll explain later," Zeke said as they rode past the back of the house.

Billy rode toward the barn as the sheriff turned to the front of the house, where he reined in and stepped down. He figured he had at least a good twenty minutes before Anderson returned, depending on what he did with the bear.

He stepped up to the house and rapped on the door.

Back in the house, Lillie was an emotional wreck. She'd seen Marsh stick his head in the door and grab his rifle before racing away, then watched out the window and seen him race on horseback out of the barn heading into his valley, followed shortly by the sheriff and his brother.

She assumed that something had happened that made Marsh fear for his life and he was making an escape. When she heard gunfire a few minutes later, she knew someone was dead, and she felt sure that it was Marsh Anderson. Now, she sat wondering what had triggered his sudden flight.

She was already fretting as she stared out the window and spotted the sheriff and his brother trotting by, and began to walk to the front of the house to see if they had gone, but spotted the sheriff walking onto the porch, and heard him knock.

Again, she made the mistake of assuming that because John was a lawman, she was safe, so she smoothed out her dress and stepped to the door and opened it.

John tipped his hat and smiled at her.

Before he could speak, she asked quickly, "Is Marsh all right?"

"Yes, ma'am. He took out a big old grizzly bear up there. The biggest I've ever seen. He gave us each a giant bear claw, too. He's probably up there getting ready to bring it back."

Lillie exhaled and smiled in relief.

John then said, "Mrs. McCallister, I did some thinking while we were riding out there, and I'm pretty sure that if we just release that deed to you, no one will really care much because it's just the right thing to do."

Lillie was genuinely excited to hear the news and asked, "When can we do that? It is Sunday, after all."

"We can do it right now, if you'd like. It's in my office, not with the county courthouse."

"Then can I accompany you back to town? I'll have to saddle my mare."

"I'll have Billy saddle her for you. You might want to grab your things, because after I give you the deed, I'll take you out to your ranch and I'll personally toss Zeke Chambers and Steve

Bristow off the property and threaten them with hanging if they return."

Lillie beamed as she said, "I'll be right back."

She trotted quickly back to her room and began emptying the drawers and tossing the clothes haphazardly into the two bags. She felt like singing as she finished, then picked up the two bags and hustled out of the room to where the sheriff waited. She thought about leaving a note, but there wasn't time and besides she could come back and visit him tomorrow as the owner of the Double M ranch; and as a propertied woman, perhaps make a better impression.

In her trust of the sheriff, and the thrill of getting her ranch back and getting rid of those two men, Lillie had overlooked a large discrepancy in his story. If he gave her the deed, or destroyed it, he would be destroying evidence in a possible murder trial.

She was making the biggest mistake of what would be her shortened life.

———

Marsh reached the bear and in a loud voice said, "Mrs. Shipman? The sheriff and his brother are on their way back to Missoula. I'm Marsh Anderson and this is my valley, so you're safe. You can come out now."

Rachel had watched the sheriff and the deputy removing the bear claws, and had seen Marsh wipe away her footprints as they did, so she wondered whose side he was on. First, he tells her to hide, then he brings the sheriff up to the bear and acts like they're friends. But she really had no other options, especially with her pistol in the little cave, so she had to trust him. She took a deep breath and slowly left her hiding place behind the trees and stumbled down the incline toward Marsh.

Marsh heard her coming and watched for her appearance from between the trees. He hadn't paid that much attention to her appearance while he was frantically trying to get her to go and hide as she had been wearing a wool hat and a heavy coat anyway; but he had seen her bright blue eyes and her height, both of which were remarkable.

Rachel finally emerged from the trees thirty feet away and Marsh, despite having heard how pretty she was, was still taken aback. The dark wool hat she was wearing accentuated her golden hair that surrounded her oval face. She was quite stunning, despite her dress and dirty appearance. He had only been affected this much from seeing a woman once before in his life, and that was when he had first set eyes on Clara and wondered if it was for the same reason.

He found it difficult to speak as she slipped and slid closer, her blue eyes boring into his trying to take a measure of the man and determine if he was friend or foe.

Rachel made her determination quickly, and then almost melted when she saw Marsh looking back at her. It wasn't one of those looks she got from men all the time; it was something else. He wasn't examining her; he was reading her. He was looking into her soul as she was doing the same to him.

Marsh finally spoke, saying, "Mrs. Shipman? I've been hoping to meet you just to hear your side of the stories that are keeping all the biddies in Missoula awake at night."

For all the horror that Rachel had experienced in the last forty-eight hours, including two close brushes with death, hearing such a simple, mildly funny statement released all the built-up tension that had never left her and she smiled.

"I came here because I knew you lived alone, and I thought you could help me. Will you?" she asked.

"Honestly? I want to hear what happened. If I believe you, then I'll help you; but I will tell you before you start talking, that I'm not on friendly terms with any of the Shipman brothers, so that will be in your favor. You can come back with me to my house and tell me."

"You'd let me use your house?" she asked, disbelievingly.

"Why not? I don't think the sheriff will be back anymore. He's made two searches already. If he comes again, I'll demand a warrant."

"I have my things over in a small cave over there," she said as she pointed.

"Let's go retrieve them and then we can go back to the house. Did you want to ride double or walk?"

"I'd rather walk, if that's all right. I'm not saying that I don't trust you, but I want to enjoy just walking through the open without worry of someone seeing me."

"If you didn't trust me, that's understandable. After having lived with the likes of Frank Shipman for more than ten minutes would make you not to want to trust another man for the rest of your life."

Rachel found herself smiling again as they reached the cave.

Marsh reached down and picked up the Webley, released the hammer and said, "A Webley Bulldog. I'm impressed, Mrs. Shipman. It's a good weapon, but you know you didn't have to cock it. You could have just pulled the trigger."

He then offered it to her and she shook her head and said, "No, please. You keep it. I've never fired a gun before."

After slipping the Webley into his jacket pocket, he picked up Rachel's two bags and they began to walk down the hill.

"Mrs. Shipman," he began, but Rachel interrupted him.

"Excuse me, Mister Anderson. Could you please call me Rachel? I don't ever want to be called by that name again."

Marsh grinned and replied, "I can understand that, Rachel. Please call me Marsh."

Rachel asked, "Is that your real name, or is it a shortened version of your Christian name?"

"It's short for Marshall, my mother's maiden name, and you just asked the same question that Lillie McCallister asked earlier today."

Rachel stopped, making Marsh try to stop, but he slid another three feet before his feet stopped moving.

"Is that Bob McCallister's wife?" she asked.

"It is. She's in my house right now and you'll meet her shortly."

Rachel shook her head violently and said, "I can't meet her. She'll try to kill me for what they said I did."

Marsh reached up, took her arm and pulled her back into a stumbling walk next to him.

"No, she won't. She understands what happened was a setup to blackmail her husband."

Rachel stopped again, but they were close to the valley floor and Marsh was able to stop smoothly this time.

"How did you know that? Everyone believes I was having an adulterous affair with him."

Marsh replied, "Not everyone, Rachel. I never believed it, and Lillie readily accepted my theory. It was the only thing that made any sense, but at least I could understand why you might have an affair. I can't even begin to wonder why you would even marry someone like Frank Shipman."

Rachel was going to respond, but bit her lip instead.

She began walking again as Marsh guided them to Sam. When they reached the gelding, Marsh tossed Rachel's bags over his back, patted him on the neck, then he began following as they began to stroll casually toward the house.

Rachel said, "I'll explain my whole situation when I get a chance. I'd rather not have Mrs. McCallister there when I do, if you don't mind. I do believe I owe you an explanation for saving my life and offering me sanctuary."

"That's what dragged me into this; my curiosity in wanting to hear your side of the story."

"Why are you helping me at all? Do you believe I didn't kill Frank?" she asked.

Marsh kept his eyes on the house when he replied, "Oh, no. I'm sure that you did. I'm also reasonably sure you had no choice. I can't see you killing him in cold blood, and knowing how ruthless and cruel all the Shipman brothers are, I'd be shocked if you had just murdered him. It was no different than my shooting that bear. He was just about to kill me, just like Frank was probably just about to kill you for somehow messing up their plans. There is one big difference, though. In my case, I could have avoided going up the hill in the first place, but you didn't have any choice at all; that and the bear had a better character than Frank."

Then he turned to Rachel and said, "Rachel, look me in the eyes and tell me that what I just said is accurate or not."

Rachel was absolutely awed how he had put all the pieces together and, just as she did when she first saw him, she locked her eyes onto his and said, "What you just told me was very accurate."

But she had another question that still bothered her and asked, "Why did you bring the sheriff and his brother up to see the bear? After you told me to hide, I thought you saw them coming, but then you went down and brought them up the hill. Why?"

"It's a man thing, Rachel. They would have come up there to see the grizzly anyway. By asking them to come up and see the bear, I was acting like a regular guy. If I hadn't, it would have been suspicious if I didn't brag about it. But by asking them to come up and see my incredible shot, it cemented my credentials as a normal man to them. When I let each of them have a bear claw, they began to see me as a buddy; someone they could trust. That will come in handy in the future, I think."

She understood most of what Marsh had done, but she didn't know him nearly well enough to trust him completely.

"What are you going to do with the bear?" she asked.

"I'll drag him down to the floor later and make use of the bounty. We'll have bear steaks for dinner."

"I've never had bear meat before," she said.

Marsh smiled and replied, "You will in a few hours. Now, how do you want to handle Mrs. McCallister?"

"I'm so filthy, I'm not sure I want to meet anyone, but I really would like you to be there."

"I'll be there, but I want you to understand that she doesn't blame you at all. She blames her husband and now the Shipman brothers. She was almost raped yesterday afternoon by Zeke Chambers, who rode with the sheriff's posse hunting for you. I happened to ride up to the ranch house and heard the commotion and she didn't want to stay there any longer, so she's staying at the house."

He then looked over at Rachel and added, "But I don't know how long she can stay here, though. She was okay until something made her mad when she was telling the sheriff what had happened. Instead of recognizing him as someone she couldn't trust, if nothing else because he was Frank's brother, she began to ask him repeatedly to give her back the deed to the ranch."

She doesn't know it yet, and I've got to explain it to her, is that she really placed her life in jeopardy by making a fuss about it. Now, she's become a danger to them; and, just to let you know, while the sheriff was explaining why he couldn't give it back to her, he said that until your case is closed, the ranch is technically yours. He said until you're either executed for murder or found dead, the deed has to stay in evidence."

Rachel sighed and replied, "So, this is going to get worse, not better."

"I'm afraid so, and now I'm in it up to my neck, too. Lillie saw to that by telling the sheriff too much and I was there to hear it."

When Marsh and Rachel reached the back of the house, Marsh took her bags from Sam's back and the horse just wandered back into the barn where oats and water awaited.

Marsh led Rachel to the porch and swung the kitchen door wide, letting her enter before he followed with the bags and his Winchester.

"Lillie! I'm back, and we have a visitor!" he shouted, expecting Lillie to come trotting out of her room, smiling.

But the house remained silent and Marsh immediately grew concerned.

"Stay here, Rachel. Something's wrong," Marsh said as he jogged past Rachel and headed for her bedroom.

Once he entered, he saw that the drawers in her dresser drawers were empty, and her bags were missing. His stomach dropped as he was certain that she had gone with the sheriff.

He turned and walked back out to Rachel and said, "She's gone. All of her clothes are gone, too. I'm really worried about her. She made that horrible mistake when she demanded her ranch back and now, she's compounded it by probably going with him. All we can hope is that she left on her own before they returned, as unlikely as that would be. I can't understand why she would trust him."

Rachel asked, "You don't think he'd really kill her, do you?"

Marsh nodded and replied, "He really doesn't have any choice now. She could go to a lawyer or the county judge and tell him what happened, and everything would just explode in his face. He not only would lose his job, he'd probably go to prison with the rest of his brothers along with Zeke Chambers and Steve Bristow."

"Is that why they were hunting for me? They were going to kill me and not arrest me?"

"I'm absolutely convinced that they were. I had guessed that was their goal when I saw the six men in the posse trying to find you and the sheriff didn't use his deputies. That guess was confirmed just a little while ago when they came to search my house again. When the sheriff and I were leaving the back door, Billy Shipman was standing there with his pistol drawn and cocked, ready to shoot whoever came out that door. He was going to kill you, Rachel. They didn't want you to get a chance to talk, but even at that, you were nowhere near the threat to them that Lillie is. She's a good, churchgoing woman that was well respected in the community. Her word would be as good as gold to a prosecutor."

Rachel then added, "As opposed to the testimony of an adulteress and a murderer who'd only lived in Missoula for a few months."

Marsh nodded and said, "Exactly."

"Are you going to go after her?"

Marsh answered, "This is going to sound incredibly harsh, but there's no point now. They're probably almost to Missoula already, if they're going that way; but they probably are going to bypass the town and ride directly to the ranch where there are no witnesses. The trouble is that I don't know where they went and if they do kill her, I won't know where they disposed of the body, and while I'm out searching for her, you'll be here alone and unprotected."

Rachel nodded and took a seat at the kitchen table wondering how it would ever be possible to have a normal life again. Then she had to laugh at herself. *When had she ever had a normal life?* She didn't know what a normal life was.

———

Sheriff John Shipman had indeed bypassed Missoula. With Lillie beside him, he had told Billy to go to the office and retrieve the deed from their safe and to meet them at the Double M ranch house. Billy acknowledged the order and turned toward Missoula to have a few beers.

Lillie had been pleased that Billy was gone because he gave her the creeps the way he kept looking at her.

The sheriff had already laid out his plan to eliminate Lillie. He needed to get her to the ranch, or more specifically, her horse needed to get to the ranch, so if anyone asked, it would look like she'd gone with her husband. Once there, he'd let Zeke Chambers finish what he started and then when Steve had used her, they could bury her somewhere in the pastures that wouldn't be noticed.

As they rode, he glanced over at a smiling Lillie and thought that maybe he'd let Zeke use her after he did, she wasn't a bad-looking woman and she was going to be dead soon anyway.

———

Zeke Chambers and Steve Bristow were sitting having coffee in the ranch house kitchen. They were the only two humans left on the ranch, the other two ranch hands having left the ranch after Zeke had told them of the departure of the McCallisters and that no pay would be coming. But before they'd gone, Whitey Jones had mentioned that he had spotted Mrs. McCallister riding off with a really big man the afternoon before; and that meant Marsh Anderson.

"We shoulda gone out there this morning, Zeke," Steve groused.

"Not yet, I'm tellin' ya. He woulda been expectin' us. He woulda seen us comin' on that damned tower of his," Zeke shot back.

Then he added, "We can go back and get her tomorrow mornin', and we can get that valley of his, too."

"Okay, but I'm not gonna wait much longer."

"You won't hafta…" Zeke began when he heard the front door open and then slam shut.

He and Steve began reaching for their pistols when they heard Sheriff Shipman shout, "Anybody in here? This is Sheriff Shipman and I have Mrs. McCallister with me. This is her ranch now."

The two men looked at each other in total confusion as they heard him say in a normal speaking voice, "Now, Lillie, I want you to understand, there's no sense in screaming. No one will come to save you this time."

They both began to smile and as they walked to the main room then heard Lillie McCallister scream.

———

Marsh let Rachel clean up in the bathroom and change into some clean clothes while he made coffee.

Rachel felt sickened by what she suspected was happening to Lillie McCallister and Marsh's inability to stop it. She partially blamed herself for delaying Marsh's return to the ranch house, but she knew that dwelling on it wouldn't help anything. She felt cleaner, but her hair was still a mess and she really wanted a nice hot bath, something she hadn't experienced in over three months, having to make do with either cold or lukewarm water.

97

Maybe she could have one later. She donned her only other dress and left the bathroom feeling better.

Marsh was at the table sipping his coffee, wondering if there had been something he could have done to help Lillie. If only she hadn't opened the sheriff's eyes to the threat she posed, or at least waited until he returned. Of course, he returned with Rachel, so that would have been worse if the sheriff had been there. He chided himself for not watching the sheriff until he had seen him leave the valley, but he was too anxious to climb the hill to talk to Rachel.

Rachel stepped into the kitchen, saw Marsh in deep thought, and correctly guessed that he was doing the same thing she had been doing; wondering what could have been done differently to prevent Lillie's departure.

Marsh heard Rachel, but only when she was very close, then he stood to get her a cup.

"Have a seat, Rachel, and I'll get you some coffee. Would you like some sugar?" he asked.

Rachel sat down and then looked up, smiled and replied, "Sugar would be nice."

Marsh nodded as he set the cup on the table and filled it with coffee. After setting the coffeepot back on the warming side of the cook stove, he took the sugar bowl and a teaspoon and set them near her coffee cup before sitting down.

As Rachel added a teaspoonful of sugar to her coffee and stirred, Marsh said, "There's nothing to gain by talking about Lillie now. I'm really handcuffed on this one. Even if you weren't here, there would be nothing I could do. I have no idea where she is or what has happened to her, so let's concentrate on your problems and what we can do to keep you safe until we make everything right."

Rachel nodded, although she believed there was nothing he, or anyone else, could do to make things right ever again.

Then she said softly, "I told you I would explain what happened, but to really understand, you need to hear how I came to be here in the first place. When I've finished, if you decide not to help me, I'll understand and not blame you. I'll just need some things and leave."

Marsh wondered what was in her past that would cause her to raise the possibility of leaving, but replied, "Alright. Go ahead."

She began slowly, when she said, "I was raised in St. Ann's orphanage in Denver. After leaving the orphanage when I turned eighteen, they found me a job as a waitress. While there, I met a man named Harry Franklin and married him when I was nineteen. He was a good-looking man who smiled at me, and I thought that was all that mattered. I was wrong, and the marriage turned into a long nightmare."

Almost three years later, he died when he slipped and fell down the stairs in our house, breaking his neck. There was an investigation, and nothing was proven, so they dropped the case and called it accidental. The house had a mortgage, and I wasn't in a very good financial position, so I went back to my job as a waitress. A year later, I married an older man named Walter Pratt, who had four children from a previous marriage; the youngest one was older than I was. The children never liked me and called me a gold-digger, but Walter was a good man and totally different from Harry Franklin."

But just seven weeks after we married, he died of food poisoning, and his children accused me of murdering their father and they began circulating stories that I had murdered my first husband as well. They even had the story printed in the newspaper. There was never any evidence of foul play, but they labeled me as a black widow, and used lawyers to block access to the bank accounts and even put stories in the paper about me."

They had me evicted from the house just two weeks after Walter died. The sheriff was smiling and seemed to be enjoying himself when he came and led me out the door. I did have a little over a hundred dollars that was household expense money that they didn't know about, but they even took all of my clothes, except for what I was wearing, so I had nothing but the hundred dollars."

Rachel was trying to stop from getting emotional, and was losing the battle as she recalled those greedy two sons and two daughters of Walter Pratt. After his death, each one had retained a different lawyer to try to get more from the estate. It was a battle of wills and power after that, and Rachel had neither. The legal battle was at a stalemate even now.

Marsh's eyebrows rose as she spoke, impressed by her honesty, yet somewhat disturbed by the story itself. She was either a multiple murderer or the victim of one set of incredibly bad situations after another. He would reserve judgement until she finished.

Then,he interrupted and asked, "Rachel, your first husband, Harry Franklin. You say it was a nightmare. How was that?"

Rachel looked at him and replied, "He was a gambler. Every spare dime we had he threw away. He'd go out to the gambling house and they'd ply him with liquor and he'd always lose, then he'd come home and take his frustrations out on me. He rarely even paid attention to me as a woman after the first three months. I was surprised he kept his job, really, but his uncle owned the bank where he worked, so I guess blood outweighed the bad character."

Marsh then asked, "Did he fall down accidentally, or did you push him down the stairs?"

He was expecting an angry denial, but instead she said calmly, "Yes, I pushed him. I didn't intend to kill him, but that night, after he had finished punishing me for another bad night at the roulette wheel, I was walking up to my bedroom and just as I reached the top landing, he grabbed me by the skirt and pulled himself close and was inches away from my face. The stench of cheap liquor almost making me ill as he screamed at me; spittle flying over my face."

I told him to leave me alone and he was reaching back with a closed fist when I shoved him away. He fell down the stairs and broke his neck. I suppose I should have been horrified for what I did, but I felt relieved, even though I knew that even if I wasn't punished for killing him, I'd have nothing and no place to go. When the city marshal arrived, I said he was drunk and fell down the stairs. When he asked if I had pushed him, I lied, but he believed me and wrote it that way. The prosecutor interviewed me as well, and I lied to him, too. The lying bothered me more than pushing him down the stairs."

Marsh didn't comment, but simply said, "Okay. You can go on now."

"Where was I? Oh, yes. After Walter died, I lived alone in an apartment for three months, and the money was almost gone when Frank arrived from Missoula. He had placed an ad in *The Rocky Mountain Times* saying he was seeking a wife to return with him to Montana Territory. I went to the address listed and found six other women already there. Frank wasn't the best-looking man I'd ever seen, and frankly, I didn't really like him very much, but I was almost out of money and prospects were slim because I had been so tainted by the black widow rumors. Many men sought my company, but it wasn't for marriage. It was as if I was walking around with a sign on my back reading 'Bed, but do not wed'."

Rachel paused and took a sip of her coffee, then sucked in a deep breath and pressed on.

"When I was interviewed by Frank, I thought it was odd when the first thing he asked was if I had any family in the area and I told him that I was an orphan. When he asked if I'd been married before, I knew he'd never heard the black widow stories, which gave me some hope. When I told him I was a widow, he smiled and offered me the position, which is how he seemed to view it, as opposed to a marriage. I packed up my things, we were married by the justice of the peace in Denver, and we left for Missoula the next day."

Marsh stood, refilled his cup and showed the coffeepot to Rachel, who nodded. He filled her cup and then took a seat again.

Marsh asked, "Why would he go all the way to Denver to find a wife?"

"He said something about there not being a very good selection in Missoula or even Cheyenne, and he wanted a wider choice," she answered.

She continued, saying, "We were technically newlyweds, but the day after we started back, I knew something was wrong when Frank never consummated the marriage, which surprised me, because I could see the lust in his eyes. When we arrived in Missoula he introduced me to his four brothers, and they all eyed me like a slab of bacon. I thought they were planning on assaulting me whenever they were in the mood, but none of them did, including Frank, who never touched me; at least not as a man is supposed to touch a woman."

But after we moved into his small house, Frank began beating me, usually with his heavy belt. He told me that he wanted to make sure I understood my place, and that if I ever disobeyed him, it would be much worse. I was shocked, to be honest. Compared to Frank, even my first husband was a saint. He still never consummated the marriage, for which I was grateful, but confused, as much as he looked at me. I figured out later that they didn't mess with me because they didn't want me to get pregnant and ruin their plans. John was the only one who seemed to have a job, and I thought it was odd that he didn't hire his brothers as deputies."

Marsh interrupted by saying, "The deputies were there before he became the sheriff. I'm sure he would have fired them and hired his brothers if he could, but the current deputies were too popular. He was worried about appearance right after he took the job and after that, he discovered that if they didn't have to wear badges, his brothers do more of the things they enjoyed doing without legal interference."

Rachel was surprised that Marsh knew so much, as Doris made him out to be almost a hermit.

Rachel took another sip and said, "Then, a month ago, Frank and Billy introduced me to Bob McCallister and I thought he was just a casual acquaintance of theirs. But then, Frank invited him to dinner; not once, but three times. I thought it was odd at the time, because Frank never invited anyone else to the house except his brothers, or John Chambers and Steve Bristow, who may have well have been his brothers as well. They were all the same sort. But when Bob was in the house, Frank treated me like a woman and not a bad dog. Bob McCallister was one of those men who pretend not to be looking but made me feel naked in front of him. He was very disturbing to me."

103

Her coffee gone, Rachel held the empty cup in her hands and stared into the ceramic bottom.

"Then, two days ago, Frank told me he wanted to consummate the marriage at two o'clock in the afternoon and when he came home, he wanted me on the bed in my nightdress with it pulled up to my waist leaving me naked and I was to keep my eyes closed while he took me. I thought there was some other reason for the odd demand, but by then, I knew better than to argue."

It was only later that I realized that he had needed me to wear the nightdress to cover my top half because that's where all the bruises and marks were. I had never noticed that he only stuck me and used his belt on my back and chest. So, that's how Bob McCallister found me; humiliated with my eyes closed and my nightdress hiked up above my waist. I guess that he'd been sent a note telling him to come to the bedroom and I'd be waiting, and he needed to be silent while he enjoyed himself."

Throughout the telling, Rachel's eyes had been watering as the images of the events began flashing in her mind. When she reached this part of the story, the tears began to drip onto the table, but Marsh could only listen, knowing he could do nothing to stop her pain.

Rachel took a deep breath again then exhaled and in a shaking voice, said, "He began kissing me and fondling me, and when the front door slammed open, I looked and saw Bob McCallister on top of me. I was shocked and didn't make a sound, as he jumped up in surprise at the loud noise. Then Frank came in brandishing his pistol and calling me a whore and other things, pointed the gun at Bob McCallister and threatened to kill him. Frank then told me to wait as I was, and he'd deal with me when he returned. Bob began to beg him not to kill him, and Frank acted like he had second thoughts after Bob promised to make it worth his while. Frank then told him to get dressed and come out to the kitchen."

I couldn't hear what they were saying, though. I sat on the bed with my nightdress pulled down and my forehead on my bent knees waiting for the further humiliation and the beating that I knew was coming. It wasn't ten minutes later after the kitchen door opened and closed, that I heard him coming and I began to shake when I heard him removing that belt. I thought he was going to whip me again first, but instead, he pulled me to my feet, then ripped off my nightdress and threw me onto the bed and took me like an animal. When he was done, he administered the beating that I had been expecting."

Marsh was torn between wanting to hold Rachel and digging up Frank and killing him again.

Her tears continued to puddle on the tabletop as she placed the cup down and began to wring her hands slowly before continuing, her breathing getting faster with each word.

"That evening, all the brothers came over to meet with Frank in his office. They met there often since I arrived, at least twice a week. I was in the kitchen preparing dinner, and Frank had come in before they arrived and told me to stay there, or else, as he usually did before their meetings, but I felt I had to find out what they were planning on doing to me because I knew I was excess baggage after they had trapped Bob McCallister."

So, this time, after Frank had gone, I snuck into the main room and listened outside the office door. They had been planning this for a while as a simple blackmail scheme, but had been surprised when Bob offered them the ranch, and now, they were planning on using me as a common whore for all of them because my use as a lure was done. I decided then to run away from the house before they could do anything, but I made a mistake. I hadn't noticed that they had stopped talking, by the time I did, I had to run to the kitchen quickly, but one of them must have caught me spying, because when they were all leaving the house, John told Frank to take care of the problem. I was the problem and was about to find out what the 'or else' was that Frank had promised me if I misbehaved."

There was a butcher's knife on the counter that I had been using to make dinner, so when Frank came walking in, snapping his favorite weapon, his thick belt, I knew what I had to do to survive. Normally, he'd hold the buckle in his hands and beat me with the leather, but he had it backwards this time and that heavy buckle was going to be part of the beating that he'd give me. He even told me just how badly it was going to be. He said, 'This is going to be the last beating I'll ever have to give you'. He was going to beat me to death, so I grabbed the knife, and when he was getting ready to take his first strike, I plunged it into his gut."

She stopped talking and took several deep breaths as the vision of the knife sliding into Frank and his horrified eyes bulging in disbelief overwhelmed her senses.

Marsh said quietly, "It's okay, Rachel. You don't have to continue if you don't want to. I've heard enough."

Rachel shook her head violently and replied, "No! I need to finish this! After he fell to the floor and the blood pooled everywhere, I knew that his brothers couldn't let me escape for what I did, and I knew if I left then, they'd see me leaving, so I had to wait until nighttime. I packed some things, waited until it was late, and just walked out into the dark, walking north. I had no place to go and remembered that Doris told me that you lived in a valley to the northwest, so I just walked until I found the wagon tracks leaving the road. I walked past your house and into your valley where I hid. I saw them arrive to search for me yesterday morning and I decided to wait. I didn't know you, so I was afraid that you might just turn me in to the sheriff."

"I don't blame you for not trusting anyone, Rachel. It sounds like you've had a horrible time of it for most of your life, but do you know what would help to make all of your troubles fade away?"

Rachel shook her head and asked, "I really wish there was such a thing."

"There is. What you need is a long, hot bath and let the water soothe your spirit."

Rachel sighed, recognizing her need for just that, and replied, "I have to admit, that does sound wonderful. Do you mind if we heat up the water before dinner?"

Marsh smiled and said, "I have a surprise for you, Rachel. One of the most incredible things you'll ever see, but I won't be able to show it to you until tomorrow. I still need to go and harvest the bear and return the meat and fat right now, and it'll be too late after that."

Rachel's interest was piqued, as well as her curiosity as she asked, "What is the surprise?"

Marsh broke into an expectant smile as he began to tell her of his pond.

"When I bought the valley, I knew there was a big lake at the far western end. I fish there and in the creek that feeds it from the mountains to the west. The same creek then exits on the other side running east all the way out of the valley. I was here over a year before I walked to the southern edge of the lake and saw a pond about two acres in size a few hundred yards south behind some trees. On the southern edge of the pond, I could see some steam rising and was surprised that I hadn't notice it before. There was a hot spring in the corner of the pond, Rachel. I trotted over to the pond and found that the water near the spring was near boiling temperature, but the further I was from the spring, the cooler it was. I picked a spot about twenty feet from the spring, and marked it. Over the next few days, I searched the valley for flat rocks and began to build a patio at the spot and then used my mules and my back to move some large logs around two of the edges to act as benches. I even built a box for the patio and covered it with a slicker for towels and soap. I can't describe what it's like, Rachel. Imagine having a bath that never grows cold. You'll be able to enjoy that soothing warmth as long as you wish. You don't have to wait for the water to get heated and you don't have to let it drain afterwards. In the summer, I bring a bedroll out to the patio with me and after I'm squeaky clean, I'll lay out there and let the sun keep me warm. It's nothing short of heavenly, Rachel."

Rachel had listened with growing interest and watched Marsh's eyes glow with excitement as he described the pond. His enthusiasm was infectious, and she wanted nothing more in this world than to try the waters of the hot spring. Her mind's images of the pond replaced the horrifying images she had just created and brought her into a more peaceful place.

"It does sound fantastic, Marsh. But how do you protect yourself from the wild animals?" she asked.

"Generally, they stay away from the pond because it has a mineral taste to it. The lake, on the other hand, is clear and cold, so they use it instead. The pond doesn't have any fish in it, so the bears ignore it, but I keep my Winchester nearby anyway. Which reminds me. I need to show you how to shoot a gun."

"Is that really necessary, Marsh?" she asked.

"Even if you didn't have those worthless humans after you, it's good to have one with you. Now, the Webley you were carrying wasn't a small caliber pistol like most revolvers you can fit in your pocket. It shoots the same cartridge that I have in my

Colt and in the Winchester '73, so it packs a good wallop for a small gun. It only has five shots as opposed to six in my Colt, but that shouldn't be a problem, but here in my valley, especially when you're on the west end, you'll always want to be armed. In fact, when you ride, you should have a rifle with you, too."

Rachel realized that he was telling her that she could stay, but needed to hear him say it.

"Marsh," she asked softly, "does that mean that I can stay?"

Marsh smiled and replied, "As long as you want to stay, Rachel. If you choose to leave, I'll make sure you have everything you need."

Rachel felt the rush of relief flood her as she took in a long breath and blew it out slowly.

"Thank you, Marsh," she said with a small smile.

"You're welcome, Rachel."

Then she asked, "Marsh, why didn't you ask if I had murdered Walter Pratt? I had just admitted to murdering my first husband and lying about it and then you know I murdered Frank, but you didn't ask about Walter. It also doesn't seem to bother you that I murdered two men and lied about one of them."

Marsh replied, "You cast all doubts about your honesty aside when you admitted to killing your first husband and even admitted to lying about it, which you didn't even have to tell me. Your lies were fully understandable, though. You hadn't intentionally tried to kill him, so you didn't murder him, yet you knew that if you said to the marshal or the prosecutor that you had pushed him, you would have hanged. Ironically, if your first husband had beaten you to death and thrown you down the stairs, they probably wouldn't even have asked him that question. Your killing of Frank was even more blameless. You had the right to protect yourself. So, that's why neither of them bother me."

Then, she asked, "I know why the marshal and the prosecutor chose to believe me, and I need to know if your decision to believe me and help me don't have the same motivation."

Marsh honestly didn't know and with raised eyebrows asked, "Which is?"

Rachel sighed and looked down at her coffee cup replying, "They both saw me as a vulnerable woman with a good figure and a handsome face and thought by being nice to me, I might be inclined to give them my favors."

Marsh asked, "Did they ask?"

"Yes," she answered quietly, not saying whether she gave in or not.

"Have I asked, or even implied such a thing?" Marsh asked.

"No, you haven't, but I wanted to know why you're helping me. Would you help me if I looked like a troll?"

Marsh laughed, "You mean like Miss Featherstone, who teaches at the high school? She does look the part, and has that gruff voice that would be right at home under a stone bridge. I'd like to believe that I would help you even if you were troll-like in appearance, and I'll admit that your good looks make it easier to make that decision, but it is far from my main reason. What they did was wrong, and I want to make it right. It's that simple."

Rachel watched his eyes as he spoke and was sure that he didn't fall in line with the prosecutor or the marshal in Denver, who had had both propositioned her. But in this case, if Marsh had asked, she would have acquiesced. She had pushed away the attempts of the marshal and the prosecutor, but she couldn't afford to push away Marsh Anderson. She was too close to being killed.

"Thank you, Marsh. And to answer your unasked question, neither the marshal nor the prosecutor fulfilled their fantasies."

"I wasn't going to ask, Rachel."

Then Marsh put his hands behind his neck and leaned back in the chair, balancing it on its back legs.

"Rachel, there's something that you did that amazed me. How did you manage to elude capture? Most people on the run would just panic and run away, leaving an easy trail, but those six men in the posse spent a day looking for you and hadn't a clue where you were."

Rachel replied, "Before I left, I took three pairs of Frank's heavy woolen socks and put them all until I had thick pads on my feet, and just left in the darkness and walked north. When I saw your wagon tracks in the moonlight, I knew that's where I needed to go, but stayed on the opposite side and walked here, but never stayed very close to the tracks."

Marsh shook his head and smiled. "That was brilliant, Rachel. How did you come up with it?"

Rachel laughed lightly, and answered, "It just seemed like the thing to do."

"Rachel, I need to go back and harvest that grizzly. Will you be all right in the house by yourself? I want you to lock both doors after I'm gone, but I don't think the sheriff will be back anymore, so you'll be safe. Can you do that?"

"I'm a lot better now, Marsh. I feel like a horrible weight has been lifted from me. I'll never be able to thank you enough."

"You just stay safe and I'll be back in a few hours. I'd invite you to come along, but I think you'd rather stay here."

Rachel nodded and replied, "I would. I'll make some fresh coffee for when you return."

Mark said, "That'll be good. I'll be gone about two or three hours, and we'll have bear steak for dinner."

He smiled at Rachel, turned and left the kitchen, taking his Winchester as he walked out the door.

Rachel stood herself and walked slowly to the windows and watched as Marsh entered the barn, then returned to the table picked up her empty coffee cup and refilled it before going back to her spot in front of the glass windows and continued to watch the barn and sip her coffee.

Marsh Anderson was a fascinating man, and easily the best man she had ever met. She had certainly noticed the effect he had on her when he first looked into her eyes, but it was his manner and gentle way with her that made her trust him with her life.

Marsh hitched up Wilbur and Claude to his wagon, stepped onto the seat, snapped the reins, then drove the wagon down his valley to harvest the grizzly.

———

Sheriff Shipman had Zeke Chambers and Steve Bristow dig a grave for Lillie's body in the remuda corral, where the ground was already churned up and new dirt wouldn't look out of place. It took them over an hour to dig the deep hole and dump her body into it. After filling the hole and packing it down as hard as they could, they spread the remaining dirt around. By tomorrow, no one would see the difference in dirt color.

The job done, John told them, "I want you two to go into Missoula and stay there. I want folks to see you for a good alibi. If anyone asks, you tell them you never saw Mrs. McCallister. Our only problem now is Anderson."

Zeke said, "John, me and Steve were already talkin' about that. Now, we know he's got that tower of his, but if we ride out there tomorrow morning and stay on the road, passing that cutoff of his, but then swing around and come in from a different direction and just watch the tower, he won't see us comin'. We can split up, so Steve will have his Winchester aimed at the front door and I'll just mosey up to the door like I wanna talk to him. I knock and step back a bit. Then, when he comes out, I'll smile and tell him that Lillie wants to see him. He won't know she's dead, so he'll wanna talk. Then Steve will be able to take a shot and we get his stuff."

John scratched his neck and thought about it. Zeke had surprised him. It sounded like a good plan and with Anderson gone, no one would know that Lillie hadn't gone with her husband.

He nodded and smiled as he replied, "You know, Zeke, that's a good plan. He's alone now and hasn't got any reason to expect visitors anyway. You go ahead. When you're done, come to my office and we'll figure out what we'll do after that."

Zeke smiled, winked at Steve, then said, "Okay, John. We'll see you tomorrow."

John grinned back. Loose ends were beginning to disappear. With Anderson gone, there would only be three left. Rachel, who he was convinced was dead, Zeke Chambers and Steve Bristow. He and his brothers would eliminate the other male loose ends after they killed Anderson.

———

It took Marsh almost two hours to slide the bear down the hill and dress it. The moving wasn't hard, as he was assisted by gravity, but the enormous size of the bear took a long time for him to carve out the meat, separate the fat and then skin the animal. He still left a lot of food out for the scavengers before he had the wagon loaded. The furry hide was spectacular and after it had been scraped and treated, would make a fine rug.

After he returned to the yard, he started his smokehouse fires and began hanging most of the meat on the hooks inside, saving some nice steaks for eating over the next two or three days. He cut out the fat, making sure there was no meat included and tossed them all into a large iron pot nearby for rendering into bear fat, which he used for many things, including taking care of his saddles and other leather items, and even for cooking.

By the time he was finished, he knew that more than three hours had passed, and the sun was low in the sky. He walked to the house with the bear steaks and his Winchester, and had to tap on the door with his toe to let Rachel know he was there.

Rachel was expecting him and opened the door quickly and added a big smile as a welcome, which was appreciated.

"I brought dinner," he said as he stepped into the kitchen.

"Those are enormous steaks," Rachel said.

"I like bear meat, but this is my first grizzly bear. I've had brown bear, and a grizzly is really just a giant brown bear, so we'll see how the meat tastes."

Marsh laid the meat on the counter , pulled a sheet of butcher paper from a cabinet and began to wrap each steak until there were only two left. He put the others into the cold room before returning to the kitchen.

"I'll cook it if you'll tell me how, Marsh," Rachel offered.

"It cooks just like a regular steak. I'll get some potatoes and onions."

An hour later, Rachel was in heaven eating a nice, hot meal and the steaks were every bit as good as Marsh had said they'd be.

"After dinner, Rachel, I'll show you how to hold and use a pistol and a Winchester. Tomorrow we can do some target practice. I have a range set up behind the cabin."

"Okay. I've got to tell you, Marsh, this is really good meat," she said.

"You cooked it much better than I do. I tend to have them turned to charcoal on the outside and still bright red on the inside."

She smiled and replied, "It's not difficult, but I'm glad I was able to be useful. It seems like you're doing all the work."

Marsh took a big bite of steak, chewed and then swallowed, before saying, "Do you want to know the truth? Since I finished the house almost two years ago, I don't feel like I'm doing enough work. I always feel like I've got to do something."

Rachel smiled and said, "I for one, am very grateful that you decided to go after the bear. You'll never know the feeling of incredible relief I felt when I heard your voice and watched as the bear dropped and turned toward you."

Marsh looked at Rachel and said, "Rachel, when I saw the bear, I didn't know you were in that small cave. When I first spotted you walking toward me, I was shocked. I then knew you had been there and the bear was coming at you. When I found the Webley with its hammer cocked, I understood that you must have been in that hole in the rock with your pistol ready to fire, but you didn't."

I'm guessing that you were aware that the sheriff was nearby, and the pistol's report would let him know you were there. You held off firing, Rachel. When I saw the revolver, I knew how much courage you had shown to face that bear and not fire. Every other person I've ever met, man or woman, would have panicked and pulled the trigger, but you didn't. You are a very brave woman, Rachel."

Rachel glowed from his praise inside, but said, "I was scared to death, Marsh. I was going to die one way or the other. I was even thinking about ending my own life rather than feeling the bear ripping at me, but when I watched as you held your fire until the bear was only twenty feet away it astonished me. That was the most courageous thing I'd ever seen."

Marsh laughed and replied, "If you don't think I was a small fraction of a second away from wetting my britches, you'd be wrong. I was terrified, Rachel. Let's let it go and say that we're both lucky we didn't have to change our underwear."

Rachel laughed, enjoying the sound that hadn't escaped her lips in a long time. She was already getting very comfortable with Marsh Anderson, and was beginning to think that if anyone could make her problems go away, it would be him.

After cleanup, they stayed in the kitchen drinking coffee while Marsh began her firearms instruction. She was sitting close to Marsh as he demonstrated loading and firing of the Webley, and then one of his Winchester '73s. She eventually graduated to dry firing in the kitchen with Marsh showing her how to hold both the pistol and the rifle. She practiced levering the Winchester and began to feel better about using the guns tomorrow.

As he had been showing her how to stand with her legs spread apart to make a more secure platform, they had been very close, and Rachel had felt her pulse rise as Marsh had to touch her arms or hands.

Marsh had actually tried to avoid contact as much as possible. If he had been worried about how Lillie might have caused him some physical difficulties, Rachel was much worse because not only was she beautiful with a voluptuous figure, he had been very attracted to her from that first look into her eyes. It was even beyond what he had felt when he met Clara.

Rachel had the power to consume him, and he needed to avoid letting his feelings show or to let her think that he saw her that way. After listening to her tell about her life, he thought any suggestion along romantic lines would put him in the same category as the Shipman brothers. Then after she had told him her problems with the marshal and prosecutor in Denver, those concerns were magnified.

But after the weapons were returned to their room, Marsh and Rachel went into the main room, where Marsh started a fire in the fireplace rather than the heating stove. Rachel had handed him logs, and when he sat on the couch facing the fireplace, she sat next to him rather than on a chair, which had surprised him.

Marsh was finding himself a bit awkward when sitting so close to Rachel; but was surprised when he realized that she seemed more relaxed by being close to him.

Rachel asked, "What was it like growing up with your family?"

Instead of giving Rachel the standard answer that he had give Lillie and others, he felt that he wanted her to know him better.

"Like most, I suppose. I was the youngest of three brothers, and all of us were expected to work for my father's construction company. Because I was the youngest, I wasn't going to be important to the business, so I was allowed to go out and work with the construction crews and I loved that. My oldest brother, Sean, was a natural at business, but after he died in a kiln explosion, Nate, was put in charge. He wasn't nearly as good as Sean, but he did okay. Nate was crushed by a runaway wagon, and I assumed his duties, and my father was actually surprised that I did well. He'd really never paid too much attention to me, but now, as his only son, he treated me like I was made of glass, which kind of irritated me. When he died, I took over and I already told you the rest."

Rachel asked, "What about your mother? You haven't talked about her."

Marsh shifted slightly so he could see Rachel better, then replied, "I never really knew my mother. She died when I was four giving birth to my sister, who died just three days later. I only remember that she had blonde hair, much like yours, and blue eyes. I was the only one of the boys to have her eyes, and light brown hair. Her name was Catherine Anne."

"So, you grew up without a woman in the house?" Rachel asked.

"No, although I wish I had. My father remarried when I was five to a woman name Ida Hoover. She was younger than my father by ten years or so, and I'll give her credit for being pretty, but she was a stern taskmaster who laid down the law. Because my brothers were older and knew our mother better, they rebelled much more than I did. There were some real screaming battles between Ida and my brothers, but only when my father was at the office. Ida lasted six years before she finally had enough of the fights and set down an ultimatum to my father. Either his sons behaved, or she'd leave. I believe my father had long regretted marrying Ida, so he told her that his sons were more important, and Ida just left. She had access to the family bank account, and took some of the money, but not enough for my father to care. So, that was the end of womanly influence in the house. We had a cook and a cleaning woman, but no more mothers."

"What was your father like?"

"I never spent too much time with him when I was young, as he devoted most of his time to work and my older brothers. I spent more time with Vince Cirillo, who was a foreman of one of our crews back then, even though he was only six years older than I was. He impressed me a lot, which is why I made him manager when I took over the company. We didn't have one before that. My father was one of those dominant men that seem to always expect other men to follow his orders immediately, and hadn't wanted an intermediary. Of course, I only knew him when he had his own company, so he might have been less overbearing when be was younger. He showered most of his attention on Sean, which was natural, really. I didn't mind because I could do what I wanted to do."

He wasn't a very big man, about five feet and eight inches. Neither were my brothers for that matter. Why I'm so big, no one had any idea. I guess I'm lucky I didn't have red hair, or my mother's fidelity might have been called into question. He did have a big head and it looked larger because of his huge crop of hair and whiskers that just about covered every inch of his face. He had these enormous eyebrows, too. I suppose, though, except his ownership of a company, he was like most fathers."

Then Marsh asked, "Rachel, how did you wind up in the orphanage?"

She shrugged and replied, "I don't know. I was left there as a baby. It was all I ever knew."

"How bad was it?"

"You know, if it's what you grow up with, it never seems that bad. Looking back, I know the food wasn't very good, the rooms were cold in the winter and hot in the summer and there were always other girls who would bully the others; but it was all I knew, so it wasn't so bad. In fact, I didn't want to leave because I was so afraid of living on my own and having to provide for myself. They got me the waitressing job and that wasn't much fun. I had my behind pinched so many times each day that when I got to my room each night, I wasn't sure which ached more, my feet or my behind."

Marsh laughed and said, "I can understand how that would happen, though."

Rachel leaned back and grinned, replying, "Oh? You do, do you?"

"Sure. Walking around all day, carrying things back and forth. I imagine your feet would be miserable by the time you finished your day," Marsh replied with a straight face.

Rachel glanced at him, then laughed. She hadn't had a normal conversation like this in a long time, and the return to typical human behavior was welcomed with relish.

"Where did you meet your first husband?" Marsh asked.

Rachel replied, "It was at the café. As soon as I began working there, I received almost as many proposals as I did pinches. Most of the men were either joking, old, or simply thuggish. Harry Franklin was none of those things. He was well-dressed, in his early twenties, and quite good-looking. He began coming to the café more and more and asked if he could call on me."

I was young and inexperienced, and so flattered and impressed that I jumped at the chance. He told me how his father was the president of the bank and he'd be taking over soon. After we were married, I found out that his uncle owned the bank, and even then, he was just a clerk at the bank. I was shocked at the lie and wondered why he hadn't progressed higher as his uncle was the boss. He made decent money, but then, he bought a house with a mortgage that put us in a bind financially. So, I went back to being a waitress, still wondering why he was a clerk and not getting enough money. It became a nightmare after three months when money became a bigger problem because he was gambling so often and drinking. He blamed me for his problems and began to knock me around. That went on for almost three years until he fell down those stairs. Even though I wasn't prosecuted for his death, after Walter's death, it was easy to blame me, which was how his children's lawyers were able to kick me out with nothing."

Marsh then asked, "But you didn't have any children?"

Rachel lips tightened as she answered, "No. I think Harry did all he could to avoid having children while adding to our financial difficulties and Walter had difficulty in consummating the marriage."

"I'm sorry, Rachel, I didn't mean to get so personal."

Rachel said, "No, it's all right. I'm placing a terrible burden on you and you should understand things that you might wonder about."

Marsh shook his head, and said, "You haven't had much luck in life, have you?"

Rachel replied, "No worse than other women that I've met, although I'll admit that these past few months have been worse than most."

"Things will be better now, Rachel. I'll make sure of that," Marsh said letting his eyes drift into hers.

She smiled and said, "I know they will, Marsh. Thank you."

There was a ten second pause and Marsh felt himself beginning to lose control, so he suddenly sat back.

Then he said, "I suppose we need to get some sleep. Tomorrow, you'll be doing some target practice and after lunch, I'll introduce you to the pond."

Rachel nodded, a bit surprised by his sudden shift away from her.

"That's probably a good idea. Are you going to sleep in your own room tonight?" she asked.

Marsh replied, "No, I'll be sleeping in the cabin like I did last night."

Rachel bit her lip and then said, "Marsh, I'd feel safer if you were in the house. I don't mind having you nearby."

Marsh was amazed at her request, so similar to Lillie's, and was going to object, but he didn't feel the same danger he had felt with Lillie, so he said, "Alright. I'll sleep in my room tonight. If you have any problems, just knock on my door."

Rachel smiled and said, "Thank you, Marsh."

Marsh stood and waited for Rachel.

Rachel slid from the couch and walked to the bedroom where Marsh had dropped her things, closing the door behind her.

Marsh stood, then began blowing out the lamps in the main room. When the only light in the room was from the fireplace, he headed for the hallway. It had been a close call for him. Having Rachel that close for so long and just talking was a test of willpower. He just didn't know how much longer he could hold out and thought maybe he should take a plunge in the frigid waters of the lake or the stream.

He finished extinguishing all the lamps and entered his bedroom, closed the door and stripped down to his pants before laying above the covers and locking his hands behind his head to think about everything. Normally, he wouldn't have stopped at the pants, but in case Rachel needed something quickly, he didn't want to shock her.

As Rachel lay on her bed in her nightdress, she wasn't thinking about Marsh so much as something he had asked her. When he had asked her about children, she had told him everything, but now, she began thinking about something else. Frank had taken her just two days ago. *What if he had impregnated her?* She absentmindedly slid her hands to her lower belly and prayed that it wasn't true. The thought of having that monster's baby repulsed her more than the memory of killing him. It was with that worry plaguing her mind that she drifted off to sleep.

Marsh didn't sleep at all. Aside from the mental anguish of knowing Rachel was sleeping just fifteen feet away, there was the overriding concern of how he could protect her when they found out she was with him; as they would sooner or later.

————

Rachel was back on the hill with the grizzly, but it wasn't a grizzly bear, it was a giant Frank with sharp teeth and giant claws instead of fingernails. She knew he was going to kill her this time and kept backing up into the small cave. She began reaching for her gun, hoping it would stop him, but when she reached into her pocket, all she had was a knife.

Frank was getting closer, and had blood dribbling from his teeth.

"I'm gonna make you pay for what you done to me, Rachel," he snarled in a deep, grinding voice.

"I'll kill you again if you come near me!" she shouted brandishing the knife.

Frank tilted his head back and emitted a howl, followed by a maniacal laugh before returning his stare with his black, lifeless eyes.

"You can't kill me again, you bitch. But I can leave you with my spawn to curse you for the rest of your days."

He ripped open his bloody shirt with his clawed fingers, exposing a giant hole in his gut that gushed a seemingly endless supply of blood.

Rachel dropped the knife and covered her face to hide her eyes from the sight as she heard his heavy feet claw the ground to get to her. She could feel his hot breath against her hands and the hot, horrible stench of death reach her nostrils as he began to pull at her clothes. Unable to contain her despair and anguish, she finally screamed.

Marsh was out of his bed like a shot and raced to her bedroom even as Rachel sat up with her eyes wide yet still screaming. He quickly sat on her bed and wrapped her in his arms. She held onto Marsh tightly as she shook with the memories of the still real nightmare bubbling in her mind.

"It's all right, Rachel. I'm here now. You're safe. Nothing bad is going to happen," he said quickly.

Rachel was still shaking violently as the images still clung to her awakened mind. She continued to shiver for three minutes as Marsh slid his hand over her head to try to calm her.

Still trembling, Rachel stammered, "It was Frank. He was the bear and he was bleeding. He was going to kill me! He was going to take me again and make me carry his evil spawn!"

Marsh continued to stroke her hair as he said, "No one is going to kill you, Rachel. That was just a wild concoction your mind put together. You're safe now."

It was another minute before the horror of the Frank-bear began sliding from her mind as it was replaced with the very real touch of Marsh holding her and his hand on her hair. She realized that she was holding onto his naked chest, and let his masculinity take her away from that place where the inhuman Frank-bear had been.

Marsh felt her relax and pulled his arms away, but she continued to keep her grip.

"It's okay now, Rachel. You'll be all right," he said softly.

Rachel sighed and released him.

"I'm sorry, Marsh. It was such a horrible nightmare. Thank you for coming."

Marsh smiled and touched her face gently with his fingertips.

"I couldn't just let you scream, Rachel. It will be better now. You need your sleep. Just try to think of something pleasant, but I'll be close if you need me."

Rachel nodded and slowly lowered herself back to the pillow. They looked at each other for a few seconds, then Marsh stood and left her room, not bothering to close the door.

Neither could find sleep for a long time, but eventually they both nodded off and Rachel used her recent, and now most pleasant memories of Marsh to ward off any more visits by Frank, or any other denizen of the dream world. But before she finally found peaceful sleep, Rachel had already concluded that she would ask Marsh for a favor that might destroy the growing sense of peace she had living in the house with him.

CHAPTER 3

Marsh was up early and fixing breakfast when Rachel passed by floating a quick 'good morning' as she hurried out to the privy.

When she returned, Marsh asked, "How did the rest of the night go, Rachel?"

She smiled and replied, "It was much better. I had a very nice dream that almost balanced out that horrible nightmare. Thank you for helping me, Marsh. It really made a difference."

"Good. Are you ready for some real shooting this morning?" he asked.

"I am. Either your cooking skills have improved in the last few hours, or you were telling a tall tale about burning steaks," she said with a laugh.

"Just trying to convince you to do all the cooking, Rachel," he said, smiling at her.

Rachel said, "I'll be back after I get cleaned up and dressed. I'll try to be quick."

She didn't wait for a response as she hurried into the bathroom and closed the door.

Marsh almost had let the bacon burn after seeing Rachel in her nightdress. Unlike Lillie, she hadn't done anything to try to impress him, but impress him she did. He had finished the bacon and had just dropped the eggs into the pan when she reappeared. Her hair was still a disaster, but she was smiling as she entered the kitchen, and that was what mattered.

She set the table and then poured the coffee while Marsh slid the cooked eggs from the frypan onto another plate already holding six strips of bacon.

He placed the loaded plate on the table as he and Rachel took their seats.

"After our visit to your pond, I'll pay you back for the long bath by baking some biscuits," Rachel said as she bit the end off a bacon strip.

"And for that, ma'am, you'll earn my undying gratitude. I may be able to cook most things, but my baking skills do need some attention. I can manage biscuits sometimes, but more often than not, they have the taste and texture of a really thick cracker."

Rachel laughed and replied, "Then I'll be happy to take over biscuit-building duties."

Marsh grinned at Rachel and began to eat his eggs.

———

An hour later, they were out behind the cabin with his Winchester '76, a '73, and a shotgun leaned against the back wall of the cabin, a box of .44 cartridges, and her Webley on a shelf that he had built into the back wall for just this purpose.

The weapons were all loaded, and it was time for target practice. He pointed out the targets that were set up at fifty yards and a hundred yards.

"I only practice with the Sharps at five hundred yards, but I know it'll reach more than double that. I've heard of shots being made at almost a mile. I've never tried one, but one of these days, I might."

"Can you see a target that far away?" she asked.

"If it sticks out I can, but today, we'll be shooting much closer."

———

A half a mile away, Zeke Chambers and Steve Bristow were walking their horses to avoid making a dust cloud. They could see the house and cabin with its tall tower, and had been watching it closely in case Anderson climbed up and spotted them. So far, they'd been lucky.

"How close do you want me to be?" asked Steve.

"I'll be at his door, so you'll be off to my right about fifty yards or less. Just keep that Winchester aimed at his front door."

"What if he ain't inside?" Steve asked.

"We haven't seen him yet, so he's gotta be inside. Let's move a bit faster," Zeke replied as he urged his horse to a medium trot.

———

Marsh picked up the Webley from the shelf.

"When you fire the pistol, I don't want you to spend a lot of time trying to aim. It's more important that you grip it securely and keep the barrel steady. Your target will be close, so just point the muzzle at him and squeeze the trigger. The longer we practice, the better you'll be."

Rachel took the pistol, its wood and steel grip feeling more comfortable in her hand than it did when she faced the grizzly. Marsh had shown her how to hold it and discovered she had been doing it all wrong before.

She was about to say something when Marsh gave her a quick "Shhh!", and held his finger in the air.

She listened and heard what had prompted the sudden request for silence. Hooves were smacking the Montana soil somewhere nearby.

Marsh walked to the back of the cabin, picked up his Winchester '76 and cocked the hammer.

He turned to Rachel and said softly, "Rachel, hold on to the pistol, but press your back against the cabin."

She did as she was told and stayed close to the shelf, her heart racing.

Marsh slipped over to the eastern edge of the back wall, took off his Stetson, lowered it carefully to the ground, then stuck his head right to the edge of the cabin and peered through the gap between two of the end logs.

He spotted the two riders and instantly recognized them both. Steve Bristow had his Winchester already out of its scabbard as Zeke Chambers trotted ahead toward his house. Bristow then began angling more to the side of the house.

He was too far away to tell Rachel anything, so he just continued to watch and see what they were going to do. The front door was locked, so they couldn't get into his house that way. They'd have to come around the back if they were planning on going inside quietly, and if they did, he'd have them in his sights.

Marsh was intrigued when Bristow stopped about a hundred yards from the house and stepped down while Chambers continued to the house. Steve Bristow left his horse unhitched and began to walk closer to the house, his rifle aimed at the front. Now, Marsh had an idea what they were planning. It was an assassination, and he didn't need to spend much time to understand why they were trying to kill him. They didn't know about Rachel, so he was definitely the target because of Lillie.

Marsh was losing sight of Bristow as he continued to step closer to the house, so he stepped from behind the cabin and began to walk toward the house, keeping his Winchester leveled.

Zeke Chambers reached the front of the house, dismounted, and hopped onto the front porch. He was smiling as he pounded on the front door and stepped back, waiting for Anderson to open his door.

Marsh had kept walking slowly, revealing more of the front yard as he neared. Then, he spotted Steve Bristow off to the side, in a shooting position with his Winchester aimed at his front door.

Marsh aimed his cocked Winchester at Bristow and shouted, *"What are you doing here, Bristow?"*

Steve was startled by his shout and quickly swung himself and his Winchester toward Marsh, who was waiting for the move, and as soon as Steve began rotating his rifle in his direction, Marsh fired.

Steve had just brought his rifle's sights onto Marsh as the muzzle from Marsh's Winchester exploded with flame and a cloud of gunsmoke, and never had a chance to fire as Marsh's .45 caliber message arrived before the sound did and punched into his chest just to the right of the sternum, blowing into his lung and severing the right subclavian artery before crashing into his sixth thoracic vertebrae. He collapsed to the ground in a twisting motion, dying even as his knees buckled.

Zeke Chambers had heard the shout from his right and was reaching for his Colt when he witnessed Steve turn, take the hit, then die. He had so instinctively reached for his pistol that he failed to release the hammer loop, and after he made one unsuccessful tug, released the annoying small strap and was pulling the weapon free as Marsh rounded the corner, his Winchester leveled with a fresh cartridge already in the breech.

Marsh already expected to find Zeke Chambers at his door, unless he had gone around the other side of the house after watching his friend die, so when he cleared the house and could see the front porch, he quickly was able to bring his Winchester to bear on his new target, who was raising his Colt.

Zeke knew he didn't have much of a chance, but continued to cock his Colt and bring it level, crouching slightly as he did.

Marsh had to stop moving to aim his rifle and as he did, Zeke fired his pistol before it was fully extended. The .44 leapt from his Colt and plowed into the ground at Marsh's right foot, but the ground was hard enough to cause it to ricochet slightly, creasing the outside of Marsh's right boot, throwing off Marsh's attempt at aiming his Winchester as he automatically hopped to his left, even though the bullet had passed.

Zeke couldn't believe his luck as he cocked the hammer to his Colt, rotating the cylinder and bringing a full chamber in line with the barrel. He started to smile as he took aim.

But Marsh's hop hadn't affected his stance, it just had shifted it to the left, so as Zeke was preparing to fire a second shot, Marsh squeezed his trigger at sixty-two feet.

The gunpowder in the .45 caliber cartridge ignited and the bullet accelerated down the rifled barrel, spinning as it gained speed. In just a small fraction of a second, it passed through the light morning air and then found its mark in the center of Zeke Chambers' chest. There was no question of survival when the heavy piece of lead crashed through his breastbone, which was unable to even slow it down significantly as it literally exploded Zeke's heart. While not killing him instantly, it was close. Zeke fell backwards and crashed into the boards of Marsh's front porch, five feet to the left of his front door.

Marsh had no doubt that both men were dead, and his only concern now was Rachel. He needed to get back and tell her that she was safe and still protected.

He began to trot back and when he thought he was close enough, shouted, "Rachel! It's me. It's okay to come out now."

Rachel had been well beyond worried when she heard the first shot, and then there were two more, but she wasn't worried about herself; she was concerned for Marsh. When she heard him shout, she lowered her Webley, placed it back on the shelf, then hugged herself tightly as she began to walk to the edge of the cabin. She was so incredibly relieved, even more than she had been with the killing of the bear the day before.

Marsh was still trotting with his Winchester in his right hand when he spotted Rachel coming around the side of the cabin. On cue, they both broke into broad smiles as Rachel released her self-hug and began to jog toward Marsh.

He almost dropped his rifle as they met, and Rachel wrapped her arms around him. He held her with his left arm while still gripping his rifle.

"Are you all right?" she asked quickly.

"I think so. It was those two that were with the posse two days ago. They must have assumed I was inside, but I don't know if they were sent by the sheriff or came on their own."

Rachel released Marsh and stepped back, looking all over him for blood and didn't find anything wrong.

"Why did you just say that you thought you were okay?" she asked after she completed her inspection.

Marsh looked down at his boot and saw the ripped leather, but no blood.

"I'll have to take my boot off to make sure, but I don't think the bullet hit the ankle. It was a ricochet from Zeke Chambers, who was on the porch trying to get me to walk outside so Bristow could shoot me from the front yard."

"What are we going to do, Marsh?"

"After we get the guns back into the house, I'll get those two loaded onto their horses and take them into Missoula to the sheriff. I'll be able to get a good read on whether he sent them or not."

Rachel's eyes widened before she said quickly, "Marsh, you can't! He'll arrest you for murder!"

Marsh shook his head as he replied, "No, he won't. Both of those men have bullet holes in the front and I shot them on my land as they were trying to shoot me. If he wants to come out and investigate, he'll be able to see the blood on the ground, but I don't think he'll do that. If he sent them, then they failed, and he'll never admit that he knew about them being here. If he didn't send them, he'll be mad that they tried and gummed up the works. After I leave, though, I want you to go into the house and lock the doors, but I don't believe he or his brothers will come out here."

Rachel said, "Okay, but I'll be very nervous while you're gone."

"Nervous is all right. Can you help me with the guns? I'll take care of those two myself."

"I can help, Marsh. I can at least hold the horses steady," she said.

Marsh smiled at her, then said, "Okay Rachel. Let's get the guns in."

They moved the guns and ammunition back into the weapons room. Once that was done, they both left the house through the front door, crossed the porch ignoring the body five feet away and stepped down into the yard.

"Did you want to go and get Bristow's horse while I start loading Zeke onto his horse?" he asked.

"Okay," she replied as she trotted away, passing Steve Bristow's body.

His gelding had wandered another two hundred yards from where he had left it, so Rachel had some distance to go.

Zeke Chambers may have been a thug and a bully, but he wasn't a very large man. After Marsh put his bedroll over his gelding's saddle to protect the leather from the blood, he swung the body over the top and secured it with Chambers' own rope, leaving most of it coiled on the saddle.

He then jogged across the yard to Bristow's body. Rachel was walking his horse back to where Marsh was and didn't seem to be too badly affected by the day's events leaving Marsh to wonder just how much she could take. The amount of stress that she had already experienced was staggering; from the deaths of her first two husbands and the rumors that surrounded them both, then her being used as a pawn to arrange for blackmail, having to kill her third husband in self-defense, the bear attack, and now this. He decided he'd need to do some things to make her feel better; the pond visit among them.

She brought the horse near and held him still while Marsh pulled Steve Bristow's bedroll and tossed it over the saddle then had a bit more trouble with the bigger Bristow, but was able to get him in position as well. After tying him down, he led the horse back toward Zeke's gelding with Rachel walking nearby.

When they reached the house, Marsh said, "Rachel, why don't you go in and have some coffee and relax for a while. I'll get these two into town and I should be back in six hours or so."

Rachel asked, "Did you want to get something to eat first?"

"No, I really want to get moving. I'll go and saddle Sam and get on my way, but I am wondering about why they came out to kill me. They don't know about you being here, so they wanted to kill me. The only reason that makes any sense is something to do with Lillie. She was a big threat to them, and if they did what I believe they did to Lillie, then they'd have to get rid of me because I knew that they'd gone off with Lillie and they couldn't be sure how much she'd told me."

Rachel thought Marsh was going to be in even more danger, but said, "That makes sense, but please be careful. Don't you think you're throwing the gauntlet down by going into town right now?"

Marsh closed one eye and tilted his head, replying, "Maybe; but I think if I play this right, and act like I believe whatever they tell me about Lillie, I can at least make them delay anything. Besides returning with two of their friends like this might give them pause to try anything."

"Please be careful, Marsh," she pleaded once more.

Marsh smiled and said, "I have to be careful, because I still need to show you the pond and try some of your biscuits."

Rachel caught Marsh's eyes and smiled at him before going inside.

Marsh then led both horses to the barn where he saddled Sam and made a trail rope. Five minutes later, he was onto his trail heading for Missoula.

Rachel didn't relax much after she had entered the house. Like Marsh, she wondered if these bad things would ever stop happening around her. She had just started to feel better being alone with Marsh and nothing around to bother them; then suddenly envisioned what would have happened if Marsh hadn't heard their horses, or if they had arrived a little later. She and Marsh would have been shooting his guns at targets, unaware that the two men were there to kill Marsh and would have been overjoyed to kill her as well. *Was it always going to be like this?*

———

Marsh arrived at the outskirts of Missoula just before noon, and residents began to gawk when they spotted him. He acknowledged the ones he knew with a head nod or a slight wave. He wanted them to know he was in town and had two bodies with him. It would start some very necessary rumors. Let the gossip begin to spread about the two men's deaths because everyone knew they associated with the Shipman brothers.

He pulled up in front of the sheriff's office, dismounted from Sam, tied him to the hitchrail, then stepped up onto the boardwalk and went inside the jail, somewhat surprised to see Sheriff John Shipman sitting there talking to both of his deputies. Marsh knew both deputies reasonably well. The older of the two, Chas Robinson was about to say something when Marsh entered and all three of their heads turned toward him.

"Afternoon, Marsh. What can we do for you?", asked Lat Foster, the second deputy.

Marsh then launched into what sounded like an angry tirade as he snapped, "I've got two bodies outside, Zeke Chambers and Steve Bristow. I was out behind my cabin tending my vegetable garden this morning and heard two horses coming in. I had my Winchester nearby after that grizzly incident in case the bear's missus came around, so I grabbed the rifle and cocked it just in case."

I spotted Bristow, who had already dismounted, walking toward my house with his Winchester aimed at the door. I knew that Chambers was around there somewhere, so I shouted to Bristow asking what he was doing. Instead of answering, he swung his rifle at me, and when I saw that Winchester swinging I pulled mine and fired. He hit the ground and I rushed to the front to see where Chambers was, and found him on my porch."

He already had his Colt drawn and as soon as he saw me, he fired. He was low, and the bullet ricocheted off the ground and ripped up my right boot. He was getting ready to fire again when I got him with my Winchester. You can all check their bodies. My bullet holes are in the front. My real question is what the hell they were there for? Now, Sheriff, I know they were with you when your posse arrived the other day looking for Mrs. Shipman, but did you have any idea why the hell they would come back out there and try to kill me?"

John had been listening to Marsh tell his tale and was getting angrier with each word. *How had those two failed?* He was getting tired of dealing with Marsh Anderson.

He let his face reveal his genuine anger, and snarled, "Those lame-brained bastards! I heard them saying how nice your place was. I think that maybe showing them the bear claws made them think they could just take your valley away from you. I'm really sorry, Anderson. They got what they had coming. They don't have any kin, so you can take their horses and anything else they got for the trouble they caused you."

Then he turned to Deputy Robinson and said, "Robinson, go with him to Sweeney's and drop off those two bodies."

"Okay, Sheriff," Chas said as he stood and grabbed his Stetson from a peg.

"Did you need me to write out a statement or something, Sheriff?" Marsh asked.

"No, I know what happened. I'm just glad they didn't kill you," he replied as he shook his head.

"Sheriff, did Lillie McCallister go with you and your brother yesterday? When I returned she was gone."

The sheriff had expected the question the moment Marsh had walked in and replied, "She asked me if I could escort her back to the ranch to get something. She never told me what it was. She was afraid of Zeke, so I went with her. When we got there, Zeke and Steve were gone, so she told me I could go back to Missoula. She didn't get back to your place?"

"No, she didn't. Maybe with those two gone, she felt safe enough to stay there overnight. Maybe I'll swing by on my way back and see if she's okay."

"I'm sure she'll appreciate it," the sheriff said.

Marsh replied, "Alright. Chas and I will bring those two bodies down to Sweeney's and then I'll swing by the ranch after."

With that, Marsh and Chas left the office. Marsh unhitched Sam, then he and Chas started walking eastward to Sweeney's Furniture and Mortuary.

Marsh looked over at Chas and asked, "Does he always call you 'Robinson', Chas?"

Chas nodded and replied, "He always has. Calls Lat by his last name, too. He expects us to always call him 'sheriff' or 'boss'."

"I guess he figures he's better than you both."

Chas grinned and said, "I noticed he called you by your last name, too."

Marsh grinned back at Chas and said, "That's okay. I don't want him to think I'm his buddy or anything. Especially not after that bizarre double search of my house and valley looking for Mrs. Shipman."

Chad's face grew grim as he said, "That still frosts me and Lat something fierce. Why did he go after her with his brothers and those two you've got on your new horses? There were lot of things about that killing that don't add up. No, sir, there's something mighty peculiar about this whole case."

"Can I ask you something, Chas?" he asked.

140

"Sure."

"Now this is between us, and if you can trust Lat, you can tell him, but you've got to understand just how dangerous this is, even to you if the sheriff knows about it. Okay?"

Chas hesitated, and then said, "I'm not sure I want to know about it, then. Me and Lat are in kind of a bad situation here. We work for John, who isn't someone either of us respect, and he has three brothers, every one of them a drygulcher."

Marsh was disappointed, but understood and replied, "Okay. I really do understand, but just to let you know, those two trailing behind us tried to kill me, and in the future, it may come down to me having to shoot each of the Shipman brothers. I'm letting you know because if I have to do it, I don't want to go to jail or hang for doing what is right. Do you understand?"

Chas felt guilty for not hearing what Marsh had to say, but answered, "I do, and I'll make sure that you don't get blamed for anything."

"That's all I could ask for, Chas."

Chas then asked, "Why did you ask about Mrs. McCallister?"

Marsh replied, "Chas, it's all part of what you don't want to know; not yet at least. I can tell you that Bob McCallister ran off and left her yesterday and I caught Zeke Chambers getting ready to rape her. She stayed in my house last night while I slept in my cabin. This morning, after the search and my encounter with the grizzly, she left with the sheriff and Billy. I was just asking how she was."

Chas knew there was a lot more to the story, but as Marsh had said, it was something he didn't want to know yet.

They reached Sweeney's and one of his mortuary assistants helped unload the two bodies. Chas removed their gun belts and handed them to Marsh. They went through their pockets and found a total of $21.75. Marsh told Chas he could keep the cash, which he gratefully accepted.

Marsh waved to Chas as he left to return to the office while Marsh led the horses away from Sweeney's. Not a bad haul, Marsh thought. Two fine horses and saddles, two more Winchester '73s, a Colt Peacemaker and a Smith & Wesson Model 3. He never had one of them before and was tickled to have one now, especially with the way it had been obtained.

He was going to head back, but decided to stop at Hammond & Company. It was the second largest general merchandise store in Missoula. He didn't go there often, mainly because they usually lacked some of the things he could buy at Worden's. But today, he'd go there because it was on Front Street and the sheriff's office was way down on Higgins Avenue near Worden's.

He tied off Sam and walked inside, waved at the clerk behind the counter and headed for the clothing aisle. He didn't want to go overboard, but he approached an older woman clerk who he didn't know.

"Excuse me, ma'am. Could you help me? My sister's coming to visit and won't be bringing many clothes. I was wondering if you could pick out a few dresses and other things she may need. She's fairly tall, about this high," he said holding his hand near his eyes.

He then added, "She'll need a riding outfit, too. Would you believe she's never ridden a horse before?"

The woman, who turned out to be Mrs. Hammond, the wife of the owner, replied, "That is a bit unusual. I hope you take it easy on her."

"I will, ma'am. I can buy the other things she'll need, but clothes are out of my areas of expertise, I'm afraid."

"I'll tell you what. You go ahead and get what else you need, and I'll pick out a few dresses and other things that she may require. Is there a spending limit for how much you'll need?" she asked with raised eyebrows.

Marsh replied, "There's nothing I wouldn't do for my sister, ma'am."

Mrs. Hammond smiled and said, "I'll make sure she has everything she could possibly need."

"Thank you, ma'am."

Marsh hoped she didn't go totally over the edge as she began grabbing things off her shelves while he wandered to the men's section and bought a new pair of boots for himself, and a Stetson for Rachel. Then he walked to the toiletry section and bought scented soaps, a bottle of rose scented shampoo, a new hairbrush and mirror set, two new toothbrushes, some more tooth powder, and six more large towels.

He knew he was taking a risk in announcing that he had a woman at his house, but he knew that Rachel would need more clothes than she had in that one bag.

Mrs. Hammond came up to the counter with an armload of clothing and set them down with a huff.

"That should be all she needs," she said.

Marsh asked, "I know she's only bringing one nightdress, so is there at least one in there?"

Mrs. Hammond smiled, and answered, "Oh, yes. There are two. Is that okay?"

"That's very good, ma'am."

Marsh paid for the order and walked out with two large bags, then hung them over the saddlehorns of the two new horses and was climbing onto Sam when he spotted a shop across the street that he had never visited and tied his gelding's reins back around the hitching post and trotted across the street to L.C. Goodspeed's jewelry store.

Again, he was fortunate that Mister Goodspeed didn't know him.

"Good afternoon, sir. What can I show you today?" he asked.

Marsh looked at the displays and spotted his choice quickly.

"The emerald necklace right there," he replied as he pointed.

"Very good selection, Sir. It's a full caret emerald with a gold chain and mounting. It's not as fancy as some like, but I prefer the simple, elegant designs."

"I'll agree with you, Mister Goodspeed. How much will that set me back?"

"It's fairly expensive. I can let you have this piece for a hundred and fifteen. It would cost quite a bit more back East."

"That's fine. I'll take it," Marsh said as he reached into his pocket.

He'd have stop at the bank soon, but not today. He quickly paid for the necklace, and Mister Goodspeed carefully placed it in a dark green display box. Marsh didn't know if that one was chosen because of the emerald or because it was the color of all his boxes and wasn't about to start a conversation.

He slid the box into his light jacket pocket, shook Mister Goodspeed's hand, then left the shop and jogged back across the street to where Sam waited.

He stepped up on Sam and turned him westward, but turned at the next street so he could ride behind the sheriff's office before leaving Missoula. He didn't want John Shipman spotting him riding out of town with two bags of purchases. He might walk down to Hammond's and ask what he bought. It was a long shot if he did, but Marsh didn't want to take the chance.

He swung north at the road and then turned east on a turnoff trail that led to the Double M. He had no doubt that Lillie was dead, but he wanted to be sure, and he wanted to make it quick in case the sheriff or his brothers decided to catch him as he searched the house and grounds.

He reached the Double M, stepped down in front of the house and walked onto the porch. He knocked on the door just in case he was totally wrong, and Lillie was inside.

After thirty seconds, he went inside and immediately noticed the displacement of two of the chairs at odd angles and as he drew closer, he saw small splatters of blood. His stomach flipped at the evidence of what he was sure was the beating of Lillie McCallister.

He walked through the house and spotted the half empty cup of tea on the table, then walked out the back door of the house. He knew that they would have to bury the body, but not want the grave to be found. So, it would have to be at the far reaches of the ranch or someplace close by that already had torn up ground.

He stepped across the back porch, hopped to the ground and walked to the corral with the remuda. It was a large corral, but there were only eight horses there now, as the others were probably out in the pastures. He also heard some distressed mooing from the barn. He sighed and entered the barn and spent a few minutes milking the cows at least enough to make them more comfortable. He then led them out of the barn and sent them on their way to the herd, hoping they could find a hungry calf or two.

He spotted the saddled mare that Lillie rode to his valley and was going to turn her loose, but decided to bring her along.

Then he walked to the corral, climbed over the rails and dropped inside. He walked among the horses, rubbing their necks and patting their sides as he looked for any signs of a grave, believing that it would be hard to find, but it wasn't. The earth had settled, helped by the hooves of the meandering horses, leaving a depression in the earth.

He removed his Stetson and held it with both hands as he looked at the shallowed ground.

"Lillie, you deserved better than this. You made a mistake, but that shouldn't have had this ending. It was the greed of those Shipman brothers that caused it. I did shoot Zeke Chambers and Steve Bristow, though, and I doubt if you'll be seeing them where you are. I hope you're finally happy now and I'm sorry that I couldn't give you what you wanted, but you understand now, don't you?"

I think I love Rachel, but it's not because she's prettier or younger than you, Lillie. I can't tell you the exact reason, it just is. But now you've found the love that you needed so badly, and

I'm happy for you. I've got to get back to my valley now, so I can protect Rachel. They'll be coming now. That man who calls himself a lawman probably knows that I've figured out what they've done. I have the rest of the day to live in peace with Rachel and then they will come. I hope I don't see you too soon again, Lillie. But when I do, I'll give you a kiss."

He pulled his Stetson back on his head and left the corral, leaving the gate open so the horses could go out to the pastures to care for themselves.

He returned to the house, mounted Sam and turned him and the three trailers due west to his house and to Rachel.

His spoken admission to Lillie of how he felt about her so soon hadn't surprised him, but so his sudden urge to enter the jewelry store had. He initially thought it was just to make Rachel feel better, but when he'd seen the necklace and the wedding bands in a nearby case, he had to admit to himself his real reason for walking into the shop.

The extremely short time he'd come to that conclusion hadn't even been a factor, either. Ironically, it had been the moment she had been honest with him about pushing her first husband down the stairs that had made him realzed that he could never let her go.

———

After Marsh had gone, Rachel spent some time in the kitchen drinking coffee and thinking of what she wanted to ask of Marsh and wondering how long she could delay.

She began to think of herself as little more than a whore if she asked, but knew that the alternative was too horrible to contemplate, and Marsh was the only one who could help her. She had no doubt he would do as she asked, but in asking, could she ever live with herself again, and would he ever respect her?

She sighed and decided to put it off another day at least.

After her coffee was finished, she walked down the hallway into Marsh's bedroom. She was almost startled by the size of his bed, then realized that it was necessary for a man that tall. She shivered and hugged herself again when she remembered him holding her in the darkness of her room, his bare chest pressed against her, then felt a bit weak in the knees and sat on his bed.

Her left hand began stoking the quilt and then she lifted his pillow and slowly pressed it to her face. She didn't know what was coming over her as she let the scent of Marsh flow over her. She had never in her life felt anything close to what she felt for Marsh and she'd only known him for a single day; one, long, eventful day. Yet she already trusted him with her life, and did so gladly. *Would this feeling she had grow or like all her other relationships with men, would it end in disaster?*

She laid down his pillow, swung around and slowly stretched out on his bed, resting her head on the same pillow and letting it caress her. With Marsh heavily on he mind, she closed her eyes to let her hopes and fantasies blend into a sweet symphony of what could be.

————

Marsh saw his house in the distance and smiled, but not because of the house, but because Rachel was there. He found even as he had been riding into Missoula that he missed having her there to talk to him. He had only known her for a day and was sure he loved her. It was just like Clara, only more so. He knew then and he knew now.

He walked Sam into the barn, trailing the three horses. Once inside, he let them all drink while he began stripping them. He took off the two bags first, then went to work on the saddles. After they were all cleared, he brushed them down. All the new horses were very nice animals; the geldings, while not as handsome as Sam, were both a dark brown with black tails and manes. One had two white stockings and a star on his forehead, the other only had a white slash on his forehead. Marsh guessed their ages to be around eight or nine. Lillie's mare, though, was quite handsome. She was about seven and just a bit shorter than the geldings. Her light tan coat was accented by a blonde tail and mane. She had a slash on her forehead and no stockings. He knew who would ride the mare even as he saw her in Lillie's barn.

Once he was satisfied that they were all content, he left them in their stalls, leaving no open stalls for the first time since he built the barn, then picked up the bags and walked toward the house. He was smiling already, hoping that Rachel would be smiling a lot more in a few minutes. He just hoped that he didn't offend her somehow by giving her gifts.

Marsh hopped up onto the front porch, set down the two bags, opened the door, then stepped inside, closed and locked the door, picked up the bags again and walked into the house, expecting to surprise Rachel in the kitchen.

He was passing his bedroom and glanced inside, seeing her feet on the bed, then quickly slowed and turned back into the bedroom, tiptoeing, not wanting to disturb the peacefully sleeping Rachel.

He set both bags down on the floor and was turning to leave when he heard Rachel softly ask, "Marsh?"

Marsh turned and smiled at Rachel who was suddenly embarrassed when she realized where she was.

"I'm sorry, Marsh. I just fell asleep."

Marsh asked, "Do you mind if I sit down? I have some things to show you."

She smiled and replied, "It's your bed, Marsh. Of course, you can sit down. I'll get out of the way."

She slid her legs from the bed and sat up as Marsh sat down next to her.

"I turned in the two bodies to the sheriff who acted as if he was shocked by what they had done. I think he was angrier that they had failed, but before I left Missoula, I thought you could use some more things, so I stopped at Hammond's and picked up a few items," he said as he lifted up the first bag and set it between them.

She smiled as she spotted the Stetson that covered the top of the bag to keep it from getting crushed. She pulled it out and set it on her head and grinned at Marsh, thinking the hat was what he meant.

Marsh then reached over, plucked the hat from her head and said, "That's to protect yourself from the sun and rain, the rest is just because you needed them."

Rachel was still smiling as she turned her eyes from Marsh to the bag, when her smile vanished and her eyes grew wide.

She began pulling out the dresses, admiring each one as they were extracted. Then came the two nightdresses and three camisoles, two riding skirts and two blouses. There were even stockings in the bag. She wanted to kiss him so badly it hurt not to.

When she finally finished emptying the bag, Marsh handed her the second one. Rachel was close to tears when she removed the hairbrush and mirror set, the scented soaps and shampoo. The towels and other things were still in the bag when she set the bag down and looked at Marsh.

"Marsh," she said in a hushed voice, "I can't believe you did this. Why did you buy women's clothing and all these scented soaps and shampoo? Aren't you worried about the word getting out that you have a woman in your house?"

"No, I'm not worried. I bought them just to make you happy, Rachel. It's that simple. You deserve some happiness in your life," he said, ignoring for the moment his deeply held conviction that the Shipman brothers would be visiting tomorrow.

Rachel was speechless and was waiting for something horrible to happen.

Marsh thought she was upset about being given so much and worried about the green box in his jacket pocket.

"Are you all right, Rachel? I haven't upset you, have I?" he asked quietly and with a bit of a grimace on his face.

Rachel shook her head and said, "No, Marsh. I'm happier than I've ever been in my life. It's just that I feel like something bad has to happen from letting it last any longer."

"Nothing bad will happen, at least for a while, Rachel."

Rachel picked up one of the dresses and held it in her hands. It was so nice, she was surprised that Marsh had such good taste, and hadn't seemed to miss anything that she might need.

"You chose very well, Marsh. I'm very impressed," she said, still looking at the dark green dress.

"I confess that I didn't choose any of the clothes. I had Mrs. Hammond choose everything."

It made sense to Rachel, but his lack of knowledge of women's clothing begged another question.

Rachel sighed and asked, "Marsh, why haven't you ever married?"

Marsh dropped his eyes to look at his hands and replied quietly, "I have been married, Rachel. It's the reason I came to my valley four years ago. I've never told anyone about it before, but I want to tell you. I feel that I can tell you anything."

Rachel had been looking at his face before he dropped his eyes, and heard the sorrow in his response to her question and almost regretted asking it.

"I was twenty-three years old and running my own construction company. There were many women who had set their caps for me, probably because I was prosperous, and I'd had dalliances with a few of them, but that's all they were. Then, I met Clara LaPierre at a dance, and the minute I saw her, I was lost. She was twenty-two, rather petite, pretty, and just a joy to be around. I knew almost instantly that I wanted to be with her and without a thought of it being just a dalliance. This was real, and what I had been hoping to find. Two weeks after meeting her, I asked her to marry me. We had a wonderful marriage and I thought everything was going perfectly."

Marsh took a deep breath, closed his eyes, and said, "Then, six months to the day after we were married, she killed herself."

He began to breathe faster and rub his hands on his thighs.

"I found a short note saying she couldn't live with the shame and that she loved me. I didn't know what could have caused so much shame to drive her to take this step, but three days later, I was in our bedroom going through her drawers because I had decided it was time to remove her clothes and donate them to a local church. When I pulled out the last dress, I found an envelope in the bottom. I don't know why she didn't burn it, but she didn't. I assume it was because she wanted to keep the address in case she wanted to reply."

It was a letter from a man named George Hammersmith who lived in Kansas City. He had read about her marriage to me in an old copy of *The Rocky Mountain News* that someone had shown him. He wrote to her that if she didn't send him a thousand dollars he would expose her past life as a prostitute. The letter had been posted four days before she committed suicide. I was devastated, Rachel. If she had only told me. If she had only trusted me, I would have told her it didn't matter and that she would always be my wife and my love, but she didn't. She somehow thought it was too horrible to even think of telling me. She should have trusted me."

Rachel wanted so much to hold him, but she didn't. She just listened and let him continue.

"What made it so much, much worse, was that she had told me three weeks earlier that she was pregnant. I was so happy with the news, Rachel, and so was she. We thought our lives couldn't get any better, then that letter arrived, and she placed her shame above not only our love, but above our baby's life."

He stopped, and Rachel could feel a trembling on the bed from Marsh.

Marsh tried to speak, then quickly closed his mouth, took in a deep breath and let it out slowly.

He finally continued in a shaking voice, "I've never told anyone about this before, Rachel. I've never even spoken her name since she left me the way she did. It was a cowardly thing for her to do, and all it would have taken to avoid it was to talk to me. That was all. A simple confession and I would have forgiven her and let her be happy again."

Rachel asked in a whisper, "So, then you left?"

Marsh was breathing normally now, having finished talking about Clara.

Marsh shook his head slowly, then replied, "Not right away. I took the train to Kansas City and hunted down George Hammersmith. He was easy to find. When I caught up with him, he was in one of his three whore houses that he called gentlemen's clubs. He knew who I was as soon as he saw me because of the picture in *The Rocky Mountain News*."

He didn't know that Clara had killed herself, and he thought I was there to just threaten him. He laughed and told me to get out or his bouncers would throw me out. I almost don't remember what happened after that, but when I walked out of there, he and his two bouncers were bloody messes on the floor. Hammersmith was the worst by far, with two broken arms, a broken leg and a non-working nose above a mouth with eight fewer teeth. I never heard about it because men like him couldn't go to the law. I returned to Denver and threw myself into my work for a while, then left the company in the hands of my manager and came west looking for solace and privacy. I found my valley and spent two years building until I had worked out of my despair and returned to being me again."

Marsh finally lifted his head, exhaled loudly then turned to Rachel with a tight smile across his lips.

"Now you know, Rachel. You haven't been in Missoula long enough to understand that my life living alone out here is one of the great mysteries in the city and the theories run the gamut from an escaped prisoner to a deposed king."

Rachel smiled, placed her hand on his and said, "Oh, I've heard many of the rumors, and most of them were being bandied about by women who wish they could come out here and warm your bed."

Marsh then said, "I know. I didn't tell you that Lillie had already tried, even though she was still married. It was why I slept in the cabin."

He paused briefly before saying, "Rachel, after I left Missoula, I went to her ranch and found where they had buried her. They hadn't cleaned the house, so I know where they did it. I even found a half full cup of tea on the kitchen table. I talked to her where they buried her for a little while and told her that two of them were dead. I apologized for not giving her what she needed to push away her loneliness, but I promised to give her a kiss when I saw her again. Then I tried to explain why I couldn't sleep in the same house with her."

Rachel, like Marsh had believed that Lillie had been murdered, but his discovery of her grave still saddened her.

"Why couldn't you sleep in the same house? Were you afraid of her?" she asked.

"No, not afraid, so much as worried. I haven't been with a woman since Clara, and it's very difficult for me to deny myself what nature demands of me. When I entered the kitchen yesterday, Lillie was wearing her nightdress and it was plain what she was trying to do. Despite her being married for ten years, from what I could tell, she was still a lonely woman and wanted me to help her end that loneliness. I'll be honest, Rachel, if it was just a matter of satisfying her physical urges, I would have probably given in, but for Lillie, she needed much more than that. She needed to be loved, and I wasn't about to give her false hopes that would lead to heartbreak. That's why I was worried."

"But you slept in the house last night," she said quietly.

"I know," he replied simply.

Rachel was so close to asking him her question, but stopped herself.

Marsh though, wanted to let Rachel know the difference between her and Lillie, so he put his right hand in his pocket and gripped the velvet box.

"Rachel, I bought something else for you in Missoula. I wanted you to have something special because I think you are special. When you appeared out of those trees yesterday, and I saw your eyes, I had a feeling that I haven't experienced in over four years, only more intensely. It's why I felt you should know about Clara, and even about Lillie. It's why it's important to me that you understand why I don't worry about being in the same house as you."

Rachel's heart was almost beating its way out of her chest when she barely whispered, "Why?"

Marsh didn't reply, but pulled out the green velvet box and when Rachel's eyes left his to drop to the box, he opened it slowly revealing the emerald necklace which caught a ray of sunlight and the deep green of the stone seemed to glow.

"Marsh!" she softly exclaimed, "It's so incredibly beautiful!"

"Then you don't mind that I bought it for you? I was worried that you might think I was trying to buy your affection or worse."

"No, Marsh, I'm not in the least offended. You keep making me happier every second I'm with you. I know my hair is a mess, but could you put it on for me?" she asked.

"I'd be honored, Rachel," Marsh said as he stood and waited for her to stand and face away from him.

She did and then lifted her tangled golden hair from her neck as Marsh removed the necklace from its case and raised it above her head and slowly lowered it down to her throat and then managed to secure the clasp, despite his enormous hands.

She turned slowly while he was close and finally decided it was time to ask her question.

"Marsh, I'm going to ask you for a favor that could make you angry, and I don't want that, but I have a terrible worry that has been bothering me and only you can make it disappear. I wouldn't want anyone else to help. So, please don't be angry. Okay?"

Marsh replied, "I'm not sure if I could ever be angry with you, Rachel, but go ahead."

Rachel sighed and said, "Last night, you asked me if I had any children, and I told you why I hadn't, but then I realized that Frank had taken me just before I had to kill him, and now I'm scared that I may be carrying his child. If I am, I don't want to grow up hating my own baby. I was going to ask you to make love to me, so I could look at my baby and know it was yours and I could love my child as a mother should. Is that a terrible thing to ask? It makes me sound like a whore, but I don't want to hate my baby."

She closed her eyes and felt the tears begin to wind their way down her cheeks. Asking the question had been more difficult for her than facing the bear, but now that she had asked, it was up to Marsh.

Then she felt his strong arms wrap around her gently, but she needed more; she needed him to tell her that he would help her. She placed her hands on his broad shoulders as she kept her eyes closed and the tears continued to fall.

Marsh slid his lips to be near her ear and whispered, "Rachel, it's far from a terrible thing to ask. What you are asking shows a kind, loving soul that only wants to provide that same love to a newborn child. I will make love to you, Rachel, but it will be just that. I will love you, not just bring you to our bed and release four years of denial. I want you to feel every bit of happiness then and as long as I can give it to you. All I ask is that you always trust me and know that no matter what happens or what has happened, you can always come to me for comfort and love."

Rachel was overcome with a blend of every positive emotion possible; including unbridled joy, complete contentment, and fulfilled peace, and it was all wrapped in bonds of love.

In one short day, Marsh Anderson had taken Rachel from the depths of despair to the peak of happiness. She was absolutely certain now, when she whispered back to him, "I will always trust you, Marsh. Always."

Marsh then leaned down and kissed Rachel gently.

Rachel had never felt anything remotely as passionate as that soft kiss, and pulled herself closer to Marsh and kissed him more deeply.

Marsh wanted Rachel so badly he was already aching when he pulled back slightly, looked at her face and said, "Rachel, I think it's time we both took a bath."

If there was one thing that Marsh could have said to delay what they both wanted so desperately, it was that.

"A bath sounds very nice," she replied in a husky voice that echoed how she felt.

"I'll go and saddle the horses. Don't forget your soap and shampoo," he said as he continued to hold her.

"I won't. Please hurry," she pleaded.

Marsh finally stepped back, said, "I hope I don't forget something, like the saddles."

They exchanged deep smiles before Marsh turned and trotted out of the room, then down the hallway and out of the house.

Rachel wasted no time packing her soap, shampoo, hairbrush and mirror set and the new towels back into the bag and thought about taking off her necklace, but decided to let Marsh have the honor before he took off everything else she was wearing.

She felt so vibrant and full of life as she stepped out of his bedroom; their bedroom, she corrected herself, knowing she would no longer be sleeping alone. She would be kept warm by Marsh and she would be loved by him as often as possible.

She felt like giggling as she left the back door and waited on the porch, looking into the barn. Then, she had an idea, so she left the bag on the porch and trotted over to the cabin and began to climb the tower. She'd stop every few rungs and look around, especially back toward Missoula. When she reached the top, she stepped into the parapet and was thrilled at the panorama before her. She turned slowly looking for anything that could interfere with their plans. Finding nothing, she began to climb down, almost missing one rung and after she caught herself, hoped that the misstep was the only bad thing that could slow down the tidal wave of happiness that flooded her.

Marsh led the new gelding and mare from the barn just as Rachel hopped down from the tower, and was smiling at the sight as she turned, spotted him and broke into a big smile and began jogging toward him. Marsh caught sight of her bag of things on the porch and walked the horses over there just as Rachel arrived.

As he turned he caught Rachel as she almost bowled him over.

"Hello," she said cheerfully as he held her face just three inches from his with her arms around his neck.

"Hello, ma'am. Pleased to make your acquaintance. Could I interest you in a ride on your new mare down to the hot spring pond for a session of cleanliness followed by debauchery, or perhaps the other way around?"

Rachel kissed him as an answer and Marsh pulled her off her feet and felt her softness against him.

Rachel felt his strength and let herself enjoy every moment of being airborne before the kiss ended and she asked quietly, "How fast can those horses go?"

Marsh laughed, set her down, picked up the bag and held her hand as they walked to the two horses.

Rachel saw the horses and turned to Marsh asking, "Where did you get the mare?"

"It was Lillie's. They left it in the barn saddled so I brought her here," he answered, "She's your mare now."

"In that case, let's go take a bath."

Marsh tossed the bag over the gelding's saddle horn and mounted as Rachel hiked her dress up to her hips, exposing her long, shapely legs, then stepped up and swung her leg around the mare's saddle and lowered her skirt as far as it would go, which wasn't far.

Marsh had thoroughly enjoyed the show and Rachel glanced his way to be sure that he had, then they both tapped the horses' flanks and had them up to a fast trot in seconds.

The anticipation of reaching the pond made the three and a half mile ride seem like thirty miles, but they reached it after only twelve minutes of fast riding and arrived on the tree side of the pond.

Marsh stepped down quickly, took the bag, his bedroll, and watched as Rachel repeated her leg exposition in getting down as he tied off the horse on a branch. He was still grinning as he tied off her mare, then took her bedroll from the horse, and they walked the hundred yards to the pond.

Rachel was brimming with anticipation, the original purpose of asking Marsh to make love to her long forgotten. It would serve that purpose, but satisfy her much more deeply held need to be loved.

When they reached the patio, Marsh set her bag down, unraveled the two bedrolls and then turned to an expectant Rachel. Their eyes were locked as he approached and took her gently into his arms.

Rachel intertwined her fingers behind his neck as they shared a passionate kiss that was a precursor to what lay ahead.

Marsh was much more experienced in true lovemaking than Rachel, who had only been the recipient of what was nothing more than rutting, so he wanted this to be special for her, so she could feel much more than passion.

Yet, it was difficult to contain himself with a woman like Rachel. He soon was kissing he neck as she pulled her golden hair aside and held him while she felt the thrill of being treated like a woman and not a pillow. When she felt his touch begin to slide over her, she let her hands wander across his body.

She was in ecstasy already as he began to undress her. Each touch, each kiss told her that he loved her as she began unbuttoning his shirt and soon felt his powerful muscles under her fingers.

Then Marsh began to ask her what she wanted him to do to her, which surprised her at first, and she was hesitatant to tell him what she really wanted; but he told her that this wouldn't be true lovemaking unless he could give her all the pleasure she could wish for.

So, Rachel began talking as he pleasured her, and soon began asking for more and then telling him things that she enjoyed and then asking him what she could do.

Soon, the quiet spring air was shattered by the unlimited sounds of passion after Marsh lowered Rachel to the bedrolls and he was able to do even more to make her cry out in pure pleasure.

Marsh was surprised he had held out as long as he had, but he was so intent on making Rachel happy and fulfilled that he focused on her alone. But after Rachel had begged him to take her several times and then grabbed him by his face and with fire in her eyes, ordered him to make her his, he happily fulfilled her demands and joined with her.

Rachel was so out of control, she didn't know who was shouting those profane words and writhing like a held snake in the afternoon sun but didn't matter. She was somewhere she had never been before and hoped she could stay. Yet even when she thought it was beyond her to feel any more of the total ecstasy, everything exploded, her eyelids fluttered, and she thought she would pass out from the sheer release of overwhelming lust.

As they lay on the bedroll, neither could believe that they had known each other for such a short duration and felt not the least bit of regret as they lay together in the afternoon sun, bathed in sweat.

"Rachel," Marsh said as he felt her heart beating against his chest, "as completely content to be laying here with you, would you care to take a bath in our pond?"

Rachel agreed with the complete contentment part of his question, but admitted to her desire to indulge in the second part as well.

"One more kiss and then we can bathe," she purred.

"Oh, no. No kiss. That would only start us going again. Let's head into the pond and you'll be able to finally get your hair washed."

Rachel laughed softly, still finding her new circumstances simply unbelievable. Then she rolled slightly to her left and they both stood. Rachel held her hair up as Marsh removed her necklace and laid it on the patio, as she bent over, opened her bag and took out a bar of soap and the shampoo while Marsh watched her before he turned, then opened his box and took out his bar of white soap. Rachel placed her shampoo on the water's edge of the patio, and then smiled at Marsh as they joined hands.

Then they slowly began walking into the warm water. With each step, the water rose higher until they were almost to Rachel's neck in the water.

"Marsh, this is amazing!" Rachel exclaimed as she exulted in the water's embrace.

"Want to swap bars of soap?" he asked with a grin.

Rachel didn't reply, but held out her scented soap to Marsh while he gave her his. They walked back toward the shore until they were mostly exposed, and each began to lather the other. Some areas were soaped more than necessary, but cleanliness wasn't the primary purpose in that case.

When they were both completely covered in suds, Marsh turned and tossed her soap onto the patio, and Rachel did the same.

Then, Marsh wrapped his arms around a slippery Rachel and said, "I love you, Rachel. When we can both go into town again, will you marry me?"

Rachel laughed slightly and replied, "This has to be the strangest marriage proposal in the history of mankind, so how could I say no? Marsh, it's been such a short time, but you've made me so happy that I'm waiting to awaken from this dream. I love you so very much."

Marsh kissed her quickly to avoid tasting too much soap, then they returned to the warm water and let the bubbles float away as they immersed themselves completely.

Rachel had to return to retrieve some shampoo while Marsh successfully played the part of voyeur.

After Rachel cleaned her hair, they spent more time in the water, enjoying its warmth and each other.

———

Sheriff John Shipman was talking to his three brothers in Frank's office.

"He's a real problem now. He's got to know what's going on. Maybe not all of it, but enough to start trouble, so we've got to come up with a plan to kill him. He doesn't come into town often enough for us to wait, so we have to get him out there. We have to get out there at night, so he has no chance of spotting us from that damned tower. The question is do we try to do it at night or hit him early in the morning?"

Lou said, "We go out at night and get into position. When he gets up, he's gotta use the privy, so we wait for him to come out and we shoot him then."

John nodded then said, "That's a good idea, Lou. I don't think we need to all go. In fact, I think this is a one-man job. The more of us that are out there, the more likely he'll spot us. Who wants to go?"

Lou quickly spoke up, saying, "I'll go. It was my idea."

Al said, "Lou, you're not that great a shot. I'll do it."

Billy chimed in, saying, "I've been out there more than you two. Let me kill him, John."

John knew why each of them wanted to go. After Anderson died, the shooter would have the first shot at rummaging through his house, but it was Lou's idea, and John thought he should have the job.

"Lou, you go. Get some sleep early and leave around midnight. You need to be in position by the predawn in case he gets up really early."

Lou grinned over his victory and said, "Thanks, John. I'll come back and let you all know he's dead and we can all take what we want from his house."

They all nodded, but Billy and Al were definitely displeased.

————

Marsh and Rachel spend another hour and a half on the bedroll, which necessitated another dip in the pool. Now dressed again, they sat on one of the logs while Rachel brushed the tangles out of her hair. Marsh just watched her with a constant smile on his lips and in his eyes.

"Marsh," she said as she brushed, "this can be addictive."

"Which part can be addictive?" he asked.

Rachel laughed but continued brushing, replying, "Both, of course, but I'll put bathing in the pool a distant second."

Then she asked, "Marsh, how long do we have before they come?"

Without hesitation, he replied, "Tomorrow. Once I asked about Lillie, it was almost like ordering the sheriff to come after me. He'd have to go and talk to his brothers and come up with some type of plan, so I knew we'd have this day for ourselves. It was important to me that you knew that I loved you, Rachel."

She stopped brushing and asked, "Why do you think it happened so quickly, Marsh? Most people court for months after they'd known each other for years. We've managed to squeeze it all into less than two days. I didn't think you'd believe me that I could fall in love with you so quickly, and was concerned that you'd think I was some loose woman after being married three times and then asking you to bed me after knowing me so soon."

"I never thought of you as anything less than an innocent victim of bad situation. As to the almost instant love we share, I have no idea how it works. I knew almost from the first moment I saw you when I looked into your eyes that you were the one woman that I should be with. I just knew, and every minute I've been with you since then has reinforced that belief. When I rode off this morning to Missoula with those two, I missed you as soon as I started riding away. I don't feel complete if you're not near and I never want to be away from you again, Rachel."

"I feel the same way. Do you know why you found me sleeping on your bed? It was because I was there being as close to you as I could after you'd gone. I guess we'll just have to accept that we were meant to be together and hope we can stay that way."

"I think we need to get back and do that target practice that was interrupted while we still have some daylight."

Rachel stood, smiled and said, "And I have some biscuits to bake."

Marsh was laughing as he gathered up their things. He had waited until Rachel had finished brushing her hair before putting her necklace back on, and still felt a rush when she held her hair up and he hung the emerald about her throat. As soon as Rachel lowered her hair, she turned, Marsh held her close, and kissed her tenderly.

"Rachel, I want nothing more than to stay here with you and love you, but it will take all we have to keep our dream alive."

Rachel replied, "And we will do it together, Marsh."

He smiled at Rachel, then they left the patio and walked to their horses.

An hour and a half later, they were back behind the cabin after having a quick meal.

Rachel had her Webley in her hands and had already fired three shots, only one hitting the target, but it had been a good start. She hit the target again with the fourth and fifth shots, missing the two-inch bullseye by only four inches at fifty yards.

"You did really well, Rachel. Now, we'll try the Winchester. I'm going to give you one of the 1873 models. The '76 has a brass plate on the stock, so you can tell easily which one doesn't use the same cartridges as the Webley. It has more of a kick than the '73, so you'd probably be more comfortable with that rifle anyway."

He handed Rachel a '73 and let her take aim at the fifty-yard target first.

Rachel felt steadier with the rifle. Marsh hadn't told her that it was the carbine version and not the longer-barreled rifle, but she had noticed the shorter barrel and asked. That took a few minutes while he explained the reason for the shorter barrel and that if she wanted to impress a man, tell him she was shooting her carbine. She said there was only one man she wanted to impress, and he already knew the difference.

When she fired the carbine, she thought it was very smooth, and hit the target, but barely. Marsh let her lever in a new round and she soon had fired six more at the fifty-yard target, all within nine inches of the bullseye. She asked if she could fire at the hundred-yard target and Marsh told her to go ahead.

Rachel was enjoying herself much more than she thought she would. The Webley was okay, but she found a real affinity for the Winchester. She never missed with her remaining eight shots, so Marsh began handing her new cartridges and watched her reload her carbine.

After firing all fifteen, she set her smoking Winchester against the cabin and asked with a guilty smile, "Marsh, could I try your '76?"

Marsh shook his head, grabbed his '76, with its six inches of additional barrel length and handed it to her.

"Thank you, Mister Anderson," Rachel said with a grin.

"You're welcome, Mrs. Anderson," he replied.

Rachel held the rifle and asked, "Could you say that again, please?"

"You're welcome, Mrs. Anderson. As far as I'm concerned, you are my wife and always will be. I don't need a ceremony, piece of paper or a ring to tell me that. You are my wife in my heart and in my soul, Mrs. Anderson."

"Then thank you for that even more, my husband," Rachel said as she let her eyes smile at him.

Then she turned and faced the hundred-yard target and cocked the '76's hammer. She aimed, held her breath and squeezed the trigger. The more powerful round didn't drop as much as the '73 did, so she was high by six inches. She felt the sharper kick of the rifle as well, and her second shot was dead center.

Rachel found that despite the added jolt from the more powerful '76, she found the accuracy to be worth it. She fired three more rounds, all close to center before lowering the rifle and turning to Marsh.

"This is more accurate than the '73, Marsh. Is it because of the bigger cartridge or the longer barrel?" she asked.

Marsh grinned and replied, "Lordy, what have I turned you into? It's a combination of both. The rifle barrel probably makes the biggest difference, but the added power of the bigger cartridge reduces the drop of the bullet because it leaves the muzzle faster."

"Can you shoot further with this one?"

"You can. It has a graduated sight in back that allows for longer ranges, but if you angle the barrel up enough, you can hit that five-hundred-yard target, but the bullet will have almost no punch left by the time it arrives."

After he'd finished, she asked, as Marsh knew she would, "Can I try it?"

"Be my guest, ma'am."

Rachel grinned again as she turned and took a few steps. For someone who'd never fired a gun before, it should have been totally impossible for her to even do as well as she had, but Rachel, although she had never pulled a trigger before today, had an uncanny ability to almost visualize the trajectory of the bullet; her mind understanding that air and gravity worked against the bullet's forward motion and both wanted to drag it to the ground. She didn't know the math, but had an innate understanding of the physics behind the ballistics.

She levered in a fresh round and held the Winchester straight at the target, then flipped up the graduated sight and used it as a guide as she angled the barrel higher until she felt it was right.

She squeezed the trigger and the gun popped her in her shoulder as it spewed clouds of smoke, a loud report and the bullet.

Marsh had been concentrating on the target, and was stunned to see a small black pinprick appear a second after she had fired. It was at the bottom of the target, but she had definitely hit where she had aimed.

Rachel couldn't see through the rifle's smoke and thought she had missed.

She turned to Marsh, shrugged and said, "At least I tried."

Marsh turned to Rachel, his mouth still agape and said, "Rachel, you didn't miss. You hit the bottom center of the target. If you had raised the barrel another half an inch, you might have hit the bullseye."

Rachel beamed in her triumph, turned to Marsh, then set down the rifle on the shelf and hugged him.

"This was a lot more entertaining than I expected it to be, Marsh. Thank you again."

Marsh kissed her on her forehead and said, "You are the most amazing person I've ever met, Rachel. Let's get these guns back to the house and I'll show you how to clean them. Then you can bake while we talk about what we'll do to welcome the Shipman brothers tomorrow."

They gathered the weapons and returned to the house, where Marsh gave Rachel a quick lesson in cleaning the guns. After she'd gone to the kitchen, Marsh did a complete cleaning and reloading of each weapon before going to talk to Rachel.

He filled the coffeepot and set it on the cook stove while Rachel was kneading the dough.

"How do we get ready for tomorrow, Marsh?" she asked.

"First, we lock up the house, and go to bed right after we clean up. I'll set my pocket watch alarm to three o'clock. It'll still be dark, and I don't want any lights on yet. I'm going to climb up into my tower with my Sharps and one of the '76s. I'll want you to stay in the house with the other '76 and with a '73 at each door and a shotgun at each end of the hallway. You'll have the doors locked. Around six o'clock or so, go ahead and turn on a lamp and make yourself some breakfast. You may not have noticed it while you were in the tower, but there are slits between the middle logs. They're not big enough to be able to shoot through, but you can look through them. I think maybe they learned their lesson about approaching in the daytime. The sheriff would probably know I'm ready for them, too; but they don't know you're here. If you start cooking, they'll see the smoke and think I'm inside. When they make their move, I'll start firing."

"So, I'm just a decoy," she asked, slightly miffed.

"No, you're basically a feint. You'll get their attention and give me a chance to pick off one or two of them. Once they know I'm in the tower, they'll think that I had just started the cookstove before I climbed the tower. They'll concentrate their shots at me, leaving you with a clear shot."

Rachel felt better, not wanting Marsh to do this alone; she wanted to help preserve what they had found.

"Okay, now I understand. I'm sorry for being sulky. I like your plan. Do I have to know anything else?"

"If you have to fire, take the shot and move to a different location. They'll see your smoke and know where you are. Don't cock the hammers to the shotguns until you're convinced they're trying to come into the house. Don't worry about damaging the house, either. I can repair the house, but I don't want to have to repair you. You are more precious than the house, the valley and the rest of this world to me."

Rachel replied, "I'd hug you for that, but my hands are caked in flour."

Rachel slid her tray of biscuits into the oven as Marsh poured her a cup of coffee while she washed her hands, then dried them on the towel near the sink. She took the coffee and after he filled a cup for himself, joined her at the table.

"Tomorrow may end this, Rachel. When they're all gone, you and I will ride into Missoula, we'll tell the whole story to Chas Robinson and get it all cleared up. Then, Mrs. Anderson, you and I will officially be married and then return to our valley."

"What will we do after that?" she asked.

"That's a good question. We don't need any money because my company's still doing well, and I don't want to turn the valley into a ranch. I've been thinking about starting a new construction company in Missoula, but they already have two, so I'll have to come up with something while you lounge around and have our babies."

Rachel reached over and smacked him on the shoulder.

"I'll do no such thing. I'll have our babies, but I won't be lounging around," she said with a smile.

"I know you won't be, but you won't be doing any housework either. I'm not going to have my wife turn herself into a slave. I watch other women work from before sunrise until late at night. They cook, clean, do laundry and take care of the children and never get a break. I'm not going to let you work yourself to the bone, Rachel. I'll hire a cleaning woman and I'll take the laundry into Missoula to Lee's Laundry once a week. If you don't want to cook, I'll hire one. I'll help as much as I can with the children, too. I'll do everything I can to make the rest of your life as happy as I can."

Rachel sighed and took his hand as she said, "I know you will, Marsh. You already have and we're just starting."

"I hope they all come tomorrow, Rachel. I want this whole evil episode done and finished, and I want every single person in Missoula to know just how wonderful you are and not the despicable person they believe."

"I think your decision to marry me will tell them something. You're very admired in the town, you know."

Marsh laughed, then said, "If that's true, then they don't know me very well, Rachel."

"I've been here less than three months, and it seemed that every place I went, someone would bring up Marsh Anderson, and I'll admit that most of them were women, especially Doris over at Worden's. I think I'll make the female population of Missoula jealous and then they'll all break down in tears."

"I doubt it, but I know I'll have every male in town green with envy when I parade down Main Street with you on my arm."

After the biscuits were out and cooling, Marsh and Rachel set about readying the house for defense. He gave her a Winchester '76 that he told her was hers now, then took the Sharps and the other '76 out to the tower, covering them and their spare ammunition with a slicker before returning to the house, where Rachel had already moved two of the '73s near the front and back doors and the two shotguns to their locations at each end of the hallway. She was wearing Chambers' gun belt that Marsh had modified slightly to fit the Webley better, just to get a feel for the gun's presence.

"We're ready now, Rachel. Let's have some dinner and then head off to bed."

Rachel raised her eyebrows and commented, "But not to sleep yet, I hope."

"Bed, yes. Sleep, no," he replied with a grin.

They barely made it through the meal, despite the rushed cooking and eating, and it was during the cleanup that the delays began; but they managed to get the dishes and pans cleaned before taking a long, convuleted trip down the hallway, banging into the side walls as they clutched and groped at each other while they kissed.

They didn't walk into the bedroom as much as fall into it when an expected bump into a wall turned into a controlled fall past the open bedroom door, but they made it to the bed more or less clothed, and began a much longer, more impassioned session of lovemaking now that Marsh's long drought was over and his previous tantrums were down to mere urges again.

Marsh was able to take more time with Rachel, and despite the less exotic surroundings, discovered that the absolute privacy allowed her to express herself as loudly as she wanted, and found that the vocal part of their lovemaking added to the pleasure they each felt.

By the time they finished almost an hour later, Rachel was totally exhausted from releasing so much energy while Marsh laid on his back, breathing heavily as Rachel laid on her right side with her left leg bent across Marsh's hard stomach with her dark golden hair spread across his chest as her head lay on the pillow and his shoulder. She was still almost numb after returning from that ultimate peak of passion and recalled after her first time with Marsh believing that the experience couldn't get any better, and after they had bathed and enjoyed each other the second time, she thought the same thing.

Now, there was this and she didn't bother thinking it couldn't be any better, but thought if she experienced even the least bit more pleasure, she might die. *But what a way to go!*

She didn't move but asked softly, "Marsh, do we have to get dressed now?"

"Not unless you want to put on a nightdress. I'd just as soon slide under the quilts when you start to get chilled. My pocket alarm will wake us in plenty of time to get dressed. We already have our clothes laid out. Sort of. They're spread out flat on the floor."

Rachel snickered as she buried her face into Marsh's neck.

"When I get cold, I'll let you know, but right now, I can't imagine another place I'd rather be."

Marsh kissed her on the top of her head and gave her a gentle squeeze.

They slid under the quilts twenty minutes later and made love once more before falling into a much-needed sleep.

CHAPTER 4

Marsh's alarm was dinging, and he had to blink a few times before he realized what it was, then reached over and pressed the small button to silence the watch.

Rachel was beginning to stir as he kissed her softly then slid out of bed, walked to the dresser and took out some clean underpants, shirt and socks and grabbed his boots and pants before leaving the bedroom. He walked into the kitchen, set his clothes down and walked out the back door still naked, into the crisp, but still dark, morning air. He didn't bother walking all the way to the privy, but stepped to the edge of the porch and relieved himself there. Then he returned to the kitchen, closing the door behind him and began pumping some water into the sink, took a small towel, soaked it, then washed himself quickly. He then pulled on his underpants and socks, followed by his shirt, pants and boots. He wasn't going to wear his hat today. This was going to be a serious day and he needed to present a small target.

He had just pulled on his first boot while sitting at the kitchen table when a naked Rachel scooted past and disappeared out the door. Marsh had to admit, it was one helluva way to start the day.

He had pulled on his second boot and started the cook stove for some coffee by the time she returned. He expected her to run quickly past, but instead, she walked to him, put her arms around his neck and pulled herself up to him, kissing him warmly.

Marsh ran his hands down the length of her curvaceous body and said softly, "I suppose we've got to stop here."

"I just wanted to let you know how much I love you, Marsh."

He ran his fingers through her hair and replied, "I know. I hope you know that I'm rather fond of you, too."

She took a deep breath through her nose and said, "I do. I'll go and get dressed now."

He tapped her on her behind when she began to leave, eliciting a head turn and a big smile from her before she trotted down to the bedroom, Marsh watching her leave in total disbelief that any man could do anything but love such an incredible woman.

He had his gunbelt on and was hastily swallowing a cup of coffee when Rachel returned.

"I'm going to get up there now, Rachel. Wait for my first shot before you do anything, and don't get too close to the windows so they can see you. And don't forget to lock the doors."

"I won't. I'll see you when this is done, Marsh."

Marsh gave her a quick kiss then trotted back to the door and went outside.

Rachel knew the front door was locked, but she walked quickly to the main room to make sure. She belted on her pistol and grabbed her Winchester before returning to the kitchen, locking the door, then poured herself a cup of coffee and began to cook herself some breakfast.

Marsh made it to his tower and despite the darkness, scanned the area for anything that was out of place. He'd been in the parapet enough times at night that he'd be able to see something that didn't belong, but everything looked normal, so he sat on the floor and placed his back against the wall logs waiting for the Shipmans.

Lou had been on the road since three o'clock, having overslept a bit, but only an hour, so he wasn't concerned. He'd still get there before the predawn.

He made the turn to the valley before four and then went cross-country a bit to avoid arriving in Anderson's front yard. He knew where he'd set up for his shot. He'd be in a prone position near the southern side of the barn, which would give him an excellent angle from the back of the house to the privy.

It was still chilly when he set out, and the cool air had penetrated the light jacket he had worn rather than his heavier jacket. He regretted his choice as he began to feel the cold, and his only source of heat was his horse. *It was June, for God's sake!*

Lou rode his horse closer to the barn than he had planned but the place was dark, so he thought he was okay, and it might not have mattered if he was walking his horse on soft turf; but the ground outside of the valley's mouth did have a large amount of rocks, and those rocks would cause loud clicks whenever they made contact with the horseshoes. Lou heard them of course, but didn't think they carried that far.

In the still hours just before dawn, the sound traveled a long way, and Marsh, still sitting peacefully in his parapet and despite his occasional drifting into visions of Rachel, couldn't help hearing the rhythmic sound in the distance, even at a half a mile.

His senses on high alert, Marsh risked putting his head above the four-foot high wall and made a scan of the area, not seeing anything at first. But the steady clicking allowed him to focus at its source and he soon picked up the shadow of a horse and rider.

"That's one," he thought.

Now, he needed to find the others. He guessed they'd be coming from the other directions, so he stayed above the wall watching until the sky began to lighten as the predawn whispered its arrival.

Marsh dropped again to avoid any chance of being seen, and using the viewing slit, kept an eye on the one shadow he had spotted, feeling annoyed with himself for not seeing the others.

Lou thought he was close enough and dismounted, ground-hitched his horse, and pulled his Winchester from its scabbard. He crouched and jogged to the barn and quickly flopped to the ground, extending his Winchester out in front of him. The ground was not only cold, but damp with dew, making Lou even more uncomfortable. He finally rested his head against his right bicep and waited.

Marsh could see Lou plainly and wondered what their plan was. He had gone to the other slits and continued to search for his three brothers, but didn't find one, and it made him nervous. He wanted to know where they were and how many he was going to have to face; he wanted them all, but he had to know where they had positioned themselves. He could use the Sharps for any that stayed away from the house and the Winchester for those that were closer; like the one near the barn, who was probably around a hundred and twenty yards out.

Inside the house, Rachel had finished her breakfast and sat nursing a cup of coffee wondering if they had arrived already, or were on their way. Maybe they weren't going to do anything today at all, which kind of irritated her because it was time that she and Marsh could have spent together.

The sky was getting brighter as the predawn was being pushed into oblivion by the dawn. It was just a few minutes after five when the sun first made its grand entrance, sending its rays across the landscape at almost a right angle, creating long shadows across the yard.

Lou had been almost dozing when the sun arrived, then his left eye caught some of the early morning sun and alerted him to the task at hand. He cursed when he spotted the cookstove smoke and wondered how long Anderson had been awake, but he knew one thing; he hadn't used the privy yet. But there was that other thing that was bothering him about his idea; what if Anderson didn't bother using the privy the first thing in the morning?

All his thoughts of privies reminded him of his own needs, so he looked around, stood and trotted a few feet and relieved himself on the side of the barn.

Marsh watched him and wanted to shoot him as he did it, but still didn't know where the other three were. He had good light now and he still couldn't see any sign of them, and even more noticeable was the absence of any horses, so he finally began to believe that Lou was the only Shipman brother to make the assassination attempt, and decided to wait another ten minutes.

While he waited, he began to work out a plan to take out Lou. He'd be within his rights to shoot him where he was without warning, but he didn't like to think of himself as a drygulcher. As he sat on the floor of the parapet he began to think of a different direction, already tired of this piecemeal design that John Shipman seemed to favor.

He cocked the hammer of his Winchester and looked at Lou Shipman through his slit finding him back in a prone position and focusing his attention on the back door. He hadn't glanced in Marsh's direction since he arrived.

He suddenly stood and aimed at Lou. He could kill him in an instant, but instead just aimed right in front of his Winchester's muzzle and squeezed the trigger.

His Winchester blasted what could have been a killing round into the ground just two feet in front of Lou's nose making a large volcano of dirt explode in his face.

To say Lou Shipman was shocked would be a severe understatement. The quiet morning had lulled him into complacency; as did the absence of movement. When the loud rifle report and the .45 caliber impact arrived, every nerve in his body sent a danger signal to the brain and just about every muscle in his body contracted.

Marsh then shouted, "Lou, you've got ten seconds to drop the rifle and the handgun and then walk to my tower. I'm not going to kill you unless you go for a gun. I'm going to start counting. One…two…three…"

Lou couldn't act fast enough. He stood, tossed his Winchester fifteen feet away, and then began fumbling with his gun belt. Marsh had reached eight by the time he unfastened the buckle and let the gun belt drop to the ground and began to walk toward the tower.

Rachel had been expecting gunfire, but it still startled her when Marsh had taken the shot. Then she heard him shout and wondered what he was doing. She wanted to watch, but remembered Marsh's caution about standing near the windows, so she stayed where she was and watched from her seat at the table.

Lou had his hands high above his head as he walked slowly to the cabin. Marsh had been watching him and when he was more than halfway there, began descending quickly, his hammer loop off his Colt.

Lou had seen him coming down and gave a brief thought of turning and running to get his rifle, but he knew he didn't have a chance of making it, so he continued his walk and stopped when Marsh walked close, his Colt in his hand.

"Alright, Lou, here's why I didn't kill you, even though it would have been within my rights to do it. You tell John that I know about the whole scheme to blackmail Bob McCallister. I talked to Lillie McCallister and she told me that Bob had been set up in this phony adultery blackmail scam. It wasn't hard to figure out, either. Do you know who else I talked to? I talked to Rachel before she died."

She told me that Frank had come to Denver and married her there, and would beat her with his belt. She said how she had heard you all talking about your scheme and Frank was going to kill her, so she stabbed him in self-defense. I wish she had lived to tell the story to the prosecutor, but she had been mauled by that grizzly and there was nothing I could do to help her."

But I'm killing angry now. John killed Lillie McCallister, and he's responsible for Rachel's death. I'm not going to shame her memory with the Shipman name. You tell him this. I'm going to give all the Shipman brothers three days to get out of Missoula and not come back. If you don't, I'll write a few letters that will ensure that you all hang. If you come back here, I'll kill each one of you. I'm going to follow you to your horse and watch you ride back to Missoula with that message."

Lou was shocked by all the facts that he had just been given; obviously told to Anderson by the two women. He slowly nodded and when Marsh told him to start walking, he did, but in a trancelike scuffle.

He eventually reached his horse, mounted, then wheeled back toward the road and trotted away, not looking back for fear of triggering a response.

Marsh watched him leave and after he'd ridden a mile he began to jog to where Lou's Winchester lay on the ground. He had so many now, he might open his own gun shop. He snatched the rifle from the dirt and then angled toward the barn and picked up Lou's gun belt.

Then he began his walk to the house, hoping he had made the right decision. Either they'd come out en masse for a final showdown or they'd slink away; he didn't think there was a third choice. He preferred the showdown because when he'd been telling Lou that Rachel was dead, he had pictured what might have happened if he hadn't reached her in time and the image not only angered him; it had horrified him.

He reached the back steps and just hopped onto the porch and was getting ready to knock when the door sprang open and Rachel shot out of the door and latched onto him. He dropped both guns to the porch floor and held her close.

"What happened, Marsh?" she asked, then continued saying, "I heard the shot and then you shouted to him to drop his weapons."

"I was getting tired of waiting, Rachel. I sent a message to John giving him three days for all the Shipman brothers to leave or I'd have the whole story told and they'd hang. I told Lou that Lillie had told me about the blackmail scheme and that I knew that John had killed her. I also told him that you had told me about what had really happened before you died from being mauled by the grizzly. I didn't want them to know you were alive."

Rachel kept the side of her face pressed against Marsh's chest as she asked, "Why? I don't care if they know or not anymore. I'd like to meet those bastards face-to-face."

Marsh smiled, looked down then turned her face toward him gently and replied, "Because my sweet, sharp-shooting wife, you will be a secret weapon. It they decide to come back with guns blazing, they'll be expecting me to be alone. Once I open fire, they'll start heading toward me. Then, my love, you'll be able to cover my flank."

Rachel smiled back, saying, "Thank you, Marsh. I was worried that you might think I was some delicate creature that would tremble in my boots."

"I know better. Now, the second part of the plan is for the two of us to ride north right now and visit the Kowalski family. They own the next ranch to the north and have a big family, too. They're good folks, and I want to sit with them for a little while and tell them everything as insurance."

"That's a marvelous idea. When do we leave?"

"As soon as possible. It's very possible that as soon as Lou gets back, John will round up the other two brothers and come back for that showdown. Even if they do, it'll take them some time to come up with a plan; so I'll get the horses saddled after I get my rifles down from the tower."

"I'll get changed into a riding skirt and blouse that some wonderful man bought for me."

Marsh had a look of horror on his face when he asked, "You've been cheating on me already?"

Rachel laughed and smacked him again before she turned and headed back while a laughing Marsh trotted back to the tower.

————

Once Lou was out of Marsh's gun range he slowed down and began to think. That shot that Marsh had put into the ground in front of him had shaken him to his core. He had been twenty-four inches from death and it had a profound effect on his mind. He knew he didn't want to return to his valley, but he knew for certain what would happen if he gave Marsh's message to John. He'd want them all to rush back out there and shoot it out and was convinced that he would be the first one killed if that happened. He had to come up with a way out.

He kept his horse at a walk so he could come up with some way of splitting the hair, and by the time he was halfway back he'd come up with a solution. It wasn't the greatest answer, but it was the only one that would let him live. He had three days to leave town, and when he did, he'd leave alone.

————

Marsh and Rachel, who he thought looked spectacular in her blouse and riding skirt topped off with her new Stetson and pistol, only had four miles to ride to reach the Kowalski ranch; the Circle K. Marsh hadn't given Rachel an exact count on the size of the family because he didn't know himself. He knew there were at least eight children, ranging in age from twenty-six to sixteen, but there were also two married sons and one married daughter in that group, so it was a crowded ranch house. Technically it was three ranch houses, but two were more like cottages.

They trotted down the access road and Marsh spotted Mary Kowalski outside beating rugs while one of her daughters beat another one nearby. He waved, and she returned his wave, as did her daughter.

Marsh said to Rachel, "That's Mary Kowalski and one of her three daughters. I don't recall her name."

As they drew closer and Mary and her daughter, Elsa, stopped beating and walked toward them. Rachel was surprised that Marsh didn't remember the daughter's name. She had light blonde hair, blue eyes and a pretty, oval face.

When they were closer, Marsh said, "Good morning, Mary. Do you mind if we step down? I'd like to talk to as many of the family members as I could."

"Of course, you can set, Marsh. Who's your lady friend?" Mary asked.

As they were stepping down, Marsh replied, "This is the very innocent Rachel, who used to be known as a Shipman, but she asked that she not be associated with that name any longer."

Rachel was expecting a hostile reaction and was pleasantly surprised and relieved when Mary Kowalski, smiled and said, "Ah! The adulteress murderer that John Shipman and his hooligan brothers have been searching for. I see that you found her, Marsh."

Marsh grinned at Mary and replied, "I most certainly did find her, Mary. Just as she was about to be eaten by a six-hundred-pound grizzly."

"That must be a tale in itself. Well, please come in and have some lemonade."

Then she turned to Elsa and said, "Elsa, could you go and ring the dinner bell? It's almost time for lunch anyway."

Elsa flashed a big smile at Marsh, then said "Okay, Mama," and trotted to the back of the house.

———

Ten minutes later, Marsh had the floor in front of the nine available Kowalskis as he began by introducing Rachel and explaining how he had found her with the grizzly, which had all the men intrigued as he knew it would. Then he let Rachel tell her story, which she cleaned up a bit for the younger ears, but still had all the women ready to kill anyone with external plumbing by the time she finished.

Then Marsh told them about Lillie McCallister and where she had been buried, about Zeke Chambers and Steve Bristow's attack and then Lou's arrival this morning.

"The reason I stopped by is not to ask for your help. I'm not going to endanger anyone else. I'm telling you this, so the story will get out if they manage to win somehow. I'm going to leave a letter on the floor of my tower with the details of the story that Rachel and I just told you. We've got to return quickly in case they decide to come back right away."

Peter Kowalski, Mary's husband, said, "Marsh, are you sure you can't use any help? Me and my boys can shoot pretty well."

"I appreciate the offer, Peter, but I'd much rather that you stay with your family. I'd never be able to live with myself if anyone in your household was hurt."

"Well, if you change your mind, we'll be here, and you can bet your last dime that we'll spread that story in a few days regardless of the outcome," he said.

Marsh shook Peter's hand and then each of the other male members of the family's hands while accepting kisses from the women, especially Elsa and Anne, who suspected that was all they'd ever get from Marsh after seeing the way he and Rachel looked at each other. The men all shook Rachel's hand as well, and each of the the women hugged her and kissed her on the cheek, too.

———

On the return ride, Rachel had told him how surprised she was when they had greeted her so affably, and then expressed a genuine concern to her before they left.

"Rachel, I'll bet once the story starts circulating, not one in ten people will believe the sordid stories about you. They all know what thugs the Shipman brothers are. John just puts on a good front. Besides, you are an easy person to like, and for me, an easy person to love."

It was a pleasant ride back for Rachel as she trotted her horse alongside her man, exchanging glances every few seconds.

Forty minutes later, they were back in their valley, Marsh had made quick run up his tower, found no one on the road and took the horses into the barn while Rachel had gone into the house to cook something for a late lunch.

———

Lou arrived back in Missoula, hitched up in front of the sheriff's office and walked inside, but John wasn't there, so Chas Robinson asked, "What can I do for you, Lou?"

"Where's my brother?" he asked.

"Beats me. He never tells us where he's going."

Lou was going to ask for a gun belt and pistol to replace the one he lost, but he doubted that they'd give him one. He knew the deputies didn't like any of the brothers, including the sheriff.

He only had seventeen dollars and change on him, but he could afford a used pistol for that much, so he left the jail and headed to the gunsmith to see what he could wrangle.

Thirty minutes later and sixteen dollars lighter in his wallet, Lou wore a used Colt pistol in a used gun belt around his waist. It looked passably like his old rig, so he hoped his brothers wouldn't notice and guessed correctly that John was in Frank's house with Billy and Al, waiting for him to return.

When he walked into the house, he worked up to a big grin and walked confidently to the office.

As soon as he spotted his brothers, he almost shouted, "I got him! I even waited for him to come out of the privy, so he was happy when he died."

John was the first one out of his chair to congratulate Lou and pound him on the back, Billy and Ed soon followed.

The sheriff said, "Well, boys, our troubles are over now. Nobody else knows a thing. I found one of her dresses that she left behind, bought a chicken and cut its throat for some blood. I've let it stay outside for a while and rubbed it up. I even ripped it using that bear claw that Anderson let us take from that grizzly. We just need to wait until I present my bloody dress to the judge, and I won't be wearing it after that."

They all laughed, Lou most of all, then John continued.

"I'll go and visit the judge tomorrow and after he issues the order, I'll register the ranch and we can go about selling it. With all those cattle and as close as it is to the railroad, I'll bet we're looking at over twenty thousand altogether."

They were all smiles until Billy asked, "When can we go out to Anderson's place and start takin' stuff?"

John said, "Whenever you want. I'm gonna be too busy for a while, so I expect you to pick out something good for me."

Billy glanced over at Lou and asked, "Did you go lookin', Lou?"

Lou shook his head and said, "Nope. I wanted to get back here right away. That place gives me the creeps. I figure with Anderson's body out in the open like that, those bears and cougars will be coming out there to have dinner."

That put a damper on Billy and Al's enthusiasm, so Billy said, "Maybe we'll go tomorrow morning and let the critters drag him away."

Al echoed the idea, saying, "Yeah, that sound like a good idea."

Lou's mind was working furiously. His three days had just been whittled down to less than one. He had planned on getting out of town, leaving a note for John telling him what Anderson had said, but now he had to change his plans and change them quickly.

But first, he needed money, and that posed a problem. John was the treasurer of the Shipman clan, and whenever they needed any cash, they'd either see John or take it from someone. With John out of the question, he needed to find a quick source of some greenbacks.

———

"Do you really think they'll leave, Marsh?" asked Rachel.

"I'd be surprised if they did. They'd be wanted murderers, and whether they know it or not, I'd put a price on their heads. I'd put a thousand dollars, dead or alive, on each one of them. They'd never find peace, Rachel. Even not knowing that I'd do that, they'd have to worry that every badge in the territory would be on the lookout for the Shipman brothers. No, they'll be back and this time, they'll give it everything they have."

Rachel exhaled sharply and said, "That's what I suspected. How can we get ready for them?"

"I don't want to be trapped inside, not even in the tower because there is an easy way to defeat a shooter indoors; you use fire. You just need to keep the shooter pinned down, toss some coal oil on whatever you want to burn and set a match to it. Then you just wait for the shooter to run for his life and plug him. I'd rather we make our stand outside; in the valley."

"But what if they burn down your house?"

"Then we build a newer and bigger one for all our children. Houses, cabins or any other structures aren't important; but you are. Now there are lots of good, defensible positions in the valley, but I'd rather set up closer to the lake where we'll have plenty of water. We bring the horses and mules down there along with a lot of food. I have a tent that we can set up, too. I used it the first year while I was building the cabin. We bring all the guns and ammunition as well. We'll set up a camp near the hot springs pool. They can't see it until they reach the lake and look south, but if we go into the trees until we almost come out to the valley floor, we'll be able to see if anyone is coming."

Rachel nodded and said, "You've really thought this out, Marsh. Will we have a fire?"

"No, we won't have a fire, but we don't need one, either. We have the hot spring right there, boiling away. I'll use my fishing net, so we can just immerse the cans of beans or any other tins of food we want to heat, and the same goes for coffee. We'll bring all four of my canteens and whenever we want to make coffee, we fill one with cold water and leave it in the hot spring for a few minutes."

Rachel smiled and said, "You make it sound like fun, Marsh."

"That hot spring pond has a lot of advantages. You know what else it can do? It can stop bullets just like any other body of water. If someone is shooting a pistol or a rifle at you from even ten feet away, if you're underwater by just three feet that bullet won't even cause a bruise."

Rachel's eyes grew wide as she exclaimed, "You've got to be kidding!"

Marsh grinned and replied, "It does sound odd, doesn't it? I don't know why, but it does. I found out the hard way when I was fishing one beautiful day last summer and spotted this huge cutthroat trout. I slowly pulled my pistol, cocked the hammer and fired. The bullet exploded the water and the fish took off, but I found the bullet on the bottom of the creek in pristine condition. I was curious, as usual, because the creek was only four feet deep. I took a few more shots, and it was only when I pointed the pistol straight down that the bullet even made a mark on the rocks below. At a normal shooting angle, I figured the bullet had to go through eight feet of water or more. I had so much fun, I was even able to bounce a bullet off the water if the angle was low enough."

Rachel was listening and was thoroughly impressed.

"Marsh, that is really interesting."

"So, if I get you angry and you try to shoot me, I'm diving in."

Rachel laughed as Marsh just watched her happy face before he leaned across the table and kissed her simply because he had to.

It didn't take long for them to bump their way down the hallway like a four-footed, walking billiard ball until they fell into the side pocket, otherwise known as their bedroom.

After their early afternoon exercises, they had to return to the very real business of establishing their new camp near the hot spring pond.

Rachel began collecting food and kitchenware they would need, as well as all her clothes in case they searched the house. Marsh went outside, saddled the horses and hitched all four mules to the wagon. He found the tent in the loft and tossed it into the wagon through the loft doors startling the mules, but it was the easiest way to get it loaded; besides, it was a guy thing to do.

Then they loaded all the weapons, to keep any more firepower from the Shipmans in case they broke into the house.

After Marsh saddled the horses, and the food, kitchenware and blankets were loaded, it was time to move to the other end of the valley.

Marsh and Rachel boarded the wagon with the saddled horses and mules trailing behind and headed west toward the lake. He drove the wagon about a hundred yards from the northern edge; that way, if the Shipmans followed the wagon tracks, it would lead them to the lake. Marsh was hoping they would play it safe and stay on the southern side of the valley, away from the tracks and a possible ambush from the nearby trees.

Once they were close to the lake, Marsh turned and headed due south to the pond, crossing the wide, fast-running stream about halfway to their destination.

Marsh brought the wagon to a halt and he and Rachel stepped down and began setting up their camp. With an empty valley behind them, they knew they had at least a fifteen-minute warning before anyone could arrive, but still, Marsh wanted to be ready.

"Rachel, bring your Winchester and we'll establish a path through the trees to the valley side so we can get back and forth without wasting any time."

Rachel nodded and took her rifle from the wagon foot well, then she and Marsh walked through the trees, marking them with knife cuts every twenty feet or so until they neared the end of the trees and the valley was clearly visible.

Marsh gazed out at his peaceful valley and said, "It's about three hundred yards to our camp from here, so it'll take us a couple of minutes or so to get back if we trot. I don't think they'll be coming this soon, but if you'll watch while I set up the tent and get everything else ready, I'll come back and get you when I'm done."

Rachel hooked her arm through his and said, "It's such a shame turning your valley into a battleground. It's just so peaceful."

Still looking out over the valley, he said, "It's not my valley any longer, Rachel, it's our valley, and once this is over, it'll stay peaceful."

Rachel sighed, kissed Marsh, then said, "You go and set up the tent and make us a second home."

Marsh smiled and replied, "I'll be back as soon as it's ready," then turned and jogged back through the trees, counting as he ran to get a closer estimate on the time they'd need to make a fast return, if necessary.

———

Lou had written his note to John telling him what Anderson had said and had it in his pocket, so he could drop it off on his way out of town. He'd lead his horse across the Hell Gate River railroad bridge that night and hope there weren't any coal trains needing the tracks. They were unscheduled and passed through at all hours, but it was faster than using the ford north of town, the only danger was being caught on that bridge by a fast-moving coal train.

Now, he needed to get his money, and the best place to find it was on the seedier end of Front Street along the river. There was still a lot of daylight, but he was getting anxious and wanted to be ready to go after sundown.

He meandered along Front Street, looking for prospective victims and spotted Matt Osterman leaving Dierman's Saloon & Billiard Parlor. Matt was an unmarried foreman at Rees Brothers Construction, and Lou knew that he had just been paid the day before, so Lou began trailing Matt Osterman, hoping he'd turn down an alley.

Lou was in luck as Matt decided to take a shortcut to wherever he was going and entered the long alley that ran behind Higgins Avenue. Lou quickly trotted up behind him. Normally, he'd do this in the dark and sneak up behind his victim, so he'd remain unidentified; but this time, he didn't care because he'd be leaving town in a few hours.

He pulled his replacement pistol, cocked the hammer and said, "Stop it right there, Matt!"

Matt Osterman whipped around and spotted Lou with his Colt staring at him and growled, "What the hell do you think you're doing, Lou?"

"Just hand over your cash and I'll let you go. I need to get outta town."

"Well, you may be getting out of town, but not with my money," Matt said as he turned and started walking away.

Lou hadn't expected the outrighty dismissal but took four quick steps and cut in front of Osterman.

"I'm not messin' around, Osterman! I mean it! Give me your money!" Lou exclaimed.

"Not with an empty pistol you're not, you idiot!" Matt snapped, and reached for Lou's Colt.

Lou initially thought Matt was just bluffing, then realized that he was so anxious to get the gun that he'd never loaded it. It was too late now as Matt grabbed the useless pistol and then, he took hold of Lou's collar. Matt was bigger and much stronger than Lou, and his Colt was loaded.

"Let's go see your big brother, you bastard," he snarled as he half-walked and half-carried Lou by the scruff of the neck down the alley until he turned back onto Higgins Avenue and began to garner attention.

Lou was humiliated and growing more despondent with each step. John was going to kill him.

Matt threw open the door to the sheriff's office and all but threw Lou into the office before he entered himself.

Lat Foster was sitting behind the desk when Lou Shipman stumbled into the office and had to use the desk to keep himself from falling onto his face.

"What's all this about?" asked a startled Deputy Foster.

"This idiot tried to rob me with an empty gun!" Matt exclaimed as he tossed Lou's Colt onto the desk.

Lat had to suppress the grin that threatened to ruin his official demeanor.

"I'm guessing that you're pressing charges," Lat said.

"Of course, I'm pressing charges. Where's this baby boy's big brother, anyway?"

"I have no idea. Let's get Lou in a cell and I'll go and find him when Chas gets back," Lat replied as he stood, grabbed a large key ring and led Lou to the closest cell.

After Lou was installed in his new home, Lat had Matt Osterman make out a formal complaint and statement. When he finished, Matt tossed Lou a hostile glare and left the office.

Lat didn't care to hear any excuses from Lou, so when Chas entered the office five minutes later and spotted Lou laying on the cell's cot, Lat simply handed him Matt's complaint and left to find the sheriff.

———

Marsh and Rachel were enjoying their first fireless cooked meal and found that it was not only easier, but faster as well.

They simply chose the tins that they needed heated, tossed them into Matt's fishing net and lowered the net into the hot spring. While the cans were heating, Rachel carved some of the smoked meat that they had brought with them, in this case it was a ham.

They learned quickly to remove the net quickly when the cans began to bulge after a can of beans exploded.

As they ate on the tailgate of the wagon, it was so idyllic that it was hard to imagine that they were only there to engage in a gunfight.

"Is one of us always going to have to be watching the valley, Marsh?" Rachel asked between bites.

"No, I think it'll be both of us most of the time. At night, we'll be in the tent, but during the day, we'll stay in the trees and watch for them. I'm a bit surprised that they haven't shown up yet, but then again, if they know I'm here and waiting for them, they don't want to come rushing in, either."

"Do you think they'll just ride into the valley following the wagon's tracks?"

"If they're really stupid, they will. If I were in their shoes, once I figured out that the wagon was heading west, I'd cross over the stream and ride toward the lake on the other side of the valley to stay out of range."

Rachel saw the logic and said, "So, that's why you drove on the northern side of the valley. You want them to come to our side."

"Yes, ma'am. In this case, stupid would be the smart thing to do. The only thing that will cause us problems is if they get into the trees on our side of the valley. Once they're in among the pines, we lose our advantage, but you are our biggest advantage. They believe you're dead, so you can't fire until it becomes necessary. If they're all out in the open, hold your fire until I shoot. If they're among the trees, we may have to get out of here quickly, though. During the day, I'll leave the wagon harnessed and two of the horses saddled for a quick retreat."

Rachel nodded as she finished eating and set her plate down next to Marsh's.

"Do we have to go back to the trees now?" she asked.

"It's too late for them to find us now. We're on our own for a while. Do you have any ideas to pass the time?" he asked innocently.

"I'm feeling horribly filthy after that long wagon ride," she replied with a grin.

———

John had dismissed his deputies for the day and had let Lou out of his cell as soon as they had gone.

"Lou, what the hell were you doing? We're real close to getting everything and there's nobody who knows what happened; so, why did you do something so stupid?" John asked in frustration.

"I needed some cash, John," Lou replied weakly.

"Then why didn't you ask me?"

Lou dilemma was crushing him as he tried to come up with some way of responding that didn't wind up getting him killed and finally decided to just come clean.

"John, I screwed up. I really made a mess of things. I didn't kill Anderson. He almost killed me."

John's anger meter pegged as Lou confessed.

"Why did you lie to us?" he growled.

"He took away my guns and told me to tell you that he knew everything and that we had three days to leave Missoula or he'd kill us all; and I know he'd do it, too."

John's rage didn't lessen, but he calmly asked, "How did he know so much? I know that he talked to Lillie McCallister, but she didn't have half of it."

"He said he knows you killed Lillie, too, but he said he found Rachel on the hill and she'd been mauled by that grizzly. Before she died, she told him what had happened. He knew that Frank had picked her up in Denver and everything else, too."

John heard at least some good news in all this; Rachel was dead after all. He never questioned the truth of what Lou had told him because he expected that she'd been killed by some wild animal, so he decided to postpone the trip to the judge for now. Anderson would have buried Rachel in his valley and they'd find her grave soon enough. He needed Lou for what they'd have to do tomorrow, so he decided to play the forgiving brother.

"You screwed up, Lou, but you came clean and told me. Now, we need to get together with Billy and Al and figure out what we need to do. What happened to your guns anyway?"

"Anderson took 'em. All I got is that used Colt I bought. Lat put it in the drawer."

John slid open the drawer, pulled out the gun belt and placed it on the desk.

Then, he said, "Grab a Winchester off the rack and head over to Frank's house. I'll get Billy and Al."

He stood, started walking to the door, then yelled over his shoulder, "And load that damned pistol!"

————

Rachel and Marsh were dressed, but still lying in a now-familiar position on one of the two bedrolls in the tent.

"They'll come tomorrow, won't they Marsh?" Rachel asked.

"They surprised me by not arriving today, but I'd be shocked if they didn't show up tomorrow, and it'll be early so the sun will be blinding us as they ride in from the east. If it's all of them, then they should be spread apart so it would be harder to target more than one. My quandary is whether to use the Sharps to pick one off at distance and then let the others scatter into the trees, or wait for them to get closer and use the Winchester to try and get more than one."

"If you use your Winchester, then I can fire at the same time. By then, it won't matter if they know there's a second gun or not."

Marsh saw the advantage of Rachel's suggestion; with two shooters, it might be possible to get all four, or at least three before they can reach the safety of the trees.

"You're right, Rachel. If I start firing the Winchester, you go ahead and shoot, but everything will depend on which side of the valley they're on and how close they'll get to our position."

Rachel was pleased that Marsh had accepted her suggestion and hadn't tried just to protect her. It meant that she was a real partner.

———

"Now I don't want either of you getting down on Lou for what he did. What's important is that we come up with a way of getting Anderson, then we search for Rachel's body. I still liked Lou's original idea of getting there in the dark and setting up. This time, we get there earlier and make sure he's not up in that damned tower. If he's not up there, then we've got him. There won't be any more tricks this time."

He continued then placed three .44 cartridges on the desk.

"Now, this one is the house, this one is the cabin and the last one is the barn. We ride in around midnight, and split up a half mile before we get there. Me and Al will ride in from this direction to cover the house. Billy you ride around to the south and you'll take care of the cabin, while Lou you ride from the north and will have the barn. Once we're all in position, Billy, you climb the tower really quiet and see if he's there. We'll be there early enough that I don't think he will be. Then you come back down and check out the cabin. It'll probably be empty, but you might get lucky. Lou, take a quick look in the barn, but there's almost no chance he'll be there. Me and Al will have the house under our rifles. I think he expected us to come after him yesterday and when we didn't, he might be thinking that we're taking him up on his offer to leave town. It doesn't matter, as soon as we see any movement, we start firing. Do you all understand?"

There were nods all around.

"Okay," John said, "we'll all get some shuteye early and leave town around midnight."

They all adjourned to find someplace to flop for a few hours before they rode to the valley to cut off the last loose end.

CHAPTER 5

The four brothers rode out of Missoula in near darkness as clouds had moved in blocking the stars and moon. They rode their horses at a walk until they were past the outskirts of the town and picked it up to a slow trot.

Three of the Shipmans were confident, but Lou was still troubled by his near-death experience just hours earlier. He didn't think any of his brothers had noticed his fear, but John had been looking for it and was well aware of his trepidation. It was why he had assigned him to the least likely place for Anderson to be found. As far as John was concerned, there was only one good use for Lou now; Lou would serve as nothing but a target to give the others a better chance to kill Anderson.

By half past one in the morning, they turned on the wagon trail to the valley and around two o'clock, they split up, the loss of moonlight making their approach more difficult, but less than an hour later, John and Al were prone in the dirt outside of Marsh's house; John had the front door covered and Al had the back. A few minutes later, Billy was climbing the tower while Lou hesitatingly approached the barn using the same path he had taken earlier. He spent a few foolish minutes looking for his discarded gun belt before finally sitting down with his back against the barn wall, building up courage to enter the barn itself.

Billy neared the top of the tower and barely stuck his head higher to look into the parapet, found it empty and climbed down carefully in the dark. Once on level ground again, he pulled his

Colt and approached the cabin, stepping carefully onto the short porch. His first step was quiet, but when he put his left foot down, there was a loud creak from a weather-beaten board. He then just pushed open the cabin door and went inside, half expecting a flash and pistol report, but it was silent inside. He couldn't see anything beyond shadows, but felt for the bed and found it empty. He walked out of the cabin not trying to be quiet and returned his Colt to his holster before retrieving his Winchester that was leaning against a tower leg.

His job completed, he simply sat on the edge of the porch and waited.

If Lou hadn't been so spooked, he would have gone into the barn much sooner and discovered the absence of animals and even the wagon, but he still stayed with his back glued to the barn wall for another twenty minutes before he finally built up enough nerve to stand and slowly walk around to the front of the barn and carefully swing open the right barn door. Like Billy, he had his now-loaded pistol drawn as he fearfully entered the empty barn. Once safely inside, it took Lou a few minutes to realize just how empty the barn was before he wandered around inside for a while to be sure, then walked back outside and wondered if he should tell John. This was another dilemma for Lou, as John had told him to check out the barn for Anderson, not his animals, but he knew it meant that Anderson wasn't there. *So, did he try to find John in the dark, or did he wait until there was enough light to tell him?*

Lou decided to wait because he sure didn't want to chase after Anderson in the dark.

As a result of his decision, the other brothers maintained their vigils and their heightened level of anxiety waiting for Marsh to suddenly appear from his house.

By five o'clock, the gray sky was lighter, so Lou rose from his position, yawned, and then trotted to the front of the yard where he could see John, still on his belly with his rifle on the ground, its muzzle pointed toward Anderson's front door. John saw him coming and wanted to scream at him for being so easily spotted, but had to wait for him to arrive.

"John!" Lou loud-whispered, "The barn's empty. All the animals are gone and so's the wagon."

John thought for second that it might be a ploy by Anderson, but then with Billy having checked the tower, it would be a stupid ploy if it was one, so he stood and began walking toward the house with Lou following. He stepped onto the porch and just opened the door and walked inside.

Once in the house, he shouted, "We've come to kill you, Anderson!", but the only response he had was the echo of his voice. His first stop was Marsh's weapon's room, and wasn't surprised to find it empty.

Lou was behind him and John, without turning, said, "He's somewhere in that valley of his daring us to come after him. Well, maybe we'll give him what he wants."

He then walked quickly down the hall, just glancing into each bedroom to make sure they were empty, then reached the kitchen, checked the cold room and then opened the back door. He spotted Billy still sitting on the cabin porch and waved him in, did the same to Al and then returned to the house, tossed some wood into the cook stove and started a fire for some coffee and breakfast; it was going to be long day of killing in front of them.

———

Marsh was taking the canteen of coffee from the hot spring while Rachel was taking some of her biscuits from a waxed paper bag and had already set butter and strawberry preserves on the tailgate.

Marsh had his Sharps and Winchester leaning against the side of the wagon alongside Rachel's Winchester, and had to hold the hot, coffee-filled canteen with a towel as he filled the two cups and set the canteen down.

As he bit into his biscuit, Marsh said, "We'll get into position as soon as we finish. We'll be able to see them soon after they pass the house. Then, you can move behind your tree and we just wait for them to arrive. I still don't have any idea how they'll do it, though."

"I'm ready, Marsh," Rachel said.

"I know you are, Rachel," Marsh replied, then smiled warmly at her.

They finished their breakfast, including one more cup of coffee before they picked up their rifles and walked into the trees.

———

The brothers had just eaten their much larger breakfast, and were having more coffee while John explained how they would take out Anderson.

"The good news is that he took his wagon, so we'll know where he went, which is almost a guarantee that he went west into his valley because he knows it better than we do. Now, because all his weapons are in that wagon, I don't think he'd just abandon it, but he probably is using some fakery to lure us into a trap. We find his wagon tracks and stay at least a hundred yards away. Keep your eyes peeled for any sign of movement in the trees, mainly on the side that we'll be using; but if we don't see the wagon, the odds are we won't see Anderson."

He must know of a hiding place for the wagon, so sing out when you see those tracks take a sudden turn. Once we see it, we hunker down over our horses' necks and set them to a gallop in the direction of the tracks. Don't follow a straight line, either; make short little cuts along the way. Expect him to start firing, and then open fire at his smoke. If nothing else, it will keep his head down until we can really pour the lead into him. Everybody got that?"

There were nods and murmurs of agreement from his younger brothers.

"Okay. Let's have another cup of coffee and get this thing started."

———

Their rifles were leaned against the same tree as Marsh and Rachel stood side by side staring into the eastern horizon. At the almost three miles distance, the house was like a tiny box.

Marsh had his arm over her shoulder as he said to Rachel, "See the smoke coming from the house? I think the boys either had breakfast or wanted to warm up a bit. They'll be coming soon."

"Marsh," she said, "I'm afraid. I know you're going to tell me that you are, too, but it won't make me any braver."

Marsh put his arms around her and held her close.

"It's all right to be afraid, Rachel. Just remember that I'm here with you. When you see them, remember what they tried to do to you and get mad. Let the anger fill you and overpower your fear, but don't let it overwhelm your common sense. Just like when you faced the bear, you were afraid, but you still were rational and that is what saved you."

Rachel had her arms around him and felt his warmth as she said softly, "You saved me, Marsh, in every way it's possible to save someone. I'll be okay."

"I know you will, sweetheart."

He gave her a warm, soft kiss and then smiled at her.

"Let's get ready," he said.

Rachel smiled back, picked up her Winchester and trotted thirty feet to the tree she had chosen for cover. It had the advantage of a small branch on the right side that was the right height for her to use as a stable support for firing.

Marsh's tree didn't have a suitable branch, but he chose it for the view it gave him through the other trees. It was still twenty feet behind the start of the tree line, but the placement of the other trees gave him a perfect view all the way down the valley to the house and he could still see Rachel behind her tree to his right.

He knew that they were deep enough into the trees that unless they saw the muzzle flash, the gunsmoke wouldn't help them at all to find their location.

They were ready for their visitors and wouldn't be rolling out a red carpet when they arrived.

———

John was on the right side of the four brothers as they had their horses moving at a medium trot down the valley; the wagon tracks about a hundred and fifty yards to his right and the northern edge of the valley was another hundred yards beyond the tracks.

The stream that flowed close to the center of the valley was another six hundred yards to his left and the southern edge of the valley was another eight hundred yards past the stream. The valley was almost exactly a mile wide, with both climbing edges covered with Ponderosa pines.

In any other situation, one would marvel at the natural beauty of the setting, but this morning was not for sightseeing or a nature tour; today was a killing day. Those pines weren't beautiful examples of arboreal perfection; they were masks hiding a man with a long rifle capable of reaching them from over half a mile.

The only one who had seen the Sharps was John, but he had bragged about the rifle to his brothers, and laid claim to it once they decided to kill Anderson. Now he was scanning those trees on the northern edge for the sudden appearance of a cloud that would warn him of the pending arrival of a .50 caliber killer. Whether or not Marsh ever fired a round with the Big Fifty, having the Shipmans aware of its presence was already having an effect on how they made their approach.

Lou was petrified at the idea of being shot, and nervously glanced left and then right again without really seeing anything. He knew that as soon as the lead started flying, unless Anderson was shot right away, he'd bolt. He didn't care if anyone called him a coward; he didn't want to die.

Billy and Al were almost oblivious to the danger as they trotted along. They were watching the wagon tracks, expecting them to turn quickly to Anderson's hiding place. They had already passed several spots where the wagon could have turned into the trees, but the tracks continued west toward the lake.

Each man had a fully loaded Winchester '73 and all of their Colts had all six chambers filled with cartridges. Eighty-four .44 caliber bullets should be enough to kill one man.

———

Marsh had been watching them ride toward them for a few minutes and was sure that Rachel had as well. After the target practice, he concluded that her eyesight was probably better than his; and his was very good. Even as he stood behind the tree watching the four men riding towards him, he marveled at the woman thirty feet away; yet still couldn't comprehend how anyone her talent and ability had to endure what she had. Maybe if she wasn't so physically gifted as well, he could understand, but the entire Rachel package was nothing less than awe inspiring. He was just grateful that he would be able to be awed for the rest of his life.

Rachel had seen them before Marsh did, and her only concern was that they were on the wrong side of the stream. Marsh's hope that they'd want to put as much distance between them and potential Sharps rounds hadn't worked. She still smiled when she remembered that he had said he didn't think they'd be that stupid. She'd ask him about that when this was over. She was surprisingly calm as she watched them ride closer, not sure if it was Marsh's influence or just her own confidence and knowing that she now had something to live for.

They were about a mile out now, so Rachel picked up her Winchester and cocked the hammer.

———

It was John who finally showed that he wasn't that stupid, when he said in a medium voice, "I think he wants us to stay on this side of the stream, so he can get at least one of us with that Sharps. Let's move to the southern side for a while."

He changed his horse to the southwest and began heading directly at Marsh and Rachel and his brothers followed his lead.

————

Marsh couldn't understand what had triggered the sudden shift, but he appreciated whatever it was. He would hold off his decision of which rifle to use until they rode closer. Both weapons were cocked, and he had another six rounds for the Sharps in his jacket pocket; the same pocket that had held Rachel's emerald necklace just two days earlier.

Rachel had her Winchester laid across the branch and braced against the trunk. She wasn't sighting yet, but could sight and fire in just seconds. Marsh had told her that he would take the leftmost rider first and she should target the one on the right. After that, it would be a free-for-all.

————

Because of the change in direction, the brothers were no longer riding abreast, but in a staggered line as they drew within five hundred yards of the tree line.

John knew they were coming to the end of the valley and was getting nervous. *Where was Anderson?* The lake was another half a mile northwest and he hadn't found the wagon yet, so he began to look at the northern edge of the lake but there were trees that not only stopped him from seeing the edge, but would have prevented the wagon from getting past as well.

They were still riding closer to Marsh and Rachel as John kept scanning the lake from those trees on the north along the shoreline going to the south. They passed the two-hundred-yard mark when John spotted the slightest opening to the south of the lake at the end of the tree line then suddenly knew where Anderson had driven that wagon; and it was right in front of them. He then made that horrible connection that if the wagon was on the other side of those trees then Anderson was probably waiting for them in the…

He shouted, "He's in the trees! Get down!"

Marsh opened fire, his Winchester announcing his position with a blast and a cloud of gunsmoke, but it was back in the trees far enough that only the sound and bullet escaped from the tree line. It was Al who discovered where Marsh's Winchester was aimed, when the .45 caliber round thumped into his abdomen, ripping apart intestines and smashing into his right kidney. He dropped from his horse into the lush grass of the valley, still alive, but bleeding extensively, screaming as he left his horse; then continued to screech after he had hit the ground, smashing his right shoulder into the dirt, snapping the collarbone. He stopped screaming a few seconds later.

John had begun to lean forward to minimize his exposure just as Rachel's shot arrived, grazing the back of his head, blowing his hat off as the bullet ricocheted slightly off his occipital bone. John fell from his horse awkwardly, rolling several times before stopping with his face in the grass.

Marsh had levered in a new round as Lou and Billy both fired blindly into the trees before accelerating their horses westward toward the gap between the tree line and the lake, each man hunkered down over his horse's neck making poor targets.

"Let's go!" Marsh shouted as he and Rachel bolted to get back to their camp, following their preset path.

———

John was stunned more by the fall than the bullet, but when he tried to stand, he suddenly felt the effect of the glancing shot on the back of his head when he felt everything spin and he fell to his knees. He waited until the spinning subsided somewhat and slowly managed to stand, but braced himself with his knees locked and his feet spread apart. He spotted his horse and Winchester a hundred yards away but ignored both and decided he had to get to Anderson now.

He began to walk unsteadily toward the trees as he pulled his Colt from its holster. He let his anger overtake his sense of survival as he walked drunkenly into the trees, daring Anderson to shoot him. He had to lean against a tree to remain upright as another, but less severe wave of dizziness struck. When it passed, he spotted Marsh's Sharps leaned against the tree and saw his heavy footprints leading into the forest.

He blinked several times to try to clear his head and began a shuffling walk following Anderson's heavy steps, not noticing the smaller, shallower footprints just a few feet off to the side.

———

Billy and Lou had ridden in a panic toward southern edge of the lake, wanting to put as much distance between them and Anderson, but not about to give him the broad target of their backs when he had that Sharps. They had both been so shaken by the loss of their brothers that they hadn't noticed two separate shooters. They had only expected Anderson, and assumed he had shot twice quickly, but now, their only hope was to get to the lakeshore safely, dismount and use the decline of the shoreline for protection. Billy believed they still had a two to one advantage.

The sun began to fight through the overcast by then and streams of sunlight appeared where it had achieved victory over the clouds, making an odd mottled landscape that also more easily exposed the expanding view of the land to the south as they neared the lake.

When Billy and Lou cleared the edge of the tree line, the wagon, mules, horses and tent were all bathed in bright sunlight just a few hundred yards to their left.

Billy pointed at the campsite and shouted, "There's his stuff! He's gonna be heading there! Let's beat him to it!"

Lou was still torn about making his escape, but behind him was death and he didn't see any threats in front of him, so he followed Billy's lead as he turned his horse sharply to the left to run the last few hundred yards to the campsite.

But then Billy warily brought his horse to a slow trot to make sure Anderson wasn't there, and Lou caught up with him.

"What's the matter, Billy?" Lou asked.

Billy grimaced and replied, "I'm not sure. I don't think he's back yet, but I'm kinda spooked. Let's go, but keep your rifle cocked."

Lou nodded and levered in a new round.

———

Marsh and Rachel both heard Billy's shout and Marsh slowed them both down. The last thing he wanted to do is to pop out of the trees and into their rifle sights.

He and Rachel each had their hammers cocked as they began to walk carefully for the last hundred yards.

———

Billy was watching the trees in case Anderson appeared, but thought they were so far ahead because they were on horseback that they would have a minute or two before Anderson showed. He had failed to realize that he and Lou had to shift to the northwest to ride around the tip of the tree line, so they had to make a much longer, roundabout path than Marsh and Rachel. Then he and Lou had slowed down when they first spotted the camp, adding further delay. He and Lou had some time advantage; but it was only seconds, not minutes.

Marsh spotted the two from inside the tree line and glanced over at Rachel, who nodded, indicating that she had seen them as well. Marsh signed that he would take the shorter of the two, who happened to be Lou. Rachel nodded again, and they separated by ten feet, each picking a tree to provide cover as they waited for Billy and Lou to dismount.

Billy had been studying the trees expecting Marsh to appear any second, but no one came.

So, he turned to Lou and said, "Let's get ready for him to show up. He probably doesn't know we're here."

Lou nodded, but without conviction, then waited until Billy had quickly stepped down with his Winchester before he swung his leg across his horse's rump and stepped down. He was turning toward Billy when Marsh's shot rang out and his .45 smashed into the left side of Lou's chest, just below the clavicle, ripping the lung apart and leaving his body a fraction of a second later. Lou spun counterclockwise, his rifle leaving his hand and somersaulting ten feet away as he screamed.

Billy had been waiting for Marsh, so when he saw Lou get hit, he fired his Winchester at the smoke even as Rachel fired her rifle. He saw her muzzle flare in the darker woods and was shocked to think he'd missed Marsh even as her shot took him in the center of his chest, killing him almost instantly.

His .44 had been on target, but had smashed into the tree that Marsh was using for cover. He and Rachel stepped out from the trees and kept their rifles on the brothers. Billy was unmoving, but Lou was still alive and in pain as blood poured from his chest.

Marsh approached him and lowered his rifle. Lou was no longer a threat; if he had ever been one to start.

Lou's vision was beginning to fade as he looked up at Marsh and croaked, "I wanted to run away, but John wouldn't let..."

Then his eyes rolled back into his head and he died. The silence was overwhelming after all the gunfire that still echoed through the valley.

Rachel stepped up beside Marsh and asked, "Is it finally over, Marsh?"

"Almost. I still have to collect those other two bodies and then take all four into Missoula. I want you to come along, so we can straighten this all out once and for all."

Rachel took in a deep breath and let it out slowly as she and Marsh walked hand-in-hand back to the wagon. They set their rifles on the wagon bed, and Rachel took off her gun belt and set it alongside.

They were heading toward the patio when John emerged from the trees, his cocked Colt pointed in their direction. He was still walking unsteadily, and the shock of seeing Rachel with Anderson added to his confusion.

Neither Marsh nor Rachel had seen him step out of the trees, but as they reached the pond side of the patio, John took aim at Marsh from thirty feet and fired, shattering their illusion of safety. The loud report startled them, but Marsh quickly recovered, grabbed Rachel by the waist, spun, and like a hammer thrower, hurled her into the pond.

Not surprisingly, John's first shot was wildly off target, as he struggled to overcome his dizziness. He had continued to walk toward Marsh, cocked his hammer for a second shot, and was stunned as Marsh turned and charged at him, quickly closing the gap.

John had expected Marsh to go for his pistol, giving him another shot at a stationary target, but the sight of the oncoming huge man caused him to rush his second shot, and with the wooziness still there, made it a wasted effort.

Marsh would never be able to explain his instant decision to attack John Shipman rather than pull his Colt, but when he struck the sheriff, his massive size and speed knocked the already unsteady man off his feet and sent him rolling into the pond, his Colt arcing away as he spun.

He was scrabbling with his hands to stop his rotation as the lower half of his body plunged into the water, almost exactly where the water from the hot spring bubbled from the molten rock hundreds of feet below the earth. It took a fraction of a second for his legs to scream to his brain that they were being boiled and his arms and legs began churning to try to escape the hot liquid.

Marsh had to scramble to his feet after crashing into John and ran to pull him from the pond. He grabbed hold of John's clutching hands and in one mammoth yank, jerked him free of the water, but those few seconds immersed in near-boiling water had done its damage.

John's pain was beyond excruciating as he screamed for Marsh to kill him and end his suffering.

Marsh listened to the horrified pleas from this poor excuse for a man who had ruined other people's lives and murdered Lillie, all while hiding behind the badge that was supposed to protect those very people he had harmed and thought it would be just punishment to let him suffer.

But in the end, he decided it wasn't his decision to make. He'd end the sheriff's life on earth and let God decide what punishment he deserved. So, he released his hammer loop, slowly pulled his Colt, cocked the hammer and pointed it directly where his heart should be; if he had one. He squeezed the trigger, and John's screaming ended even as the loud report rolled across the pond's steaming water.

Marsh holstered his pistol and slowly turned to see Rachel, who was stepping out of the pond, her clothes and hair streaming water as she reached the patio.

Rachel had witnessed most of the confrontation with John Shipman, and knew why Marsh had to do what he did and wasn't sure if she would have been able to do it.

Marsh reached her on the patio, and despite her being soaked, put his arms around her and said, "I'm sorry to toss you in the pond, Rachel. I just needed to keep you safe."

Rachel replied quietly, "I know. I knew what you were going to do before you did it, too. Now, it really is all over, isn't it?"

"Yes, Rachel, the bad part is over. It'll take a while to clean up all the mess, but we'll need to get the bodies into Missoula and talk to the deputies and maybe the county prosecutor. Did you want to get changed?"

"I'll be back in a little while," she said as she kissed him quickly and walked to the tent to put on some dry clothes.

Some time had been saved by having the team already in harness, and the wagon was empty, so it would be easier to load the bodies in the wagon than drape over their horses; so Marsh began hauling the three brothers near the camp to the wagon. He did John first as he was the closest, then he threw Billy's body and then Lou's into the wagon's bed. He stripped the gun belts from each man as he did, tossing them into the wagon's foot well, but had to hunt down John's pistol.

Rachel stepped out of the tent and asked if he needed help with anything, and Marsh said she could go and get Billy's horse while he tracked down Lou's.

After they had all six horses trail-hitched behind the wagon, they climbed into the seat and set off back toward the lake and then swung around the tree line and rolled east toward the house. They had to stop and load Al's body, add the two other horses to the string, and find the dropped Winchesters, before Marsh trotted into the trees to get his Sharps and they could restart their trip to the house.

Once there, Marsh let all the horses into the corral and then trotted into the barn to retrieve the tarp. He left the four brothers' gun belts and pistols in the barn, and their Winchesters in their horses' scabbards. After the bodies were covered with the tarp, they started toward Missoula.

Two hours later, just before noon, they entered the town and Rachel began getting a bit self-conscious when people began to stare at her; the adulteress and murderer.

Marsh could feel her discomfort, pulled her close against him and put his arm over her shoulder. He was telling all the judgmental spectators that he wasn't bringing Rachel in as a prisoner, but as his woman. He noticed that those that had already had convicted and sentenced her in their minds probably believed he was guilty of some mortal sin as well, but he also counted more folks who were smiling as they drove past.

Rachel glanced at Marsh, smiled and realized it didn't matter at all what anyone else thought.

They reached the sheriff's office and stepped down, Marsh making a point of assisting Rachel down from the wagon even though she surely didn't need the help.

Inside the office, Chas and Lat were discussing where else they could search to find Lou. Chas had arrived earlier than usual to get some breakfast for their prisoner and hadn't been all that surprised to find him missing. He had gone to John's apartment and didn't find the sheriff there, so he had returned to the office and waited for Lat Foster to arrive. Then they had both searched the town looking for any of the Shipman brothers and found none of them.

They had only returned to the office twenty minutes after their futile search and knew where the brothers had gone. Chas felt horrible for not having listened to Marsh and done his job as a lawman and had just told Lat about his meeting with Marsh when the door opened and they both turned.

Their mouths dropped as Rachel stepped inside followed by Marsh.

"Mrs. Shipman!" exclaimed Lat, as Marsh pulled out a chair for Rachel.

"Don't ever use that name in front of Rachel again, Lat," Marsh said, "I've got all four Shipman brothers in the back of my wagon. They came to my valley early this morning intending to kill me for what I knew and didn't know that Rachel was with me. I need to get the bodies dropped off at Sweeney's and we'd probably be better off meeting with Mister Crawford, so he can hear the story at the same time and make a decision about prosecution."

Chas then turned to Lat and said, "Go ahead and drive the wagon down to Sweeney's and leave it there. Tell them we'll need death certificates on each of them as soon as possible and to bring the wagon back here."

Lat replied, "Okay, but could you wait until I get back before starting?"

Chas nodded, then Marsh said, "Tell the mortician that the reason for John's unusual appearance is that he slipped into a boiling hot spring, and was in incredible pain. He kept begging me to end his suffering, so I did, as much as I wanted to let him feel some of the pain he had inflicted on others."

Lat's eyes were wide as he listened but then just nodded and dashed out the door.

While Lat was gone, Marsh and Rachel gave Chas a short summary of what had happened that morning. When Deputy Foster returned, they all left the office and walked next door to the county courthouse to see Mister Edmund Crawford, the county prosecutor.

After ten minutes of conversation, the meeting moved to the chambers of Judge Davis at the recommendation of the prosecutor as it involved a lot more than just a gunfight. It was a long meeting; lasting over three hours. The court reporter, James Litchfield, was called in after the first few minutes to make a record of the proceedings.

The death of Lillie McCallister seemed to have a bigger effect on the judge than all the other deaths, although he was outraged at the treatment of Rachel by the brothers. Because the story was the only thing that made sense of all of the odd aspects of the whole affair, the prosecutor and the judge both accepted what Marsh and Rachel said as accurate. The prosecutor recommended that all of the Shipman brothers deaths, including Frank's, be ruled as justifiable homicide and the cases closed. Judge Davis agreed and also issued an order declaring that the Double M ranch sale was valid, and that Rachel was the legal heir of Frank Shipman making her the new owner. He mentioned that he wished he could issue an arrest warrant for Bob McCallister for deserting his wife which resulted in her death, but acknowledged it was outside the scope of the law.

After handshakes all around, Marsh and Rachel left the judge's chambers and stopped at the land office and gave the clerk the judge's order. It only took a few minutes for Rachel to be listed as the legal owner of the Double M ranch, then given a copy of the new deed which ended the legalities in the Shipman case.

When Marsh and Rachel finally left the county offices, Rachel was a bit disappointed that Marsh hadn't asked the judge to marry them while they were there. It would have put a wonderful end to a horrible day, but she still clung tightly to his arm as they stepped out into the now sunny Montana day.

"Where do we go now, Marsh?" Rachel asked, as she stepped up into their empty wagon.

"First, we stop at Goodspeed's for some wedding bands; then, my love, you are going to Worden & Company and you will find a wedding dress, and not just an ordinary dress, a white satin affair. You will have it tailored to fit and we will then go to the Methodist Church and see the reverend and schedule a wedding in a week. I'm going to stop at the Missoula Times and have them run an announcement of our upcoming nuptials and that it is open to the public."

Rachel was aghast and asked, "Marsh have you lost your mind? I thought we'd have a quiet ceremony and was disappointed that you didn't have Judge Davis marry us today."

"No, Rachel. I want everyone in Missoula to know that you are not only innocent of the whispers that had been spread about you, but the most perfect woman God has ever allowed to set foot on His earth."

Rachel wanted to kiss him again, but thought it was inappropriate in the busy street with so many pedestrians.

Marsh saw her smile and didn't care about the pedestrians, riders, or drivers. He put his arms around Rachel and kissed her as if there wasn't a single set of eyes to witness the shameless display of public affection.

He then sat back, flicked the reins and began driving the wagon as if nothing unusual had happened.

Rachel was blushing as they started, but incredibly happy that Marsh was going out of his way to let everyone know that he was her man now.

After they found a nice set of wedding bands at Goodspeed's, they stopped at Worden's and Doris was told the basics of the case and despite a tiny bit of envy, gushed to Rachel how happy she was to find out that she was innocent and going to marry Marsh, then added that she knew all along that Frank was up to no good.

They found a wedding dress and Rachel tried it on in the back room and found it only required minor changes, and didn't even have to be hemmed because of her height. She said she'd handle the alterations and Marsh paid for the dress.

The meeting with Reverend Fairly took a bit longer because he had to hear more of the story, but once that was done, a wedding date was set for June 7th at ten o'clock.

That left two more stops; the first was to the newspaper, the *Missoula Times*. There were two newspapers in town, but the *Times* was the daily paper and more widely read. As it turned out, Marsh didn't have to pay for an announcement. The editor, Harrison Spaulding, took down the basics of the wedding and rushed out of his office to go to the county offices to read the official transcript of the events.

The final stop was to the Windsor Hotel and Hall. Marsh arranged a large buffet that would be open to the public after the wedding. J.E. Williams, the proprietor, after being given the story, was more than happy to oblige and be part of the story.

Before they left Missoula, they ate a large lunch at the International Restaurant on Front Street, attracting the attention of many of the other diners. Marsh whispered to Rachel it was because she was easily the prettiest woman in the place.

On their return ride, Rachel asked, "Marsh, isn't this going a bit far for our wedding?"

Marsh put his arm around her waist and replied, "No, Rachel. I am doing nothing less than celebrating the joy you have given me. I want to share it with everyone and I want everyone to understand just how much I love you."

They were out of town, but even if they were on Higgins Avenue with hundreds of onlookers, Rachel didn't care anymore, as she twisted in front of Marsh and kissed him passionately.

The rest of the ride to the valley was a testament to how well the mules knew the way to their barn without human guidance.

By the time they returned to the house, Rachel, despite her amorous intent, was exhausted from the excitement of the day and the lack of sleep the night before. Marsh told Rachel to go and take a nap while he took care of the mules. She thanked him, stepped down from the wagon and entered the back door while Marsh drove the mules to the barn. He left them in harness because he still had to go back to the camp and retrieve everything, including the guns and tent; and had to unsaddle all the horses before he joined Rachel, too.

By the time he finally entered the house after taking care of all of the horses, removed his gun belt and Stetson, and walked down the hallway, it was almost an hour later. He stuck his head in the bedroom and found Rachel curled up like a six-year-old and looking every bit as innocent.

He wanted to hold her, but she looked so peaceful, he turned around and walked back to the kitchen, pulled his hat back on and belted on his pistol.

Before he left, he wrote a quick note letting her know that he'd gone to retrieve the tent and other things from the campsite.

He returned three hours later, stopped near the back porch and began unloading rifles and pistols. He left the food and other things that Rachel had packed on the porch, then drove the wagon to the barn, unharnessed the mules and put the tent back in the loft.

Marsh stepped onto his weapon-laden porch and opened the door to the kitchen finding Rachel standing there with a smile on her face and a cup of coffee in her hand.

"Welcome home, Marsh," she said.

Marsh accepted the coffee and the smile and stepped inside. They walked to the table, where Marsh set down his cup and latched onto Rachel. He had been trying to focus on all the things that needed to be done and most were complete now, and he could finally devote all his attention to Rachel.

He didn't kiss her, but simply held her close, knowing how near they were to losing everything just a few hours ago when John Shipman stepped out of those trees. He had invested every bit of his heart and soul into this incredible woman he had engulfed in his arms and the thought of having her taken from him was simply beyond his ability to comprehend.

Rachel felt the security and love while she was being held and knew she could never find it anywhere else. This was her home; not the house or even the valley. Her home was in Marsh's arms.

After holding her for another two minutes, he kissed her softly and said, "Now, Rachel, we can really begin our lives together."

"Can I seduce you now, Marsh?" she asked demurely.

Marsh smiled and replied, "I'm not going to give you a chance, Mrs. Anderson."

She laughed as he scooped her into his arms and carried her still laughing to their bedroom.

———

The next morning was the first time that Marsh and Rachel had a normal awakening without fear of being discovered or shot. It was a glorious sensation to simply revel in each other's company with no inhibitions or worries. They didn't leave their bedroom until almost eight o'clock and then, it was a mad dash to the privy for Rachel, while Marsh took the gentlemanly prerogative by walking out the front door.

After breakfast, Marsh spent almost an hour cleaning and sorting all the rifles and pistols. It was getting to be a very large inventory, especially with Winchester '73s and Colt Peacemakers. When that was done, Marsh and Rachel saddled their horses and rode north to visit the Kowalskis.

Marsh doubted that they received either newspaper, so he wanted to make sure that they had all the news, including the wedding and celebration afterwards.

Peter and Mary Kowalski greeted them like old friends and the entire family was soon in the large main room to hear the story.

"We heard gunfire yesterday, and Mary had to keep me from rushing over there with my Henry," said Peter.

"Peter, I happen to have a few spare Winchesters and Colts that I'm sure you can put to good use. Why don't you and your boys come over some time and I'll set you up with some ammunition, too. If you want to, we can do some practice shooting on my target range."

Not only Peter, but his four sons and son-in-law, all seemed as if Father Christmas had arrived in the form of Marsh Anderson.

"Do you mind if we stop by tomorrow, Marsh?" asked Peter before consulting with Mary.

"Not at all, come on by in mid-morning so you'll have plenty of time to get back and do your work."

His work comment seemed to have mollified Mary, as the male side of the Kowalski clan all thanked Marsh and said how anxious they were to try the Winchesters.

————

When Marsh and Rachel returned to the house, Marsh set aside six of the Winchester '73s and six boxes of .44 ammunition, along with six gun belts.

"You sure made friends of the Kowalski men," Rachel said with a smile.

"We sure don't need the guns, and I think it'll be kind of fun to do some practice shooting tomorrow."

Then she asked, "Marsh, what will I do with the ranch? I don't want it. My life is here with you."

Marsh shrugged and said, "Then sell it. Right now, there are no ranch hands to manage the herd. I'm not even sure how big it is. Just by looking at it, I'd guess around six or seven hundred. Between the ranch itself and the cattle, you'd probably be looking at well over twenty thousand dollars, but before we do anything about the ranch, we need to go to Sweeney's and have them exhume Lillie's remains from where they buried her and give her a proper burial."

Rachel asked, "Marsh, do we want to have a family cemetery built here in the valley?"

"I was thinking about that. I think Lillie deserves to stay here, don't you?"

Rachel smiled softly and replied, "I do."

Marsh then said, "Something else I want to build now that it's quiet. I'd like to build a cottage down near the pond, so we can spend time there by ourselves. What do you think?"

Rachel's face lit up at the suggestion, answering the question before she replied, "I think that's a marvelous idea, Marsh."

With their immediate plans set, Rachel and Marsh finally separated when Rachel said she was going to make her wedding dress alterations, and Marsh wandered out to the corral to look at the new horses. While he was there he wondered about the Double M's remuda. He had no idea how many were there because he'd let the horses and two cows loose so they could graze.

As he watched the horses, he began to think about his own future now that he had a wife. He didn't doubt that they'd have children, he just hoped that Rachel didn't have to worry about the possibility of the first one being Frank's. He knew that she would love the child, but having that slim chance would bother her all through the pregnancy. All he could do would be to reduce the odds, a task he found utterly delightful.

But what would he do for a living? There were already enough construction companies in Missoula, so that was out. Money wasn't a problem, so it wasn't a question of working because he needed the cash. He needed to be useful and that meant work.

He'd been corresponding regularly with Vince Cirillo over the years, and would send him a telegram when they went to Missoula letting him know of the wedding and that he'd be writing him a letter with all the details. He'd also invite him to bring his wife, Lucy, with him for the ceremony and be their witnesses. Maybe Vince would have an idea of what he should do.

He sighed and left the corral and decided to climb his tower just for pleasure this time.

When he stepped into the parapet, he found the letter he had written just yesterday with all of the details of the Shipmans' crimes. *Was it only yesterday? And how many days has it been since he met Rachel?* So many things had happened in such a short amount of time, everything was a blur.

He slipped the letter into his pocket and scanned the horizon in the early sunset. He looked north and saw the Kowalski ranch and the roadway and adjoining railroad tracks disappearing over the horizon almost twenty miles away. Looking east, he could make out the Double M ranch house and the massed herd of cattle in the pastures. Then southeast was Missoula and the Hell Gate River crossed by the fading Northern Pacific Railroad tracks. It all looked so peaceful and he wondered how long it would stay that way.

He climbed back down his tower and headed back to the house. After he entered, he started a fire in the cookstove and began to cook dinner.

Rachel made an appearance a few minutes later saying she had completed her dress modifications and would take over the food preparation without an objection from Marsh.

Later that night, as Marsh held Rachel close to him, he said, "This is our first night when we can really just relax. Are all your worries gone now, Rachel?"

She sighed and replied, "Almost. Just that silly one that you're helping to make me forget."

He kissed the top of her head, but couldn't respond. Only time would heal that concern.

CHAPTER 6

Peter Kowalski and his four sons; Jacob, Adam, Carl and Simon, and his son-in-law, Will Draper, arrived just before ten o'clock. Marsh and Rachel had been up and ready for some time and had the Winchesters and gun belts on the back porch.

As expected neighbors, they didn't need permission to step down, so Peter drove the wagon near the barn, pulled it to a stop, and everyone unloaded, their eyes drawn to the tower, as would be expected.

"Good morning, gentleman," said Marsh as he and Rachel exited the house, each carrying a Winchester '76.

"Howdy, folks!" replied Peter as he and his male relatives approached.

"Would you like some coffee, or do you just want to shoot guns?" he asked.

Before Peter could respond, his oldest, Jacob replied, "If it's all the same to you, Mister Anderson, we'd kind like to try those Winchesters."

Marsh smiled, and replied, "I understand, and the name is Marsh. To answer your next question, it's short for Marshall, which was my mother's maiden name. Let's go over to the porch and you can each select your own Winchester and pistol. Take a box of cartridges as well. I've already put a couple of boxes of cartridges for target practice on the shelf behind the cabin. There are cleaning kits for the guns next to the cartridges."

In deference to their father, the eager young men let him select his guns first, then it was by age until the youngest, Simon, took his weapons. Will Draper took the final Winchester and gun belt. They were all in excellent condition, so the order really didn't matter.

None of them commented on Rachel having a rifle as they walked toward the cabin, probably because they thought she was carrying a spare for Marsh's use. That conception would change in a few minutes.

As they walked, Marsh gave them a basic lesson in operating the rifle and the differences between it and the Henry; the only repeater that the Kowalskis had at their ranch.

Once they were behind the cabin, Marsh pointed out the two targets.

"Peter, did you want to start at the fifty-yard mark with the Colt, or the hundred-yard mark with the Winchester?" Marsh asked.

Peter opted for the pistol range and after he fired his five rounds, the others emptied their pistols as well. They did reasonably well for first time pistol shooters, each one getting at least one round into the target.

Rachel pulled out her pistol, and Peter looked over at his sons with a smile as she took aim and squeezed the trigger, missing low and right by four inches off center. She fired the remaining three rounds, all within two inches of center, including one dead center shot.

"And that, gentlemen," Marsh said proudly, "is by a woman who had never shot a gun until a couple of days ago, and her Webley has a shorter barrel than those Colts, so it is supposed to be less accurate."

Rachel holstered her weapon and smiled shyly at the men, as if she was just lucky while Marsh rolled his eyes.

Marsh tried the Smith & Wesson, trying to get a feel for the pistol. He didn't do quite as well as Rachel, but it didn't damage his self-esteem.

When they shifted to the rifle range, the men did better, but were all expecting Rachel to outshoot them, which she did convincingly. Marsh was surprised that he shot better than Rachel, and would ask her later if that was intentional on her part. He suspected that it was because when she finished shooting, she smiled at him as if she had just given him a gift.

After they had finished shooting, Rachel asked, "Peter, I'm the new owner of the Double M ranch, and was wondering if you could help me. Neither Marsh nor I are ranchers and it's empty of people now, so I'd like your advice about what to do with it."

Peter's eyebrows shot up and he replied, "You have the Double M and that big herd with nobody watching it?"

"I'm afraid so. We just found out about it and registered the deed yesterday. I'm concerned about leaving it unattended."

Marsh had been listening and said, "Why don't we all go inside, have some coffee and try to work something out."

Peter replied, "That's a good idea. I may have a couple of suggestions."

Everyone wandered to the house, the Kowalskis leaving their gifted guns in the wagon as they passed by.

Once in the kitchen, before Rachel could do anything, Marsh quickly set out six cups, poured the coffee, then winked at Rachel, saying quietly, "This is payback for letting me outshoot you."

Rachel smiled, winked back and took a seat at the table.

Marsh was close to giggling as he sat down. *What a life it will be married to that woman!*

Peter started by asking, "Do you know how many cattle are on the ranch?"

Marsh replied, "I'm not sure, but I'd have to guess around six to seven hundred head."

Peter nodded, then said, "Prices are pretty good now, with a three-year-old steer going for $28.15. Did you want me to send a couple of my boys over there to do a count and keep an eye on them for a few days?"

"That would be marvelous," replied Rachel.

"Then, I have a proposition for you, Rachel," Peter said and soon continued.

"I'd guess that the ranch is worth about fifteen thousand plus the cattle and remuda. It's a nine-section ranch with good water and grass. So, you are probably looking at least thirty thousand dollars if you sold the ranch; but if you kept the ranch, you'd be looking at a nice income from the sale of the cattle each year. Jacob and his wife, Marie, already have two boys and need a place of their own. Now, I don't have that kind of money to spend to buy the ranch, but if you are willing to let Jacob run your ranch as a manager it would give them room to raise their children and he could hire some ranch hands to help out. What do you think?"

Rachel smiled and turned to Marsh, "Marsh?"

"I think it's a great idea. It doesn't cause any headaches for anyone and solves the problem."

Peter looked at Jacob who was already wearing a grin, and asked, "Do you think Marie would like that, Jacob?"

"I think she'd grab one boy under each arm and run all the way to the ranch," Jacob replied, his face split with a large smile.

"I think Carl and Simon would be just as happy not to have to share a room any longer, too," Peter said as he glanced at his two younger sons.

"We were planning on going over there this afternoon. Did you want to come along?" asked Marsh.

Peter answered, "I've got to do some work or Mary will roast my ears, but I think Jacob and Marie could go over with the wagon and Simon and Carl could ride along to check out the herd. When are you leaving?"

"We'll swing by just after lunch and show you the route. I went cross country and a wagon can make it without any problems. There are just a couple of creeks in between."

"Then they'll be waiting for you. I think Mary will be the happiest of them all. She would love the privacy and I think or maybe Jacob would appreciate it even more," Peter said as Jacob's ears turned red.

Ten minutes later, the Kowalskis were all waving from their wagon as they trundled down the trail to catch the road back to the Circle K.

Marsh and Rachel waved, and then turned to go back to the kitchen.

"That worked out for everyone," Marsh said, "Especially Jacob, I think."

"I know it's a load off my mind," Rachel added.

After cleaning the guns and having lunch, Rachel and Marsh rode out of the valley due north toward the Circle K. When they arrived, they found the wagon harnessed and waiting out front along with two saddled horses.

"Looks like they're anxious," said Rachel.

Just as Marsh and Rachel reached the front yard and were preparing to step down; the front door began spewing Kowalskis.

When Peter emerged among the steady stream, he waved and shouted, "We're ready to go."

For a moment, Marsh thought he meant all of them, which he wasn't sure could squeeze into the wagon even with two of them riding. As it turned out, he meant Jacob and Marie on the wagon with Simon and Carl riding alongside. Marshal and Rachel remained in the saddle as Simon and Carl mounted their horses and Jacob and Marie boarded the wagon.

Two hours later, they arrived at the Double M ranch, which was as quiet as they had expected, as it hadn't been empty long enough for any significant changes to happen. Simon and Carl rode out to the herd while Jacob and Marie stepped out down from the wagon. Rachel and Marsh had led their horses to the front hitch rail and tied them off, so they waited for Jacob and Marie to reach them.

"Rachel, give me a minute to go inside and fix something in the house. It'll only take a minute or so."

She guessed it had something to do with Lillie's death, so she just nodded, and turned to Jacob and Marie and said, "Let's go take a look at the barn. Marsh needs to fix something in the house."

They both guessed as Rachel had when he had said he to 'fix' something, so they went willingly to the barn with her.

Inside the house, Marsh quickly returned the furniture back to their original places and then walked to the kitchen, emptied out Lillie's half-filled teacup and then pumped some water into the sink, added some soap chips and dipped a towel into the water. He returned to the main room and scrubbed away the blood stains as best he could, but it would require sanding to get them out, so he just shifted the rug slightly to hide them for now.

Once that was all done, he checked the rest of the house quickly and found it free from any evidence of Lillie's violent death. As he walked to the kitchen, he wished he hadn't given John Shipman the mercy he didn't deserve.

He stepped outside, tossed the towel into the trash can, then spotted Rachel with the Kowalskis and waved them in.

Jacob and Marie were enthralled with the house. They had been living in one of the small cottages on the Circle K and the two children had already made it crowded. The ranch house would give them a lot more room for their expanding family.

While they inspected the house, Marsh and Rachel remained in the kitchen; Marsh having started a fire in the cookstove and had a coffeepot already on top.

Jacob and Marie returned a few minutes later with big smiles and asked when they could move in.

Rachel replied, "Whenever you're ready. Just to let you know, we'll be having Sweeney exhume Lillie's body from the corral where they buried her; probably within a week or so."

Jacob asked, "Where will she be buried?"

"We're going to have a cemetery built in our valley. She'll rest there," replied Marsh.

Jacob nodded; appreciating the solution to the awkward problem.

By the time the coffee was ready, Carl and Simon arrived and joined them.

"Marsh, there are seven hundred and twenty-three head of cattle out there!" announced Simon as they walked into the room.

"And twenty-three horses," added Carl.

Marsh replied, "Simon, you do realize that Rachel is the top hand here, don't you?"

Rachel laughed and said, "Come on in and have some coffee."

Marsh turned to Jacob and asked, "Now you know what you have to work with, Jacob. How you do it is up to you."

Jacob and Marie both lit up and thanked Rachel and then Marsh for the opportunity.

After they finished coffee, Marsh and Rachel said they had to go to Missoula to get some things done and if they had any problems, to let them know.

When they reached Missoula, odd things began happening as soon as they reached the outskirts of town. Folks would spot them riding and wave and smile as if they were long lost friends. It was becoming like a visit from Queen Victoria with all the waving and smiling.

They stopped at Sweeney's to arrange for the movement of Lillie's remains to the valley, and found out what had happened. *The Missoula Times* had dedicated an extra edition; the first in their short history, to the combination wedding announcement and story as taken from the official report.

It was going to get worse as the day progressed, but they did arrange for the transfer after a half an hour wasted retelling the story.

Next, they went to T.W. Longstaff on Main Street. They were the second largest construction firm in town, but Mister Longstaff was an architect, so Marsh thought he was better suited for what he wanted.

First, he told him of the immediate need to have cemetery laid out with wrought iron fencing, and was told it could be done in three days.

Next, Marsh explained what he wanted for their cottage. The design intrigued Mister Longstaff, as well as Rachel as she listened to Marsh describe what he envisioned. It took a while, but between Marsh and Theodore Longstaff, they came up with a design in just an hour. All three of them were excited with the final design, although Marsh and Mister Longstaff knew they'd be doing some tweaking as they went along.

The final job that Marsh wanted was to expand his house to add three more bedrooms, a dining room, a library, and a bathroom with an indoor water closet. It didn't take as long as it had to design the cottage, but it did take a while.

Mister Longstreet did say that the house and cottage would require the added support of Rees Construction in order to get both jobs done before the winter set in, and Marsh told him to go ahead.

He wrote a draft for all three jobs and shook hands with an almost giddy Theodore Longstaff, who hadn't had this much fun in designing a house since he'd arrived in Missoula.

After they'd left, Marsh had to send a telegram to Vince Cirillo in Denver letting him know about the wedding, which didn't take long.

The last stop before the left town was office of *The Missoula Times,* where they were given a dozen copies of the extra edition paper. Marsh had wanted to stop by and thank Mister Spaulding for getting the truth out, but the editor and owner was more than pleased, having to print over two thousand copies.

They made a waving, smiling exit from Missoula and headed for their valley. Marsh and Rachel read the newspaper on the return trip, with a few laughs along the way.

"Rachel, I do believe you have angel's wings, or at least a halo or two," Marsh said as he read and rode, letting the mules drive.

Rachel replied, "It's not as bad as you stepping down from Mount Olympus with a thunderbolt in your hand."

"Do you know how hot those things are?" he asked, grinning at her.

"Of course, not. Angels never hold anything hot," she replied smiling back at him.

When they returned, Marsh took care of the horses while Rachel trotted inside to fix a quick meal. They would have stopped at Lister's Café, but they would have wanted to eat rather than spend the time waving and talking.

Two hours later, they were on the couch, with Rachel curled up under Marsh's arm.

"Marsh, the cottage sounds so special. Each time you came up with something, I was more amazed. I think Mister Longstaff was going to break out in giggles a few times. I may never want to leave it."

"We'll have to sometime. That's why I wanted the house expanded. We'll probably have a houseful of children to catch up to the Kowalskis."

Rachel sighed, and asked, "Marsh, what if I can't have children? I know that I haven't exactly been a frequent bed partner until recently, but still, I would have thought that I might have gotten pregnant at one time or another. The first three months with Harry, he couldn't keep his hands off me. After that, it became very infrequent, but I still thought I should have conceived at least once."

"I have no idea, Rachel. One of these nights, I'll be holding you and you'll whisper that you're carrying our baby. Until then, all we can do is what we've been doing a lot of these past few days."

"Marsh, would it sound terrible if I said I hoped I didn't get pregnant this time?"

"No, I'd understand. Did you want to stop until you know?" he asked.

She looked up at him and replied, "You'd be willing to do that for me? You know how much I enjoy it with you, and I feel like I'd be depriving you."

"Yes, sweetheart, I'd be willing to do this for you. I'd be willing to do anything for you."

Rachel pulled in tighter and pulled his arm around her.

"Then forget I ever brought it up. It was a silly thing to think about," she said.

"You're many things, Rachel, but silly isn't one of them."

———

With the ranch problem out of the way and all the other preparation done, all that remained for Rachel and Marsh to do was to spend time together; whether it was down by the pool, shooting or just enjoying each other's company in the house or taking a ride in their valley.

The crew arrived from Missoula the next day to build the cemetery fence. It was a one-day job, because they were using standard fencing. The location was one selected by Rachel, and Marsh approved of her choice.

Two days after the cemetery was built, Sweeney arrived with Lillie's remains in a proper coffin and she was laid to rest in a much more serene and proper location than the corral. Marsh had them make a headstone that didn't add much, but he didn't know Lillie well enough to put anything poetic on the stone and felt it would have been phony to do so. The headstone had her name, dates of birth and death and a single word: HOPE.

On the 5th of June, Marsh and Rachel rode into town and visited the Bennett Brothers and bought a new buggy, and rented a second. They had trailed one of the brown geldings into town and designated him as their buggy horse.

After completing their transactions, they each drove a buggy to the train station with their new buggy trailing three horses. They had visitors arriving on the afternoon train.

At 2:10 PM, Marsh had the pleasure of introducing Vincent Cirillo and Lucy to Rachel. In his telegram to Vince, he had asked if he and his wife would act as witnesses for the upcoming marriage, and Vince had instantly replied that he and Lucy would be honored.

Vincent and Lucy drove the rented buggy while Rachel and Marsh drove their recent purchase. Vincent insisted that they stay in the cabin, rather than intrude on their privacy, and Lucy mentioned quietly to Rachel that Vince liked to have privacy for themselves as well, now that they had a few days away from their four children, who were being watched by his mother.

They spent hours talking about what had happened in Missoula and how the construction company was going. Rachel and Lucy became friends almost immediately, probably because of the similarities in the men they had chosen to marry.

———

On June 6th, Marsh and Rachel were on the couch again, discussing the wedding ceremony.

"Everything is going to be so different for me," said Rachel. "I'm not used to all this attention."

"Well, too bad, Mrs. Anderson. You're going to be the center of attention for the rest of your days; at least from me."

"You know what I mean," she replied as she laughed.

"It'll all quiet down after a while. We'll be just regular folks like everyone else."

Rachel looked at him and said, "You've got to be kidding. Regular folks?"

"Sure. Regular folks that have been involved in gunfights, murders, blackmail and attacking grizzly bears. They're everywhere."

Rachel just smiled and relaxed. It wasn't going to be so bad after all.

———

One hundred miles east of where Marsh and Rachel were having quiet time together, Bob McCallister was not enjoying quiet time or any other kind of time. He had two reasons for being unhappy.

The first was when he arrived and had his first visit to his favorite bawdy house, he hadn't found the stimulation that he normally did and thought it was because of all the tension he'd been under. But after it happened again the next night, he determined that the reason for his lack of enthusiasm was back in Missoula; it was Rachel Shipman.

He had never been so excited when he had been able to kiss and fondle her for just those few seconds. He never wanted a woman as badly as he wanted her, and then she was taken from him. Ever since that moment, he had been fantasizing about finishing what he had started, and the whores just didn't arouse him as much anymore.

When he heard of her murdering Frank, running away and that she had probably died, he felt empty inside.

But earlier today, some stranger had given him a copy of *The Missoula Times* and he had been horrified and then elated when he read that she was alive after all and free of any charges. But the horrible part was that he found his name in print as the fool who had fallen for the scam. Now they all knew what he was, and it angered him terribly. It also angered him to find that she was marrying Marsh Anderson. He knew Anderson, and thought he was too strange to marry a woman like Rachel.

They were being married tomorrow and would then return to his valley. He knew where it was and that was where Rachel would be.

He set the newspaper aside, then returned to his hotel room and packed his bags.

———

The day of the wedding was as perfect a day as possible, with light clouds and abundant sunshine.

Marsh donned his suit that he had worn often as the owner of Anderson Construction, while Rachel slipped into her wedding dress. Neither felt the custom of the groom not seeing his bride before the ceremony was applicable; as they were both getting dressed in the same room.

Marsh was dressed first and watched Rachel in admiration as she filled out her white satin dress. It wasn't a full wedding gown, but she looked stunning when she was finished; her emerald necklace the perfect touch.

At eight-thirty, they boarded the buggy for the trip into Missoula. Vincent and Lucy drove the rented buggy behind them at a brisk pace once they reached the road.

They arrived at the Lutheran church fifteen minutes before ten o'clock and found a packed church with an overflow crowd as the two couples both stepped out of the buggies and walked up the steps to the church.

Reverend Fairly was at the altar already, so they walked down the aisle, Marsh smiling, but still scanning the crowd for some danger. He couldn't shake the feeling that something bad was going to happen, but when they arrived before Reverend Fairly, the only thing that mattered was Rachel.

They joined hands as the reverend began a soliloquy about the joys and responsibilities of marriage that no one really wanted to hear, least of all the bride and groom, and although he only spoke for seven minutes, it seemed much longer.

Finally, vows and rings were exchanged, Marsh kissed his wife, and they were able to turn and smile at the large crowd that exploded in a deafening round of applause which echoed off the high ceilings.

Marsh, Rachel, Vincent and Lucy all had to go to the minister's office to complete the marriage certificate before they left to go to the Windsor Hotel and Hall for the post-ceremonial buffet.

The food was excellent, and managed to serve all those who took advantage of the opportunity to get free food and talk to Marsh and Rachel.

———

Bob McCallister had stepped down from the train as the crowd was at the Windsor Hotel enjoying the buffet. It was an advantage to him as not many were on the streets to recognize him, and he had gone to great pains to change his appearance, including shaving off his beloved moustache and getting his hair trimmed much more than he normally would.

He needed a horse, though, and he decided the easiest thing would be to just borrow one. After leaving the depot carrying his two travel bags, he walked down the alley behind Main Street heading west. He found a handsome gelding tied behind a building, hung his two travel bags over the saddle horn, untied the horse, and stepped up, then turned the animal west and then when he left Missoula, he headed north.

He didn't know exactly where Marsh's valley was, but like most folks, knew how to get there and soon found the turnoff, then angled his borrowed horse to the northwest.

Bob had read that there would be a free buffet provided by the newlyweds after the ceremony starting at noon and running until four o'clock. It was only three when he reached the house, so he knew it was empty, but didn't bother going near the house. He was stunned by the tower, though, and thought it was an ideal place to hide. He stepped down, took down his two travel bags and slapped the horse on its rump, watching it jog back the way he had come. Bob didn't care if it made it back to town or not, as long as it wasn't visible. He had time, so he walked to the tower, left one of his bags on the ground and carried the other up the tower, feeling almost nauseous when he reached the parapet. He slid one bag inside and climbed back down for the second, returning just a few minutes later. After sliding the second bag onto the parapet floor, he stood in the tower and looked all around him, astonished at the view. He looked east and could see the ranch he lost. For a few minutes, he wondered if there was any way he could somehow reclaim the property, but knew it was useless and then concentrated on Missoula. He should be able to see them coming almost as soon as they left town.

He sat down with his back against the west wall and pulled out his pocket watch. It was just a few minutes after four, so they should be leaving soon. While he was sitting, he noticed the slits cut in the sides of the parapet walls. They would come in handy when they were close.

He put his pocket watch away and pulled out his Remington derringer. For the fifth time since leaving Helena, he cracked the small pistol open to verify that the two .41 caliber cartridges were there, then smiled and closed the gun.

Now, he just sat back and fantasized about when he got Rachel alone. One shot to kill Anderson, and the second to threaten Rachel. After he tied her up, she would be his at last. He hadn't even remotely considered the possibility that they might have guests with them when they returned.

———

After a full day of festivities, both couples finally drove back to the valley at four o'clock. The good news was any food preparation wasn't necessary as Mister Williams supplied them with two baskets of chicken, potato salad, pies and cakes to take home.

As Marsh drove, Rachel was pulled in close to him, sharing the occasional kiss. She was so totally content and happy, and knew that all that awaited her was more of the same. Like Marsh, she was excited about what changes they were going to make in their valley; and much more importantly, that they would be spending their time together.

Behind them, Vince and Lucy were enjoying a second honeymoon. Lucy had been inspired by the wedding and was as amorous with her husband as Rachel was with hers. Vince was anxious to return to the cabin and show his wife just how amorous he could be.

They drove toward the house first, and after the buggies stopped out front, the two women went inside while the menfolk drove the buggies to the barn to unharness the horses.

Rachel put on some coffee, and when Marsh and Vince arrived, they all sat in the main room to let the day wind down.

———

Bob McCallister had been more than just a bit annoyed to see two buggies arrive rather than one. He was peering though the slits and didn't recognize the other couple, yet they seemed to be friendly with Anderson; but when he saw Rachel in her bridal dress, he almost passed out from her perfection. He hoped she didn't change before he took her.

So, all he could do was wait and hope the other couple left.

———

The discussion in the kitchen focused on the cottage that Marsh and Rachel were having built at the hot spring pond and, with two construction men there, it became a lively talk. Marsh suggested that Vince and Lucy take a ride down to the pond and enjoy some private time, a suggestion that they accepted quickly and only possible because of the extended length of the summer day.

Rachel supplied them with towels and soap while Lucy had to change into a riding skirt and blouse. Vince and Marsh went outside to the barn and saddled two horses and led them to the front porch as Lucy and Rachel waited.

Ten minutes later, Marsh and Rachel were standing on the back porch and waving as Vince and Lucy rode down their valley to the hot spring pond.

Marsh put his arm around his bride and led her back into the house, closing the door behind them.

Even though they knew that Vince and Lucy would be gone for at least another three hours, they decided to just relax for a while and talk about things before dinner. After dinner, it would be a no-holds barred wedding night, but for now, just letting things unwind seemed like the perfect thing to do.

———

Bob had watched Vince and Lucy mount the horses and had to switch to the west slit to watch them ride off toward the lake. *Where were they going?*

After watching them all but disappear, he had a decision to make. Did he go down there now, or did he wait until dark? That other couple would probably come back before sunset, but they were probably staying in the house, and he only had two shots. The deciding factor was Rachel's wedding dress. His fantasy had become all-powerful, and he had to have her now.

He took one last quick look to the west, saw no one, then clambered down the tower.

———

Marsh had Rachel under his arm as she seemed on the verge of sleep. He would just let her doze if she did, because she needed her rest.

Rachel wasn't close to sleep; she was just enraptured by the absolute peace that dominated her. She could never have envisioned in her most wonderful dreams that this could be happening to her, and knew that this was the way it was going to be now. Nothing could change that.

There was a knock on the door, which startled them both. *Why would Vince and Lucy be back so soon?* Besides he shouldn't knock.

Marsh unhooked from Rachel, stood, gave her a glance and shrugged as if to say, 'I have no idea', then walked to the door. As soon he swung it open, he saw a moustache-less Bob McCallister standing three feet in front of him with a derringer in his hand.

He shouted, "Bob, what are....", then Bob fired.

The .41 caliber bullet traced out of the short barrel and punched into the left side of Marsh's abdomen, dropping him to the floor. Bob quickly pulled the hammer back and pointed it at Rachel.

"You're mine now, Rachel!" he shouted happily as he saw her wearing the bridal dress.

"You bastard!" she screamed and began to rush to Marsh.

"Stop right there or I'll kill you, too!" he yelled, pointing the Remington at her.

"I don't care, you slimy little worm! My place is with my husband!"

But as she drew near, Bob dropped the pistol to grab her, and the gun went off. The bullet blasted out of the muzzle and smacked into her left calf, sending her crashing to the floor.

Bob was horrified, and he went to reach for her. He had just begun to touch her when he felt two hands grab his belt and the back of his collar. *What was happening?*

Marsh, his side burning with pain, had seen Rachel fall and McCallister reaching for her. His temper exploded and he stood, grabbed Bob's collar and his belt and lifted him above his head, listening to him scream in panic.

Marsh took two steps toward the fireplace and hurled Bob McCallister into the stone box. His screaming stopped with a resounding crunch.

Marsh didn't care if he was alive or dead, as he quickly turned to his Rachel who was bleeding from her leg and said, "Rachel, how bad is it?"

"I think it'll be okay, but you were shot in the stomach. You need a doctor!"

"We both do. I'm going to go and harness the buggy. Before I do, I'm going to go and get some towels for your wound."

"No! You need to take care of yourself!" she shouted.

Marsh ignored Rachel and trotted to the bathroom, grabbed three towels and returned quickly to her side, then took a knee. He looked at her wound and said, "It's not bad, Rachel. The bullet went clean through. I'm going to wrap it and bind it."

Rachel had given up arguing and watched as Marsh, his abdomen wound still bleeding, carefully wound a towel around her and then tied a second one to keep the first in place. He left the third towel with her and even took a second to kiss her before jogging through the open doorway.

He reached the barn, harnessed a horse to the buggy and ten minutes later, feeling light-headed, drove it to the house. He staggered a bit going up the steps but made it inside to Rachel, helped her stand, provided her support to the buggy and then assisted her inside. He was really getting woozy when he made it to the seat and then handed her the reins.

"Rachel, I don't think I can drive. Can you?" he asked as his head rolled.

"Yes. Lie down on my lap," she ordered as she flicked the reins and kept flicking them until the horse was moving at a fast trot over the rough terrain.

Marsh had his head on her lap and was drifting away as she hit the road, then had the horse at a full gallop as the buggy flew down the road.

Marsh could only think about Rachel and her leg wound and hoped she would be all right. His Rachel was such a good person. She shouldn't have such bad things happen to her. It wasn't fair.

Marsh finally lost consciousness as Rachel drove like a woman possessed.

———

Back in the valley, Vince and Lucy had been overwhelmed by the freedom that they enjoyed in the hot spring pond. They hadn't made love so exquisitely since their first two weeks of married life, and they weren't even sure that it could compare to this.

But the sun was going down and they had to ride back.

They reached the house and Vince let his wife go to the house while he unsaddled the horses. He had just reached the barn when he heard Lucy scream followed by a shouted, "Vince!"

Vince ran for all he was worth, expecting the worst and wasn't far off when he saw all the blood on the floor near the doorway. Then he saw a second pool near Lucy's feet as she pointed toward the fireplace and spotted the body of Bob McCallister crushed against the fireplace. There was almost no blood around his body other than a trail from the large pool near the doorway. He spotted the derringer, picked it up, cracked it open and emptied the cartridge cases.

"That man must have come in here and shot Marsh and Rachel. It looks like Marsh had enough strength to toss him into the fireplace. I've got to ride to Missoula and find them. Are you coming?"

"No, I'll stay here and clean up this mess. I'll leave him where he is."

"Okay, Lucy, but take one of Marsh's shotguns and keep it close in case he's not alone."

"He's alone, Vince. Men who use derringers are always alone," she replied as she stared at Bob's body.

Vince nodded, slipped the derringer into his pocket and ran back outside as Lucy headed into the kitchen for a mop to clean up the blood.

He mounted his horse quickly and set off down the trail at a fast trot.

———

Rachel was in an examining room in Sisters Hospital and had begged the doctor to take care of Marsh before he even examined her, but she didn't have to ask because Marsh was in very real danger of dying. He had lost a lot of blood and only Rachel's fast driving had given him a chance. Luckily, he was a very big man, and the bullet hadn't caused any significant damage to any organs, but he needed a lot of work to close off the bleeding blood vessels.

While the doctor was working on Marsh, Deputy Chas Robinson came in and talked to Rachel, who told him that Bob McCallister had just arrived at the door, and when Marsh opened it, Bob shot him and then, when she tried to go to Marsh, he had tried to grab her and dropped the derringer and it had gone off and hit her leg. Then, she told him with a shaking voice how Marsh, a bullet in his abdomen, blood pouring onto the floor, had stopped Bob from grabbing her and picked him up over his head and thrown him against the fireplace.

"Is McCallister dead, Mrs. Anderson?" Chas asked.

Under any other circumstances, calling her Mrs. Anderson would have made her smile, but this time, all she did was answer, "I'm not sure. Marsh even went out and harnessed the buggy and helped me into the seat. It was only when he got on board that he finally knew he couldn't do any more."

Then with tears racing from her eyes, Rachel shouted, "He can't die! My husband can't die! Not again!"

When she said it, it all came back to haunt her; four marriages, three dead so far; and wanted to die herself. *Not Marsh! Please, God, not Marsh!*

She prayed that He take her soul, not her husband's.

Chas could see how upset she was and slowly backed out of the room. He needed to ride out to the valley, but some bastard had stolen his horse. *What incredibly bad timing!*

He couldn't ask the doctor what the odds were that Marsh would live, as he and Sister Anne, the nurse, were in surgery.

He was walking out of the door of Sisters Hospital, when a man came racing up on a lathered horse and leapt down, almost running into Chas.

Vince spotted his badge and stopped.

"How is he? How's Marsh? How's Rachel?" he asked in rapid fire.

"Excuse me, sir. I don't know you," Chas replied.

"Oh. I'm Vincent Cirillo. My wife and I came up from Denver. We were his witnesses at his wedding today."

"Oh, that's right. I should have recognized you. Marsh is still in surgery with a gunshot to the belly. He lost a lot of blood. Rachel is in the examining room with a gunshot to her leg. Did you just leave the valley?"

"I did. The man that shot them both is dead. It looks like Marsh threw him against the fireplace. Here's the pistol he used to shoot them," Vince said as he handed Chas the Remington.

Chas looked at the gun and shook his head as he said, "A coward's gun. I wouldn't have expected any different from Bob McCallister."

Vince was startled, and asked, "*That* was Bob McCallister? Why did he want to kill Marsh?"

"We may never know. Are you going to go and see Mrs. Anderson?" he asked.

Vince nodded and said, "My wife is alone in the house. Do you think she'll be all right?"

"I'm pretty sure. Bob was alone," he said, then paused and added, "and deserved to be."

Vince then trotted into the hospital, while Chas took the horse to the trough, let him drink before leading him down the street to the livery to be fed and cared for. He told Joe, the liveryman, that the county would pay the bill.

Rachel was still despondent when Vince stuck in his head and asked, "Rachel, how are you?"

Rachel looked up with her wet, red eyes and said quietly, "Marsh might die, Vince. It's all my fault, too. I should never have married him. I love him too much."

Vince didn't know what she was talking about as he had yet to make the connection between Marsh's Rachel and the Black Widow Rachel from the newspaper.

"Rachel, it's not your fault. It's the fault of that bastard that shot you and Marsh."

"He didn't try to shoot me. He dropped the derringer to try to stop me from helping Marsh. Don't you understand? I'm the Black Widow that's had three husbands die, and now, that curse will cost Marsh his life."

Vince's eyebrows shot up. *She was that Rachel.* Rachel Pratt, wife of the millionaire that had married her and seven weeks later, died of food poisoning; and who's first husband had died in a suspicious fall down the stairs. She killed her third husband in Missoula, according to the newspaper story, but Marsh must have known all the stories, yet obviously loved her. Vince wasn't about to put any credence into the whole curse thing, but right now, all they could do is wait.

He waited for another twenty minutes before the doctor came out of surgery. He walked across to Rachel's examining room and didn't seem happy, which worried Vince and terrified Rachel. Sister Anne stood behind him.

"Doctor Walsh, how is Marsh?" she asked, dread filling her voice.

He was truly uncertain as he replied, "I'm not sure. The bullet missed anything critical, and I stopped the bleeding and cleaned the wound, but he lost a lot of blood. All we can do now is wait and hope there is no infection and that he can produce enough new blood to replace what he has lost. Now, I need to treat your wound, Mrs. Anderson."

She nodded and laid back down as the doctor began to work. She refused laudanum and grimaced when he applied alcohol as an antiseptic, then sutured both sides of her calf as she absorbed the pain. Rachel felt she deserved much more punishment for what she had caused and accepted the pain as part of her sentence.

She noticed as the doctor was sewing her leg that somehow, miraculously, her white wedding dress hadn't picked up a spot of blood and couldn't see how that was possible; but before Doctor Walsh finished, Rachel passed out.

———

Chas borrowed his fellow deputy's horse and had Lat man the office waiting for results about Marsh and Rachel's condition. He led Vince's horse as he rode Lat's horse to

Sister's Hospital where he retrieved Vince to go back to the valley. He needed Vince to be there when he went to the valley as Vince's wife was alone in the house.

As they turned onto the moonlit trail, Chas noticed a horse walking in the distance and whistled. The horse responded and trotted toward Chas.

"I guess I know who stole my horse now," he said to Vince as he took his horse's reins and they continued on to the house.

When they reached the house, they stepped down and tied off the three horses. When they stepped onto the porch, Vince called, "Lucy, it's me. I've brought the sheriff."

Chas didn't correct him as the door opened and Lucy said, "Come in, I've cleaned up the blood and have some coffee on the stove. I haven't touched the body."

"That was smart, ma'am," Chas said as he entered and gave a quick scan of the room.

He could still see the wet spots where the blood was and found it hard to believe that Marsh could have picked up a hundred and seventy pound man over his head while he was bleeding from a gunshot wound to the belly. He stepped over to Bob McCallister's body and stared at the crumpled mess. His head had struck halfway up the left side of the stout stone fireplace. He wanted to spit on the body, but knew it would be unprofessional. That man and the Shipmans had brought so much violence and pain to the city, and just when things were being put right, this bastard has to come here and ruin everything.

"Mister Cirillo, could you help me get the body on my horse?" Chas asked.

"Sure. I'll be right with you," Vince replied before he asked Lucy how she was.

It only took them a few minutes to drape Bob McCallister's corpse over the saddle, then Chas mounted and led the horse back to Missoula while Vince returned to the house to be with Lucy.

———

Marsh knew he wasn't dead when he regained consciousness because his belly was still hurting and his mouth was gunky and dry. It was still dark, though, and when he slowly raised his eyelids, he looked around with just his eyes and knew he was someplace medical. It must be Sisters Hospital, he thought.

He turned his head to the left and then the right. When his head was fully to the right, he spotted Rachel. At first he thought she was sleeping and then, the horrible thought filled his head that she was dead. It was too dark for him to see if she was breathing, so he needed to somehow talk to her, but his mouth was like a dried up swamp.

He began working his saliva to try to get him some moisture, but it was making him dizzy with the effort, so he slowed down just a bit and finally managed to weak rasp, and asked, "Rachel?"

She didn't move and Marsh began to panic. Not his Rachel. *How could she die from a leg wound?* His fear of losing her overcame his logic as he stared at her.

Again he croaked, "Rachel!"

Rachel was sound asleep. She had passed out when the doctor sutured her wound, but had revived just ten minutes after he finished. She had asked to be put in the same room with her husband so she could be there when he awakened.

Initially, Doctor Walsh thought it was a bad idea, as he didn't give Marsh a one in four chance of surviving; but Rachel's tenacity won the argument, so Rachel had been wheeled into the same room with Marsh. She'd managed to stay awake until almost one o'clock before giving in to her body's demand for sleep.

Now, she was dreaming that she and Marsh were in the hot spring pond, the new cottage was completed and while they sat on the patio, their children were playing in the nearby water. She looked at her children, her babies, and smiled. There were five blonde-haired, blue-eyed girls. There were no brown-haired, brown-eyed children among them. There wasn't a spawn of Frank Shipman; all her little girls were Marsh's babies. She began to cry in absolute joy, and turned and smiled at Marsh who was watching their daughters and then he looked at her and simply said, "Rachel."

It was enough. She didn't need to have him tell her that he loved her; she could see it in his eyes. She was about to tell him how happy she was when he said again, "Rachel," but his voice sounded different. It wasn't the soft, masculine voice that he used when talking to her. It was a gruff, harsh voice. She was going to ask him what was wrong when his voice said once more, even more gravelly, "Rachel."

Her eyes popped open and she saw Marsh looking at her. His voice may be different, but the joy in his eyes when he looked at her was the same and she knew it always would be. *Her Marsh was back!*

She was so incredibly happy and relieved, all she could manage was a soft, "Marsh."

Marsh had used up almost all his available strength to call to Rachel and was fighting to keep his eyes open, but he needed to tell her, so he took a deep breath and forced out the words, "I will see you in the morning, my wife."

Then his eyes closed and he fell into a sleep rather than another round of unconsciousness. Rachel just watched his face as Sister Margarite entered and asked, "Was that you, Mrs. Anderson?"

She smiled and replied, "No, Sister, that was my husband. He said he'll see me again in the morning. He'll want to have something to eat and he'll need a lot of water."

Sister Margarite turned to look at Marsh and wondered if his wife wasn't dreaming, but smiled at Rachel and said, "I'll have it ordered for him. Now, you need to get some sleep yourself, Mrs. Anderson."

Rachel smiled and replied, "Oh, I will now. I know that soon, we'll be back in our valley together where we belong."

Sister Margarite nodded her head and left the room silently, the way that only nuns can manage, as Rachel closed her eyes, took a long, deep breath and let it out. Marsh wasn't going to be the fourth one.

————

When Rachel awakened in the early hours as sun streamed through the window, she found Marsh looking at her.

She immediately smiled and said, "Good morning, my husband. You did say you'd see me in the morning."

In a surprisingly clear and strong voice, Marsh replied, "I did. I wanted to let you know that I would never leave you, Rachel."

"How come you sound so much better?" she asked.

"There were two glasses of water on that shelf near the window. I drank them both and felt much better."

"But Marsh, they thought you were going to die last night. You act like you weren't even shot."

"Trust me, Rachel, I know I was shot. How is your leg?"

"It hurts, but I'll be okay," she replied and then said, "Marsh, I watched what you did after you'd been shot and I don't believe I'll ever see anything that could match it. You were just shot and bleeding and when you saw Bob McCallister reach for me you stood up and picked him up over your head and threw him almost ten feet across the room. How on earth did you do it?"

Marsh exhaled softly and said, "I thought he was going to hurt you, Rachel. I couldn't let anyone hurt you. Never again."

Rachel sniffed twice then said, "I'd come over there and kiss you if I could walk."

Marsh smiled and replied, "You don't want to get me all excited again. I never did get to consummate our marriage, and I might try."

Rachel began to laugh and wipe away tears at the same time. Before she could say anything else, Sister Mary Joseph walked into the room and her eyes bulged as she looked at Marsh.

"Jesus, Mary and Joseph! How is this possible? Mister Anderson, we were ready to administer Last Rites to you last night and here you are acting like you're ready to leave," she said breathlessly.

"I'm sorry, Sister, but being so close to a beautiful woman is very therapeutic."

The good sister replied, "That may be, Mister Anderson, but it's still a miracle."

Marsh then added, "Having my wife here is good, too, Sister."

The nun laughed and said, "You've got a touch of the blarney, Mister Anderson. I'll have them bring you and your wife some breakfast."

"Thank you, Sister. I'm really hungry."

"The doctor said that eating will help you build your blood supply back to normal, so you'll be eating everything on your plate."

"I promise, Sister," Marsh said as Sister Mary Joseph left the room smiling.

Rachel looked over, grinned at Marsh and said, "I do believe you've made a nun blush, Marsh."

"Someone has to on occasion."

He found that talking was wearing him down quickly, so he laid his head back down and just relaxed.

———

After breakfast, the visitors began arriving. First was Doctor Walsh who was astounded by the Marsh's rapid recovery then examined both his stomach wound and Rachel's leg wound and said they'd both have to stay in the hospital for at least another week to make sure there was no infection.

Next, Chas Robinson arrived to get an official statement, then told him that Bob's body had been buried in the city cemetery, and said that the prosecutor said it was the most justifiable homicide he'd ever seen.

Vince and Lucy arrived at ten o'clock and said they'd stay for a few more days until Marsh and Rachel could go home, and told Marsh that the construction crews arrived to start both jobs and he'd keep an eye on them to make sure it was done right.

Rachel looked at Lucy, and asked how she liked the pond. Lucy didn't verbally reply, but simply winked and grinned at her.

The rest of the day was filled sporadically with more wellwishers, some that Marsh barely knew and Rachel didn't know at all.

That evening, when everyone had gone, Rachel looked over at Marsh with almost an angelic look on her face and said, "Marsh, my monthly began today. No spawn of Frank Shipman will ever be issued by me."

He knew how much it had worried her and was glad there would never be any doubt.

Then, she told him of the dream she had just as he had awakened and found him looking at her. How they were at the new cottage by the pond and there were five golden-haired blue-eyed girls playing in the water.

Then she asked, "Marsh, will you be disappointed if I never give you a son?"

Marsh shook his head slowly, smiled and replied, "Not one bit, my love. I have a great attraction to golden-haired, blue-eyed women."

———

Over the week of their convalescence, Marsh and Rachel indulged in what became the best way to make the time pass faster and better; they talked. They spoke of anything and everything, and as they did, they found why they had fallen in love so quickly. It wasn't that they thought exactly alike, but it was because despite their incredibly different paths that they took to adulthood, the way they looked at life was identical.

Rachel was up on crutches after three days, and was able to kiss her husband. Which, as he had suspected, made him wish he wasn't bedridden; as opposed to other, more useful purposes for a mattress.

Marsh was able to sit, with a lot of pain, on the same day that Rachel left her bed to use her crutches, and two days later was able to walk unassisted. He told her it was more comfortable to walk then it was to sit up, which made perfect sense to her.

On the seventh day, Doctor Walsh examined their wounds as he had done every day and told them both that they could leave tomorrow, but it would be a good idea to have someone stay with them for a week or so, so he would have Sister Margarite accompany them tomorrow when they returned home, and she would remove their sutures rather than have to return to Missoula.

Vince said he'd bring the buggy at nine o'clock in the morning, and he'd trail hitch Sam so he could ride back while Rachel drove the buggy with Marsh and Sister Margarite.

It was all arranged, so the next day, Marsh and Rachel would be returning to their valley.

———

Even as the buggy and Vince were riding back to the valley, a visitor was arriving on the train from Denver. He stepped off the platform and arranged to rent a buggy. He had a travel bag and a leather satchel, wore a bowler hat, a dark tweed suit and spats over his black oxfords. He was tall, just under six feet, but only weighed about a hundred and fifty pounds. His age was about forty, but he looked older with a receding hairline and gray streaks in what hair remained. He had all the earmarks of an attorney.

———

Marsh and Rachel, who still used a crutch, were finally able to enter their house again. The construction crews working on the house addition all waved as they arrived, and Marsh and Rachel waved back. Vince had told him that they had another two weeks to go and the cottage crew had another three weeks because of all the odd things that Marsh and Mister Longstaff had put in the design.

Sister Margarite was given a bedroom near the kitchen, and said she'd be handling the cooking as well as caring for her two patients. Sister Margarite was a young nun, having taken her final vows just three years earlier. She had grown up in Baltimore and was totally shocked by the conditions when she first arrived, but had adjusted well to life on the frontier. She had a pretty, round face, smiled a lot, and both Marsh and Rachel were happy that she had been chosen for the job.

Sister Margarite was preparing lunch, while Vince and Marsh discussed the construction company back in Denver and the job that the two firms were doing in the valley. Meanwhile, Rachel and Lucy were sitting as far away as possible, talking in low voices, and giggling as they would sometimes pass glances at their husbands.

Sister Margarite was about to tell them that lunch was ready when they all heard boots stepping onto the porch. Marsh quickly pulled his Colt and waited while Sister Margarite answered the door, not even glancing back at him.

She swung it open and Marsh knew who the man was standing at the door, as did Vince. He was Wolfgang Schliechster, Esquire, and the holder of the uncoveted title of Shadiest Attorney in Denver.

"I wish to see Mrs. Anderson, if I may. My name is Wolfgang Schliechster, and I represent the interests of the Pratt family."

Before the sister could reply, Marsh said, "Come in, Mister Schliechster."

Rachel glanced at Marsh with fear in her eyes. *What could they possibly want?* They had taken everything from her.

He smiled that phony smile that only bad lawyers and good salesmen seemed to possess, and entered the room.

"Have a seat, Mister Schliechster," Marsh said affably.

Rachel was getting nervous and wondered why Marsh was treating him so congenially.

Marsh had already guessed why he was there and what the Pratts wanted; he also had already been planning his response. This wasn't all that different than setting up to face the Shipmans almost two weeks earlier. It just wasn't going to be nearly as dangerous.

Mister Schliechster sat down and placed his satchel on the table and snapped it open, pulling out a thick legal document.

"Mrs. Anderson, I am here representing Walter Pratt, Jr., Lawrence Pratt, Patricia Pratt Longley, and Susan Pratt Harrison. They believe that you are responsible for the death of their father and have filed a wrongful death suit to bring some semblance of justice. They are seeking damages in the amount of fifty thousand dollars," he intoned blandly as he slid the papers toward Rachel and sat back waiting for her reaction.

But Marsh intercepted the documents before Rachel could take them. She looked at Marsh and saw him grow stiff as his blue eyes that had only held warmth for her, turn icy cold. The moment she saw his face, she began to feel sorry for Mister Schliechster.

Marsh made a show of reading the document, but didn't read a word. He was thinking as he pretended to read; then, after three minutes, he gently laid the papers down on the table.

"Mister Schliechster, do you believe that your clients would accept a settlement rather than have to go through a lengthy and costly trial?" he asked.

The attorney had a very good poker face, but Marsh could see the satisfaction in his eyes.

"I have received instructions from my clients about that possibility," he replied.

"Now, we don't have a lot of cash available. Do you have an alternative proposal?" Marsh asked.

Vince wondered what he was talking about, because he knew that Marsh could afford to pay the fifty thousand. He guessed that Marsh was getting ready to pounce on poor Mister Schliechster.

"It has come to my attention in a recent newspaper article that Mrs. Anderson has just been awarded sole ownership of a ranch, the Double M, I believe. After doing some research, I found that the property and livestock would be worth upwards of thirty to thirty-five thousand dollars. But accepting the ranch as payment would be subject to market vagaries and could sit unsold for months. However, they would be willing to accept the ranch as a settlement to drop their lawsuit."

Marsh sat back in his chair, took a deep breath and then asked, "Mister Schliechster, have you ever seen a grizzly bear up close? I mean a live, six-hundred pound monster, standing on his feet with his giant claws in the air, ready to attack?"

Mister Schliechster, shook his head, wondering where the hell Mister Anderson was going and replied, "No, I can't say that I have."

Marsh pointed to Rachel and said, "My wife, the one you are threatening with your nonsensical lawsuit, stood with such a bear, his claws ten feet in the air, just twenty feet in front of her, but she didn't panic. She didn't make any bad decisions. My wife, Mister Schliechster, has sand. I saw the bear and let it run at me and shot it through the mouth when he was twenty feet away and charging. Mister Schliechster, I have sand."

When four armed men, intent on killing us both, invaded our valley, that woman that you think will just bow down and let you roll over her with your legal threats, stood with me, firing her Winchester, and we killed all four of the bastards. We were both shot a few days ago, yet here we sit. Now, you come in here and honestly believe that you can scare either of us? I believe you seriously underestimate both me and my beloved wife."

Mister Schliechster began to tap his fingers on the table as his nerves ticked up a notch.

Marsh continued in his cold, intense voice, saying, "Now, Mister Schliechster, I'll tell you a few things that maybe you don't know. Perhaps you've heard of Anderson Construction?"

"Yes," he replied, then suddenly made the connection and knew he would have a serious conversation with his investigator when he returned to Denver for missing that critical tidbit of information.

"I own the company, as my good friend and manager, Vincent Cirillo can verify. Now, those bastard boys of Walter Pratt, and his bitchy daughters, used newspapers and lies to portray my innocent wife as a Black Widow and essentially threw her out of her house and even took her clothes just because they are selfish, greedy moneygrubbers. She had no power, no contacts, and was an easy target for you and those useless clients of yours."

So, Mister Schliechster, here's what I'm going to do. I'm going to tell you to go ahead and file your silly lawsuit if you so desire. I'm instructing Vince that when he returns to Denver to initiate a suit for slander, libel and defamation of character against your clients. You know what makes this an interesting legal duel this time, Mister Schliechster? This time, it will be Rachel who will have all the power. I have the resources and the contacts; I'll hire Pinkertons to investigate the sources of those stories that appeared in the newspaper and threaten them with libel unless they cooperate. My firm has a permanent retainer with Whitcomb and Harper, and I'm sure that you're familiar with them. Now, your clients don't have access to the Pratt estate or moneys because it's still in probate. You and their other attorneys are operating on the premise that they will be awarded the estate by the probate court. If they don't win, you don't get a dime. Now, Rachel, on the other hand, has the backing of much more liquid assets."

Mister Schliechster was beyond nervous. He had expected a short negotiating session and walk away with the deed, which would satisfy the legal bills of all of the attorneys of the Pratt children. But now, not only was he not going to get that settlement, he knew he was in deep trouble. It wouldn't take a lot of investigating by the Pinkertons to find the links to the newspapers, and, even worse, the bribes paid to the judge who issued the eviction order. He needed to make this go away and get back to Denver.

"Mister Anderson," he began, "I don't believe we need to create such a legal turmoil. I believe I can convince my clients to drop their lawsuit just as a gesture of conciliation."

Marsh glanced over at Rachel, who's eyes were dancing, then glared at the beaten attorney.

"Mister Schliechster, you obviously misinterpreted what I just explained to you. You are viewing everything in convoluted legal terms, but I'm speaking in terms that are much more direct. I view what you are doing as nothing less than an attack. In your case, you are attacking us using fancy words, phony smiles and a nice leather satchel with intentionally obtuse papers."

But to me, an attack is an attack, whether it's by a viscous grizzly bear, four armed killers, a crazy man with a pistol, or a smooth attorney wearing a nice suit and bowler hat. I have no intention of negotiating with you, Mister Schliechster. Tomorrow, Mister Cirillo will return to Denver and he will initiate exactly what I outlined because the only way to defeat an attacker is to kill him. I intend to financially destroy you and your clients. Now, I suggest you leave our valley and return to Denver. You may be wise to leave Denver and practice your brand of law in the sewers of some other city in the East."

Mister Schliechster opened his mouth to respond, then thought wiser of it and just took the legal papers back, slid them

274

into this satchel, closed it and then with as much dignity as he could manage, stood, and left the room and the house. When he stepped into the buggy and started moving, the room resounded in applause, with even Sister Margarite loudly clapping.

After the applause died down, Marsh turned to Vince and said, "Did you get all that, Vince? Rachel will give you all the details, including the judge's name and dates and times. Engage the Pinkertons and let Charlie Whitcomb know the legal issues we'll need to confront. I think he has a young firebrand in his office who would be perfect for this case. I think his name is Johnson or something like that."

Vince smiled and said, "His name is Paul Johnson, and he's not just a young firebrand anymore. He's a partner now, I just didn't want to correct you. He's still got the fire in his belly though. You're right, he's the man we want."

Marsh nodded and turned to Rachel, "Sweetheart, we'll sit down with Vince in a little while and he'll take down everything you can remember. In a few months, we may need to go to Denver to finish it."

Rachel replied, "Marsh, I don't need or want the money. I'm so very happy here with you."

"Rachel, it's not about the money. It's just what I told Mister Schliechster. They attacked you just like the grizzly did. Even if they backed down this time, they may come back later. I think the only reason they even did this was because they needed quick cash to keep funding their legal battles. The only concern I have, and this is for you, Vince, is if Mister Schliechster gets back before you do and tells the Pratt brats that they need to drop their infighting and get the probate court to make their decision."

Vince nodded and replied, "I can ride into Missoula and send a telegram to Paul Johnson and tell him we're retaining the firm to represent Rachel Pratt, now Rachel Anderson, in the probate of Walter Pratt and that new information will be presented to the court."

"That's great, Vince. Can you wait for a response?" Marsh asked.

"Sure. I'll get that done right now. Can I borrow Sam?"

"Go ahead. You need to get back quickly, though, so you and Lucy can relax in the cabin," Marsh said with a grin.

Sister Margarite giggled and returned to the kitchen to reheat lunch.

———

Forty minutes later, Vince was riding to Missoula to get the message sent to Denver. When he arrived, he spotted Chas Robinson and waved him over. He stepped down and explained what Mister Schliechster was doing, described him, and suggested that if there was a way to delay his departure, Marsh and Rachel would appreciate it.

Chas smiled and said he'd see what he could do.

Vince sent the telegram and waited for a reply. It took over an hour, but when he received the message, he read it and smiled. It turned out that Paul Johnson was very familiar with the Pratt case, as were many attorneys in the city. In his message, he said he'd take on the case, and awaited Vince's return for details.

He rode back to the valley willing the horse to go faster. When he arrived, he let the horse go into the barn to drink and rest as he trotted quickly to the house. He leapt over the steps and crossed the porch quickly, but didn't knock and just entered the house, spotting Lucy and Rachel talking and Marsh watching his wife. They all turned and saw his big grin.

He read the telegram and then told them of his brief talk with Chas.

"Great job, Vince," Marsh said with a grin to match Vince's.

Vince then spent almost an hour taking down the details of the situation from Rachel.

Once she was done, Vince looked over at Marsh and said, "I can't believe they got away with this. I remember all those stories in the paper. They painted Rachel as a money grubbing, manipulative tart that sold herself to better her station. I even remember the picture that they put in the paper. It wasn't very flattering."

Marsh said, "Well, we're going to change that, Vince. When Paul Johnson mentions libel to the newspaper, make sure that they have a copy of the Missoula Times with our wedding picture and suggest that a follow-up story might reduce or eliminate their liability, depending on how well written it is. They'll be able to link it to the hardships that Rachel has had to face."

Vince nodded, but Rachel seemed distraught as she said, "Marsh, I'm uncomfortable having that Black Widow story brought up again."

"That's just it, Rachel. I never want to hear that name applied to you ever again. If we have to travel anywhere, I don't want anyone to even think of you as someone other than who you really are; the most extraordinary woman I've ever met."

Rachel smiled grimly and squeezed Marsh's hand, hoping that it worked out that way.

With the excitement of the day finally over, Vince and Lucy left the house and walked to the cabin to enjoy their last night in the valley, and the two invalids were able to make their way to their bedroom after Sister Margarite turned in.

———

The next morning, things were a bit hectic as Vince and Lucy had to make the 10:40 train back to Denver. Breakfast was automatically eaten, bags were packed and farewells made. By 7:40, Vince and Lucy were leaving in their rented buggy, waving as they disappeared down the trail.

Marsh provided the crutch for Rachel as she limped alongside heading back into the house.

It was a twist of anatomical engineering that Marsh was more mobile than Rachel even though his injury had been life-threatening. Once the danger from blood loss and infection had passed, the only injury Marsh had sustained was the same as Rachel; muscle damage. With Marsh, as long as he avoided tensing his stomach muscles, he was all right. Rachel couldn't walk on her leg yet, although it was healing rapidly. In another day, Sister Margarite would remove their sutures and then it would just need more time to complete the healing.

That day, the construction crew doing the house addition had to go into the house to cut two doorways to the new rooms, so Marsh and Rachel, accompanied by Sister Margarite, moved to the cabin for the day.

After they were in the cabin, Sister Margarite asked why the men were digging such a large hole near the new addition, and Marsh explained the purpose of the septic tank and, naturally, began talking about their cottage that was being built at the other end of the valley.

Rachel joined in excitedly talking about the hot spring pond, leaving out what she and Marsh did while enjoying its relaxing waters.

Then Marsh abruptly changed the subject as he sat on the porch in the afternoon sun with Rachel sitting next to him and Sister Margarite beside her with the hammering and sawing noises emanating from the house.

"Rachel, there are a few things about Bob McCallister's return that have me puzzled. I can understand why he came back despite having to face the humiliation that drove him away in the first place, because you are most assuredly worth that and more. But where was his horse? How did he get here? Was he planning on leaving or thinking he could take the valley with a derringer? He wouldn't have stayed in town, so where were his basic things. Even if he was only going to stay a single day, he'd need his shaving kit and other necessities."

Rachel replied, "Maybe he was just going to do what he wanted to do, then steal one of our horses and return to wherever he was living."

Marsh scratched his chin and replied, "Maybe. Maybe he thought he could move back to the Double M. But motive and transport aside, there's the question of timing. He had to arrive in town while we were getting married and come out here either before we arrived or immediately after Vince and Lucy went to the pond. Now, if he came after they left, he'd see two buggies and think we had visitors, but he walked right up onto the porch with a two-shot derringer in his hand obviously knowing we were alone. He had to have been watching, so when they left, he knew we were alone and he could come to the house. I guess he was up in the tower when we arrived and watched until he saw them leave. He was either there or the barn loft, but if he was in the loft, he wouldn't be able to see if they had gone far enough away to give him time."

Rachel smiled and asked, "So, Mister Pinkerton, what is your motive for trying to unravel this mystery?"

Marsh laughed and replied, "The same motive that put me into the whole mess in the first place; my unquenchable need to discover why. It's gotten me into more trouble over the years than I could imagine, but in this case, my love, it led me to you."

"And I'm very grateful for that. So, how can you solve the mystery of the apparition of Bob McCallister?" she asked.

"Beats me," he replied, then looked at one of the legs of his tower a few feet away, and said, "Maybe if he got here on a stolen horse, kicked it loose and then climbed the tower to watch, his personal effects are still there. If not, they might be in the barn's loft. I think I'll go check."

As he stood, Sister Margarite blanched and she exclaimed, "Mister Anderson, you surely can't climb that tower! Your sutures haven't even been removed yet."

"I'll be fine, Sister. It's an easy climb," he said over his shoulder as he began to step up the rungs of his tower.

Both women watched with totally different expressions on their faces. Sister Margarite was horrified while Rachel watched in interest to see if he would find anything.

Marsh himself was now convinced that he would find saddlebags up in the tower and they might give him more clues as to why Bob had come to their valley, although he was pretty sure it was for Rachel, because that would be the only valid purpose. He was also prepared for disappointment as he passed the halfway point. His stomach didn't hurt at all, which surprised him, but he accepted the lack of pain as a good thing as he approached the floor of the parapet.

Then, his eyes reached the level floor and he spotted two travel bags and let out a whoop.

Down below, Rachel smiled and said to Sister Margarite, "It sounds like my husband has made a discovery."

Marsh climbed into the parapet and sat on the floor with his feet dangling over the edge as he pulled the first travel bag onto his lap and opened it, finding clothes, a shaving kit, a towel and an extra pair of shoes. He set it aside and opened the second and found more clothes, and then a newspaper. It was a copy of the extra edition of the *Missoula Times*. Bob had written along the margins and had underlined and crossed out words and sentences in the long article.

Marsh examined the scrawls and the deletions and circled words and it was obvious that Bob was obsessed with Rachel and had grown to hate Marsh for marrying her. He also circled the Double M and the valley, the wedding date and time, and written on the side: Rachel McCallister. He sadly noted that Bob had lined through Lillie's name as if he didn't care or was happy she was gone.

With the motive for his arrival solved, he carefully refolded the newspaper and set it aside to continue his exploration. It didn't take long before he ran into a large envelope and pulled it from the bottom of the travel bag. Marsh had a good idea about its contents before he opened it and wasn't surprised to see a lot of cash. He did a quick count and came up with $6,148. He slid the money back into the envelope then returned it to the travel bag with the newspaper. After closing both bags, he looked down and saw the heads of Rachel and Sister Margarite and calculated the trajectory.

He then shouted, "Look out below!", and after they both looked up, he tossed the first travel bag, with all the clothing away from the women and watched as it arced outwards a few feet and then plummeted to the ground making a large mushroom cloud of dust as it hit.

He then held out the money bag and tossed it away as well, watching it plop to the ground before swinging around and beginning his descent.

When he arrived, he retrieved both bags and stepped over to the porch and sat next to Rachel.

"Well?" she asked.

"This was a very worthwhile find, my beloved wife. Most of it was his clothes, but none of them were new, so I gather that these two bags were all he had with him when he left the Double M. It looks like he didn't go far, probably to Helena where he knew his way around, at least to the cathouses. But before we go any further, I'd like to ask Sister Margarite something."

Sister Margarite, who was used to her role as a bystander, took a few seconds to respond.

"Of course, Mister Anderson. Feel free to ask your question," she said.

"Before I do, Sister, you've got to stop calling me Mister Anderson. Call me Marsh. Okay?"

The nun smiled and replied, "Okay, Marsh."

"Very good. Now, I know that you probably have taken a vow of poverty. Is that right?"

"Yes, that's correct," she replied.

"So, I can't reward you personally for your assistance, but would I be able to donate these bags of clothes so you may distribute them to the needy?"

Sister Margarite was touched and replied, "Why, of course, Marsh. That's very thoughtful."

"Now, if there was any loose change or a few greenbacks in here, would you be able to accept them on behalf of the sisters to help them in their mission to provide physical and spiritual support for those in need?"

The nun was practically beaming now, and replied, "Yes, we have a fund for that purpose, although, to be honest, it tends to be less than we sometimes need."

"Well, Sister, I don't think you and your sisters will need to worry about that for a while. I checked and there's over six thousand dollars in an envelope in this bag."

Sister Margarite went from beaming to shocked in a flash, and even Rachel was stunned momentarily by the amount.

Rachel asked, "He had that much?"

"Lillie told me that he had emptied their bank account and about two thousand dollars from their safe before he left, so they must have had at least four thousand in the bank."

Sister Margarite finally recovered and asked, "But Marsh, is this legal? Surely there must be a legal owner somewhere."

Marsh replied, "If there is, she's sitting right next to you. The court order making her the legal heir to Frank Shipman made her the owner of the Double M ranch and all that it contained.

Now, it might be a stretch to say the money in the bank account would go to Rachel, but the money in the safe surely would be included. Now, I look at the additional money as being just compensation for what Bob did to me and to Rachel, and as the sisters provided me and Rachel with extraordinary care, I think it's only right that you accept the donation in the spirit that it is offered."

Rachel then added, "I concur with my illustrious husband in his excessively verbose method of describing the gift."

Marsh looked at his wife and began to laugh, and was soon joined by Rachel and Sister Margarite.

When the laughing subsided, Sister Margarite said she would accept the gift on behalf of the sisters and would thank Marsh and Rachel in her prayers, as would all of her sisters.

Marsh then gave Rachel the newspaper and let her draw her own conclusions, which, naturally, matched his own, and like Marsh, noted that Lillie's name had been stricken from the narrative.

———

Two days later, their sutures removed and both of her patients doing better than expected, Sister Margarite said she needed to return to Missoula, so Marsh harnessed the buggy and brought it around to the front. He was functioning almost normally already, although his stomach muscles still protested if he overdid it. Rachel was walking unassisted, but had a pronounced limp, and she worried that it might be permanent.

Marsh loaded the two travel bags on the back of the buggy and assisted Rachel into the buggy first, as she required the help. He also guided Sister Margarite into the buggy just because her voluminous habit made it difficult to negotiate entry. He boarded next to Rachel, flicked the reins and they departed the valley for Missoula.

When they arrived at Sisters Hospital, Marsh reversed the assistance to help both Sister Margarite and Rachel from the buggy and let Rachel use his right arm as an aid more than a crutch as they walked inside; Sister Margarite carrying the valuable bag and Marsh the second.

After seeing her to Mother Superior's office and leaving the second bag, Marsh and Rachel accepted the thanks of a still dumbfounded Mother Mary Beatrice for the huge gift. After a much more heartfelt thanks from Sister Margarite, Rachel told her that if she ever wished to visit, or any of her sisters wished to partake of the hot springs pond, to send a note to the valley; then she and Marsh left the hospital and returned to the buggy.

They stopped at the sheriff's office and Marsh entered alone, leaving Rachel in the buggy rather than making her walk again. When he entered, Chas Robinson was at the desk and Lat Foster was leaning backwards on a chair nearby.

"How are you boys doing?" Marsh asked as he walked through the doorway.

Lat dropped the chair down to the floor and stood as did Chas, then stepped forward and shook Marsh's hand.

"We're doing fine now, Marsh. With the Shipman boys gone, especially our boss, things have calmed down a lot," Chas replied, then added, "and we had a bit of a problem when we arrested a visitor for vagrancy and caused him to miss his train to Denver. It cost him a whole day and he said he would sue us for false arrest."

Marsh laughed and said, "I wouldn't lose any sleep over it. He'll be way too busy with the problems I'm creating for him to worry about you. I just stopped by to let you know that I found Bob McCallister's travel bags in my tower. There was over six thousand dollars in one of the two bags."

Chas said, "As far as we're concerned, Marsh, that's your money. It was left on your property after that weasel shot you and Mrs. Anderson."

"That's all right, I donated it to the Sisters Hospital. It seemed like the right thing to do."

"I'm sure they really appreciated it," Lat said.

"Did you know that McCallister stole my horse to get to your place?" asked Chas.

"That explains that little mystery. Did you get him back?" Marsh asked.

"I did. I found him when we went back to your valley."

"Well, I'm on my way back there now. I hope we've seen the last of all this excitement. A man could get killed this way," Marsh said with a grin before waving, and leaving the office.

He was stepping up into the buggy when a messenger called out to him and raced down the boardwalk.

"Mister Anderson, I'm glad I saw you. I was just gonna ride out to your place to give you this," Henry Carson said as he trotted breathlessly up to the buggy and handed him a telegram.

Marsh took the telegram and handed Henry a dime. Henry grinned, slipped the coin in his pocket and waited to see if Mister Anderson needed to send a reply.

Marsh read the long telegram, smiled and said, "I don't need to send a reply, Henry. I'm glad you caught up with me and saved yourself a trip."

"Thanks, Mister Anderson," he shouted, then turned and trotted away.

Marsh climbed into the buggy and handed the telegram to Rachel as he flicked the reins and started it rolling west down Higgins Avenue.

Rachel read the message and asked, "Marsh, what happened?"

"I believe the rats are running for cover. Vince said that as soon as Paul Johnson notified the probate court that he had new information and would be representing you in the case, the word got back quickly to the attorneys hired by the Pratts. Now, realize that the kinds of lawyers that they would have to use to pull off the shenanigans they did wouldn't be representative of the legal profession because what they did was borderline criminal. Once you were cleared in Walter's death, they had no legal standing to do those things. They called on their lawyers and social comrades to deny you, a social climber, your property as legal heir. Once they blocked your access to the bank accounts, they knew you couldn't hire a competent attorney to stop them. The judge who wrote that order is in deep trouble and will probably be removed from the bench and lose his license to practice law at the very minimum. They probably hoped you were so naïve that you didn't know that you could have probably walked into any good law firm, told them your story and they would have stopped them in their tracks using a promissory note as a retainer. You just took the hundred dollars and left, making their lives easier. Now they are going to suffer. I imagine they've all been living the high life thinking that they would be coming into a lot of money, and don't have a lot of assets to continue. Did Walter talk about them at all?"

"He did. He was ashamed of them all and swore they wouldn't get a dime because they weren't worth that much. He was providing them with allowances, and said they still complained and called him miserly. He was a good man, Marsh."

Marsh looked over at Rachel as they left the city limits and asked, "Didn't he make a new will after you were married?"

"Yes, he did. He left everything to me, but their lawyers said that I had forced him to change the will."

"But you said that they weren't going to get a dime. Where was the money going to go in his old will?"

"That's what was odd. He didn't leave it to anyone. He only specified that none of his children would get a penny. I remember sitting in the office with his lawyer when he was drawing it up and he said that at least the state wouldn't get the money."

Marsh was flummoxed by that bit of news and asked, "Then why didn't his attorney offer to represent you as the legal heir?"

Rachel sighed and replied, "Because he was hired by the oldest son, Walter, Jr."

Marsh shook his head rapidly and said, "And no one noticed that? I'm sure that Paul Johnson has, and I'll bet that he's one attorney that'll be leaving Denver soon. I can't believe all this. When you told me the story, I never thought to ask about the will. I had assumed that he hadn't changed it yet, and their arguments had some legal merit, but this is downright theft and nothing else."

Rachel sighed and said softly, "I just wish we could go back to the pool for a few hours."

Marsh smiled and replied, "You know, the construction crew leaves around five o'clock, and I'd like to go and see how the cottage is progressing. Would you like to ride down there after they've gone for the day?"

Rachel forgot all about wills, lawyers, and even her healing leg and replied, "We can have our privacy, too."

"We can have our pond to ourselves again, and in a couple of weeks, we'll have our cottage and our pond to ourselves."

Rachel squeezed in even closer to Marsh, if that was possible.

They returned to the house just after noon, so Marsh helped Rachel into the house and then returned outside to unharness and take care of the horse then roll the buggy into the barn.

He then returned he handled cooking lunch while Rachel sat at the table, irritated by her lack of mobility.

"This is driving me crazy, not being able to get around. I don't know if this thing is ever going to get better. Look at you. You're already acting as if you hadn't been shot and now I'm turning into a Whining Wimpy Witless Woman."

Marsh paused and peered at Rachel, then said, "Very impressive run of 'w' words, wonderful, witty, wild, but woefully wrong wife. You're just in the process of healing. But I think that walking isn't helping because your damaged muscle goes from doing nothing to jarring and then having to shove quickly. Now, I have just the exercise for you that will help it much more, I believe."

Rachel raised her eyebrows, smiled, and asked, "And what, as if I didn't know, is the exercise that you're thinking of?"

Marsh grinned and said, "Swimming."

Rachel was taken by surprise and replied, "Swimming? I thought you were going to go with a more pleasurable form of exercise, but that doesn't matter because I can't swim."

"Well, my love, when we go to the pond this evening, I'll give you your first lesson and I think it may lead to other, land-based exercise as well."

Rachel's mood improved remarkably as she replied, "Then I guess I'm going to learn to swim."

————

Five hours later, they were standing near the half-completed cottage and admiring the features that Marsh had wanted.

"If this had been a normal cottage, it would have been done already, but the septic tank and the hot water lines were difficult as was running the cold water lines from the stream."

"So the hot water is coming directly from the hot spring?" she asked.

"No, we can't do that because of its high mineral content. The minerals would plug up the pipes in less than a year. What we did was to run a series of loops of copper and place it near the spring. Cold water enters one end and by the time it leaves the loops, it's almost as hot as the spring. It's like a moonshine still."

"So, we'll have hot and cold running water, a water closet, and that hallway to the pond."

"The hallway has two advantages. We'll be able to use the pond almost every day, and it'll provide some measure of privacy when we're on the other side of the hallway."

Rachel smiled and said, "But not when we're naked in the water."

"No, I'm afraid not. You could get yourself a bathing suit for when we have visitors."

"I may as well go in the water fully clothed."

"Maybe you could just wear some long johns or something."

"That might work but right now, I'm going to get naked."

A few very exciting minutes later, Rachel was with Marsh in four feet of warm water as he let her slip into the water and showed her how to float first. After she began to trust that she wouldn't sink if she let the water support her, he rolled her onto her stomach and supporting her as his left hand massaged her water wings, let her dog paddle around for few seconds before releasing her to move on her own.

Rachel felt the soothing warm waters almost massage her injured calf as she moved slowly through the water.

"You're the only person I could imagine who could make the dog paddle look elegant," Marsh said as she passed by.

Rachel laughed, resulting in a mouthful of the brackish water, before she pulled up close and pulled her legs under her and stood close to Marsh.

"This is so much better than I could have hoped for, Marsh. Can you show me how to really swim now?"

It took longer to graduate to a normal stroke, but Rachel, as she did everything else, learned quickly and was soon swimming alongside Marsh as they swam away from the hot spring and back to the patio. They managed several laps before her leg began tightening and she had to stand.

Marsh and Rachel waded to the edge of the pond and Rachel sat on the very last row of patio stones so her legs could stay in the warm water.

Marsh then walked over to the other end of the patio and slid the two bedrolls close to Rachel's end and she stood momentarily while he pulled them just past the rocks, allowing her to sit again in comfort. It also allowed them to engage in more exercise.

When they were resting afterwards, and Rachel had put her necklace back on and nothing else, she said, "I think that you're right, Marsh. Swimming seems to be much more helpful than just walking. Can we come here every day?"

"Every day, and when the cottage is completed, we can stay here until you feel normal again. I noticed something else that I never mentioned before. I don't know if you noticed, but your scars from where Frank would hit you are almost gone now. I think the water helped in the healing."

Rachel just asked quietly, "Were they that bad, Marsh?"

"Not as bad as I had imagined, but you are so perfect, Rachel, any marks would be a sin. When I first saw them, I was so angry that I wanted to dig up that bastard and shoot him, but they're almost not noticeable any longer."

Rachel sighed, wondering if the inside marks that Frank and her first husband had left on her would ever be totally gone, but in the end, if they did or didn't, she knew as she lay pressed against her husband, that she would never be hurt again.

———

Over the next three weeks, Rachel's pain diminished to almost nothing and her walk returned to normal. The extension to the house was completed and then the cottage was done. Marsh had ordered furniture and a cookstove and one heat stove for the cottage and had it delivered when the work was done.

Now that the couple was mobile, they took care of the mundane things that newlyweds needed to do: Marsh had Rachel added to the bank account in Missoula, the deed to the valley, and the deed to the Double M was changed to Marsh and Rachel Anderson. Marsh had his bank in Denver send a form to add Rachel to the account there, which they completed and returned, before Marsh had a will drawn up in Missoula by Woody & Marshall. Alan Marshall was tickled when he watched Marsh write out his full name on the document.

As he had promised Rachel, they spent most of the time in the cottage and it seemed like a perpetual honeymoon. They had to go to Missoula for supplies twice and had been updated regularly in letters and telegrams from Denver. The newspaper had printed not only retractions of their previous stories about Rachel, but had two issues recounting all that had happened to her since being forced out of the city by those greedy Pratts.

Jacob and Marie were doing well at the Double M, and had brought Simon along, as well as hiring two hands to manage the herd.

It was on the 3rd of July that they received a thick envelope from Denver. They had been alerted of its pending arrival by Paul Johnson in a telegram two days earlier. Following Marsh's instructions, he had rejected every offer of settlement by the Pratts, even as they dropped to laughable offers. As he had explained to their sorry excuse for an attorney; this was a battle and he would only accept an unconditional surrender.

The probate court finally rendered a verdict naming Rachel as the sole heir to Walter Pratt's fortune. The news had hit Rachel hard, as she felt enormous guilt for Walter's death even though she knew she had nothing to do with it. The food had been purchased and prepared by his cook, and Rachel hadn't eaten any of the chicken, which turned out to be the offending dish. Yet she felt that she didn't deserve either the money or the house or other things, and it left her depressed.

The envelope was sitting on the table in the cottage's kitchen while Marsh made coffee and Rachel sat staring at it.

Marsh poured two mugs of coffee and set one down in front of her near the sugar bowl, then sat across from her so he could watch her eyes.

"Marsh, what should I do? I feel ashamed for having Walter's money and things."

"Would you rather that his children get them?" he asked softly.

"No. Never. I just don't feel right," she replied, still staring at the envelope.

"Rachel, you could do a lot of good with that much money. Remember Sister Margarite's face when she realized that the hospital would be getting the six thousand dollars? Now, with that much money, you could make a lot of people just as happy. You don't need to spend it on yourself. You wouldn't anyway, because that's not you. According to the papers in that envelope, you now have access to almost two million dollars in his accounts in Denver and Omaha, and you have stocks worth another half a million dollars. The house and grounds are worth another twenty thousand and then there are his other properties. The possibilities for you are endless, Rachel."

She looked up at Marsh and asked, "Why do you keep saying I have all this money, Marsh? You just had me added to your bank accounts and your valley and I was shocked to find that you had over a hundred thousand dollars altogether. But now, when this comes up, you say it's mine, not ours."

"Because, this is your decision, Rachel. You know, you never did tell me how you met Walter."

Rachel smiled gently and replied, "We were sent to his house to cater a dinner party. Walter hated the things and spent much of the time in the kitchen. We started talking and one thing led to another."

"Did you know that I met him a few times when I was a boy? We were hired to build a new stable for his horses and he spent a lot of time on the job site. That was when I still worked on the jobs. He would ask me about the job and talk about my father, whom he knew well. I liked him a lot."

Rachel then sighed, slid the envelope to her, removed the papers and looked at the legal documents.

"I suppose I need to sign these in ink and have them notarized," she said.

"We can go to the bank and do that. After you take some time, we can talk more about what you want to do, but just talking to you right now, gave me an idea, Rachel. Those stables we built for Walter. They were for his quarter horses. He loved his horses and showed me the corral where they stayed while we built the bigger stables. They're your horses now. Maybe we should build our own big stables and bring them here. We'd have to hire some real horse breeders and handlers, but I think it would add a sense of purpose to our lives."

Rachel smiled at Marsh and said, "I think that's a wonderful idea."

"But for now, I think we both could use a swim," he said as he stood and took her hand.

———

The next day, Marsh and Rachel went to the Missoula First National Bank where she signed and had the documents notarized and mailed them back to Denver. Marsh then sent a telegram to Paul Johnson to let him know the signed documents were on their way.

On the way home, they rode north to the Double M to see how everything was going and shared coffee with Jacob and Marie. Marie was pregnant again and Rachel said that she would arrange to have more bedrooms added to the ranch house.

When they were riding back, she turned to Marsh and said, "I guess being able to do things for people isn't too bad. Lord knows you've been doing nothing but good things for me since the day you found me near that grizzly bear."

———

They did have to make a trip to Denver to finalize all the property transfers. There were twenty-eight fine quarter horses in the stables being cared for by four staff members and Marsh asked if they wouldn't mind coming along with the horses to Missoula. Two of them were married and expressed concern, but Marsh told them he would build them all houses nearby, so they all agreed. They arranged for transfer of the horses and the men in September, which would give Marsh time to have the houses built.

The money was all transferred to Marsh and Rachel's account in the same Denver bank, and the money from the Kansas City account was transferred to their Missoula account. They placed all of the properties up for sale with any sales revenue being deposited in their Denver account.

Rachel walked through the house seeing if there was anything she wanted to bring back to Missoula, and was surprised that her jewelry that Walter had bought for her was still there until Marsh reminded her that if they walked off with anything, the others would pounce. She took the jewelry, her clothes, and a heavy coat that she liked. She placed the clothes in a big trunk and Marsh had it shipped, but she slipped all her diamonds, rubies and pearls into her coat pockets like so much cheap costume jewelry.

After leaving the Pratt estates, they went to dinner with Vince and Lucy.

"Well, we've gotten this all cleaned up now, Vince," Marsh said after they placed their order.

"It was a lot easier than I thought it would be, Marsh," he replied.

"We're having the horses and staff brought to Missoula, and I don't believe we'll be returning to Denver except to visit. When we visited Paul this morning, I had him write up papers turning over Anderson Construction to you, lock, stock and barrel. I left you thirty thousand dollars for operating expenses, so you'll be fine."

Vince glanced at Lucy and then back to Marsh, "Marsh, you can't do this. It was your father's firm."

"Sure I can. You've been running the company ever since I left four years ago. You'll do just as well now that you own it. I'd recommend you keep the name, though. It's well recognized," Marsh replied with a smile.

Vince was flabbergasted and couldn't respond, so Lucy replied, "Thank you so much, Marsh and Rachel. I know Vince will do you proud."

Rachel smiled and reached into her pockets and put two handfuls of jewelry on the table.

"Take whatever you like, Lucy. You'll need to impress your husband's new clients."

Now, it was Lucy's turn to be speechless while Vince smiled.

Rachel added, "And don't be a piker. I want at least half of those pieces gone or I'll leave them all for the waitress as a tip."

Lucy's trembling fingers began wading through the expensive gems and gold and began sliding some pieces out of the pile. When she was done, she had two diamond necklaces, a ruby brooch and a pearl necklace. Rachel slid a ruby and diamond ring across and scooped the rest into her pocket.

"I only needed ten pieces, so you keep the ring, too," Rachel said.

Marsh instantly knew where the rest would go as Lucy took the ring and slid it onto her finger, showing Vince in the candlelight.

Lucy said, "Are you sure, Rachel? I think some of these pieces would look perfect on you."

Rachel slid her fingers under her emerald necklace and replied, "This is the only jewelry I will ever wear."

Rachel turned to Marsh and smiled so intensely that Marsh thought she was generating her own light. Rachel, who never had anything to give other than herself, was discovering the joy of presenting gifts to those she cared for.

———

When they returned to Missoula, Marsh and Rachel stopped to see Mister Longstaff for some major construction work that would keep his firm and the Rees Brothers busy for two months.

Rachel watched as he explained how he wanted the trail that led to the valley turned into a roadway. Mister Longstaff told him that it would be fast and simple because it just involved common laborers.

Because he owned the three sections before the valley, he wanted the four houses along with a common barn, to be built using four different floor plans, a half a mile from the beginning of the valley.

Finally, he described a very large stable with room for forty eight horses and rooms for tack, a smithy, a large workroom and a loft for feed. He wanted heating stoves to keep it warm and a large exercise corral outside. The location would be halfway between his house and the four houses, but away from the new roadway to the south.

It took Mister Longstaff almost a half an hour to come up with an estimate, which Marsh paid with a draft.

They finally returned home at six o'clock that evening, totally exhausted from the trip and the strain of so much high finance. Rachel's trunk of clothing had arrived before they did and Marsh carried it into the house and helped her hang her clothes while he left the frilly things for her to fold and put into her drawers.

When they finally crawled into bed, all they did was remove their clothes and slip under the quilts, not caring one iota about neatness.

———

The next morning, with their tiredness gone, they didn't leave the bedroom until eight o'clock. The new extension gave them even more freedom of movement in the house with a second hallway to the kitchen past the three new bedrooms, the library and through the new dining room.

By nine o'clock they were riding north to visit the Kowalskis. Rachel had already picked out a piece of jewelry for Marie at the Double M, so now, she could give the other Kowalski women their choices.

When Rachel and Marsh arrived, they were greeted warmly as they always had been, and were sitting in the expansive kitchen with the entire family except for Jacob, Marie and Simon who were out at the Double M.

This was Rachel's show, so Marsh just stood aside and let her go.

"Mary," she began, "we just returned from Denver yesterday, and I went through the house were I lived for a few weeks before my husband died. Marsh asked me to take what I wanted, and I took my clothes because that's all I really liked. But I didn't want everything to go with the house when it's sold, so I brought some things back for you and all of the other Kowalski women. I've already selected one for Marie, so you get to choose first."

She then took out the nine pieces of jewelry and set them on the table to a combination of 'ahs' and 'oohs'.

Mary Kowalski looked up with pie eyes at Rachel, and asked "Are they real stones, Rachel?"

"Yes, Mary. They're real. I believe truly good women like you deserve something a little extra out of life."

Mary began touching the jewelry and slowly took a ruby necklace from the group and handed it to Peter, who smiled as she flipped up her hair and he lowered it around her neck and did the clasp. The rest of the family, along with Marsh and Rachel all clapped as she beamed first at Peter, then at Rachel and Marsh.

"Rachel," she said, as her eyes watered, "I never expected to wear something so beautiful. I was happy with my beautiful children, but this is so pretty. Thank you."

"You're welcome, Mary," Rachel replied, wiping away a tear of her own.

Then things got interesting as each of the other women began to argue about who was next. None of them believed they should be the next one to choose.

Finally, Mary announced that she would make the choices based on age. As she gave each daughter or daughter-in-law a piece, they thanked Mary, Rachel and Marsh and either pinned it on, had their husbands do as Peter had done if it was a necklace, or slipped it on if it was a ring. Each woman seemed overjoyed with what Mary had chosen for her.

When they were all done, Mary asked, "Rachel, could we see the piece that you chose for Marie?"

Rachel nodded and pulled out the diamond necklace. It was smaller than Mary's necklace, but still elicited sounds of awe and approval.

Marsh finally spoke and said, "Now, Peter, I want to let you know that if you need anything at all, you come and see me and Rachel. Don't ever let anything cause you problems, unless it's a baby who loses its diaper at a bad moment. That's nothing we can help you with."

They all laughed and the mood in the house was sky high as Marsh and Rachel departed for the Double M. If the gifts to the nine Kowalski women at the Circle K was impressive, Marie surpassed all of them in her absolute joy when Rachel presented her with the diamond necklace. Like Mary, she had Jacob hang the necklace around her throat.

They returned back to the valley before noon and were surprised to see work already starting on the roadway. As Mister Longstaff had said, this was the easy part. There were always laborers ready to work and with almost thirty men doing the job, and mules dragging the levelers, the three mile road would be done in just a week.

After they had lunch they were spending some relaxing time in the main room in their customary positions on the couch, with Rachel tucked in close under Marsh's arm.

"You're really getting into philanthropy, aren't you, Rachel?" he asked.

Rachel smiled and replied, "I never knew how good it felt to make other people happy."

"Well, sweetheart, you never had much to give other than the most precious gift of all that you've given to me. I'd give up every dime we have just for a minute of your love, and I know that I'll have it for the rest of my life."

"I know you would, Marsh. So, now with the horses coming and no more reasons to go to Denver, are you happy?"

"I've been happy since that day I saw you walk out of the trees, Rachel. You want to know if I'm content with my life as a man. Do I feel like I'm contributing rather than just living? I'm not sure about that yet. Having money was never the point. As long as I knew, we always had money, but when I worked with those construction crews and at the end of the day, I could see something that I helped build standing there; I felt like I had contributed. When I found the valley and built that cabin and the tower and then the house and barn, I felt the same way. I'll figure out something. How about you, Rachel? Do you feel content or are you still restless?"

Rachel thought about it for almost thirty seconds before answering. "Like you, I'm very happy. You've made me that way. You love me so much I want to give back even more, but I'll admit to being restless. I think you know why."

"I do. I think all women want to experience giving life a new beginning and to hold her new baby in her arms. You'll have yours, Rachel. I have no doubt at all."

Rachel then turned to face Marsh and said softly, "Then we should be doing something to make that happen, shouldn't we?"

He smiled back and replied, "I thought you'd never ask."

————

Over the course of the summer the spots picked out by Marsh for the new houses was a constant cacophony of hammering, sawing and workmen's cursing as the buildings went up. Each house was built on its own two acre lot with a large barn in between the two center houses for their personal horses. The huge stables were being built at the same time, and Marsh had ensured that it would have easy access to the lush grass of the valley.

Once the houses were completed, Marsh had them all furnished, which provided a lot of business for Mister Sweeney that didn't involve dead people. Rachel selected all the dinnerware and cookware for the houses, making sure none of the patterns were repeated.

After receiving a telegram that the horses were on the way, Marsh and Rachel rode to Missoula and arranged for the four pantries and cold rooms to be stocked.

The roadway had been long completed by the time the horses and their handlers arrived, and Marsh found it interesting that when the men arrived, they weren't accompanied by just two wives, but each of the four men was now married. The older wives were accompanied by three children and two children respectively.

After the horses were stabled after their long train ride, the families all met with Marsh and Rachel, who had already met the men. Each of the women, including the two newlyweds, were older than Rachel, and, of course, none were anywhere close to being as pretty. But each of the two new wives were already pregnant, which at least explained their sudden marriages.

All of them were extremely grateful for their complete new houses and Rachel was happy to have women that she could talk to without having to ride anywhere. The Kowalski women would ride over sometimes, but this would be better.

―――――

It was the last day of summer and the weather had already been cooling rapidly, which was no great surprise for locals. Rachel and Marsh had spent a lot of their time in the cottage and at first, Marsh thought it was for the simple reason that it was the nearness of the pond, but it wasn't.

They were lying in bed and Rachel was rubbing her emerald necklace that was the only thing she wore as she laid halfway on Marsh.

"What's the matter, Rachel?" he asked softly, sensing her quiet mood.

"Oh, nothing, really. I just thought I'd be pregnant by now. Lord knows we've been trying hard enough."

"How do you know you're not pregnant now? Your monthly isn't due for another week."

"I could be, I suppose, but seeing all the children and Ruth and Nellie already bulging makes me feel so incomplete."

"Is that why you don't want to stay in the house so much? You see all those empty bedrooms and wonder why they aren't full of blonde-haired, blue-eyed little girls like in your dream?"

She inhaled and exhaled softly and replied, "It is. I just walk around in the big loop down the old hallway where our bedroom is, then into the new section and it seems so sterile, just like me."

"I don't think you have a problem at all, Rachel. I believe you'll have your five daughters. In fact, I think we should come up with five girls names right now and save the time."

Rachel laughed softly and said, "You do, do you? Well, I can guess the first one will be Clara and the second Lillie."

"And you would be wrong, Rachel. I want our girls to have their own names and not carry the burden of someone else's lives. I want to let them be themselves. I was thinking for the first little girl, we name her Sarah Jane."

Rachel tilted her head up to Marsh and said, "You're serious, aren't you?"

He looked down at her and replied, "Very. What do you think of my choice for our first daughter's name?"

She squirmed in a bit closer and said, "I like it a lot. Can I have the second one?"

"It's your turn."

"I'd like Laura Ann."

"I like that one a lot, too. Now, for our third, I suggest Grace Louise," Marsh said.

Rachel replied, "Why, Mister Anderson, I never would have suspected you had such good taste in naming little girls. For our fourth, I'd recommend Hannah Ruth. So, how do we do the last one?"

Marsh said, "I can do the first name and you can do the second. I'd like one Katie in our family."

"So would I," Rachel said, and completed the name adding, "Katie Jean."

Marsh then kissed Rachel on the head and said, "There, we have the names and in six years, we'll have our little girls."

Rachel couldn't help but smile and reply, "Maybe Sarah Jane is already here after all."

———

As intimate as Marsh and Rachel were, it wasn't any great mystery when Rachel's monthly didn't arrive a week later, but she didn't want to get her hopes up yet, so neither she nor Marsh said a word.

The horses were all adapting well to their new home and reveled in their freedom to run in the valley under the guidance of their keepers who all were more than just a little pleased with their new location. None of them had their own homes before and their wives and children were all happy to have the room.

Two weeks after missing her monthly, Rachel was still only tentatively hopeful. Marsh had gone into the valley that day with Peter Kowalski to do some hunting while Rachel remained in the large, empty house reading as Marsh had filled their new library, giving her a wide selection.

Just around three o'clock, Marsh and Peter returned, and after a stop at the smokehouse, Marsh waved as Peter left to ride home.

Marsh entered the kitchen, set aside the meat he had obtained in their hunt, then leaned his Winchester '76 against the wall and began slicing the meat into thick steaks as Rachel walked into the room and smiled at him.

"I see you had a successful hunt, Marsh. Is that dinner?"

"Yes, ma'am. If you'll have a seat, I'll fix you a nice steak and some hash browns."

"Well, I'm not going to say no," she replied as she took a seat.

As he prepared the steaks, he talked about how well the horses were doing and then, he sprang a surprise on Rachel.

"I've been writing, Rachel," he said, not looking at her.

"To Vince and Lucy?" she asked.

"No, I mean writing as in a book. I've already written two hundred and ten pages and I'm about halfway complete."

Rachel replied in surprise and pride, saying, "Why, Marsh, that's wonderful! I know you'll do well. What's the subject?"

"It's about us, really. We've had so many things happen to us that it sounds more like fiction than reality, so I'm going to tell our story, but I won't use our names."

Rachel was so happy that Marsh had found something to make him feel like he was contributing again.

"Do I get to read it?" she asked.

"You'll be the first. I need you to correct all my mistakes," he replied with a grin as he glanced her way.

Thirty minutes later, he had finished cooking their meal and set two steaks on the plates along with a mound of hashbrowns.

He set the larger steak in front of Rachel and filled her mug with coffee.

Rachel stared at the large piece of meat and the equally large portion of hashbrowns and said, "This is too much, Marsh. I'm hungry but not this hungry."

Marsh had already cut into his steak and was chewing, so he waited until he swallowed before answering.

"I had to go hunting today for some bear meat because Sarah Jane told me that you had told her how tasty it was and she was getting hungry."

Rachel stared at Marsh for a good fifteen seconds before realizing that he didn't appear to be joking.

"Marsh," she asked quietly, "you're not joking are you?"

He looked at his Rachel and said just as softly, "No, Rachel, I'm not. It was only a dream I had last night, but it seemed so real. You were close against me and I could feel your emerald on my chest. I thought at first I was awake, but I wasn't surprised when a little girl walked up to the bed and tapped me on the shoulder and told me that she was hungry and her mama told her that bear meat was really good."

I told her I'd get her some and she said, 'Thank you, Papa,' then gave me a kiss and left. It all seemed so normal, like it was an everyday occurrence. When I woke up this morning and felt your emerald still on my chest, I thought for a few moments that the little girl was somewhere in the house. It took me almost a minute to realize it was just a dream, but I wasn't taking any chances of not providing Sarah Jane with her bear meat, so when Peter came by, off we went. Now, eat your steak and make Sarah Jane happy."

EPILOGUE

Seven months and eleven days after that conversation, little Sarah Jane Anderson arrived in Sisters Hospital in Missoula.

Rachel was in the room with Sister Margarite when Marsh was allowed to enter. As soon as he saw Rachel's beaming, but tired face, he knew that she had reached an even higher feeling of contentment than he had when his novel, *The Valley,* had been published.

Marsh stepped past a smiling Sister Margarite and sat on the chair next to the bed.

"You look more beautiful than ever, Rachel," Marsh said.

"I feel that way, Marsh. But I'm nowhere near as beautiful as Sarah Jane is. She's so perfect."

"She is all that, Rachel. But she'll have a beautiful, wonderful mother who will be there to inspire her and her sisters."

"Thank you for giving me the one gift that only you could give. Thank you for our daughter, Marsh."

"And I'll have to thank you for not only our daughter and those that will follow, but for the one thing that only you could give to me that made life worth living. You gave me your love."

He leaned over and kissed his wife softly then continued down and kissed their new daughter.

———

Over the next four years, like clockwork, Marsh and Rachel would return to Sisters Hospital and have another blonde-haired, blue-eyed little girl. What made it more remarkable was that Sarah Jane was born on the first of June, Laura Ann arrived on the second of June, Grace Louise on the third of the month, Hannah Ruth on the fourth and Little Katie Jean was born on the fifth of June.

Neither parent expected Rachel to get pregnant again, so they just continued to enjoy each other as much as they had before.

Four months after Katie Jean returned from Sisters Hospital, a very contented Rachel was with her husband in the cottage, which was a good place to spend a cold winter's day. It was a miserable ride to and from the cottage, but it was always worth the trip.

One of the many advantages of designing your own home, or in this case, your cottage, was that you could do whatever you want. In addition to the very useful hot and cold water and water closet, Marsh had a stone bath that was four feet wide by six feet long and three feet deep. He and Rachel would spend a lot of time in the bath when it was too cold to be outside, or there were visitors to the hot springs, either the Kowalskis, the horse families, as they were collectively known, or even Vince and Lucy who would visit at times bringing their brood.

It was while they were in the bath that Rachel said, "Marsh, I don't know how to explain this, but I'm pregnant again."

Marsh was surprised as much as Rachel had been and replied, "Really? I know how it happened, but that kind of ruins all that mystic dream stuff."

Rachel slid against Marsh and sighed. "Six little blonde-haired, blue-eyed girls won't be so bad."

Marsh smiled, rolled over and kissed Rachel saying, "I already have six. This will be seven."

———

But they were both wrong. The next one was not only not a girl, but he was born in July.

Marsh would have no talk of a Marsh, Junior, and he convinced Rachel that their son have his own name just as their daughters did. Rachel acquiesced and let Marsh choose the name and he went with Aaron Albert Anderson. Rachel laughed and agreed to the name and hoped he learned how to write his 'A's well.

Aaron Albert was born on the fourth of July, with the same sandy brown hair and dark blue eyes of his father, and it wasn't until he turned five that he discovered that the fireworks weren't for his birthday.

Aaron did turn out to be the last of the Anderson children, and as much as he loved his daughters, Marsh took personal interest in his son's development.

As they grew, none of the children had a clue about the enormous wealth that their parents possessed. Rachel was in charge of the charitable giving and eventually had to set up a foundation to ensure that the family still managed some privacy. Marsh continued to write, producing a novel every year or two, and bought himself a typewriter to make life easier on his publisher. He could have bought his own publishing house, but went the anonymous route and submitted his works under the pen name of R.J. Anders.

Once the children reached their teenage years, boys began to flock around the Anderson house. and Aaron became Marsh's guard, but when he reached sixteen, he became useless.

The five pretty blondes often traveled together when they went to Missoula and made quite a sight that newcomers would notice and say, "Who are those pretty blonde girls?"

They were never referred to as the Anderson girls by the locals. When asked, they replied, "Those are the Valley girls."

Laura Ann was the first to marry and was soon followed by Grace Louise. Sarah Jean waited for almost a year after Grace to wed, and Katie Jean married two months later. Each girl was presented a handsome dowery and Marsh lectured each prospective bridegroom on the dangers of making his daughter unhappy. It didn't matter, as the girls all had a strong head on their shoulders courtesy of Rachel. Hannah Ruth seemed destined for spinsterhood when she turned down suitor after suitor.

Rachel finally had a long talk with Hannah, asking her why she had rejected so many very eligible beaus, and she confided in her mother that none that she met could compare to her father, whom all the daughters worshipped.

Rachel smiled, hugged Hannah and said, "Hannah, I have been blessed to find my perfect man. He has loved me for more than twenty years now and I still want to spend every minute of the day with him, but it's not a matter of him being perfect for every woman. He was perfect for me. We each have our faults and peculiarities. I have plenty, and so does your father, but those faults don't matter to each of us. What is important is that we just blend together. When you meet someone, don't expect him to be like your father, because you will never find one. I have never met another man to even rival your father, but when you find a man that meshes with you, and makes you happy, then marry him. You'll still have your father to love you, but your husband will love you as a woman, not a daughter."

Hannah hugged her mother and thanked her for her advice before saying, "I really do like Mark Chalmers and I enjoy spending time with him, too. He's asked me to marry him three times already. I don't think I'll wait for him to ask again."

A month later, the final Valley girl was married and only Aaron remained on the valley.

Aaron decided to pursue a career in medicine, which received his parents whole-hearted support. He left Montana in 1910 to attend medical school at Harvard.

So, after all the children were gone, and they were alone in their valley again, Marsh and Rachel began spending more time in their cottage by the steaming pond. They would return to the house once or twice a week to retrieve new books and Marsh would climb his tower to see the changes that progress had brought. He had telephones in the house and cottage now and had the four houses wired as well. He could talk to the Kowalskis at the Circle K or at the Double M in seconds rather than having to ride. There was electrical power to all the buildings now, making kerosene lamps obsolete.

But none of that really mattered to either Marsh or Rachel. To them, the simple things were always the best. The two wealthiest people in the state, which was saying something as Helena, Montana had more millionaires than most large cities back East, would ride in their valley, shoot their rifles, which Marsh kept updating as new models came out, and spend many hours together in their pond or bath.

The one great advantage of having the telephones installed was that they now would get advance notice of arriving visitors.

Their daughters would visit often with their families, and Aaron would return from college during summer break.

When their twenty-fifth anniversary arrived, there was a huge celebration in Missoula for the city's most famous couple. All of the Valley girls were there with their husbands as was Aaron, Vince and Lucy and their family, and the giant crowd of Kowalskis.

After the party that afternoon, Rachel and Marsh rode their horse back to their valley, passing the house and cabin with its tower still pointing skyward, and into their valley. After they had ridden a half a mile along the northern edge, they dismounted.

Marsh held Rachel's hand as they climbed the incline and when they reached the spot where the grizzly had died. He released her hand, then Rachel smiled at Marsh and continued to climb until she was thirty feet higher, tugging on a dark green knit hat as she walked.

After she stopped and turned, Marsh shouted, "Ma'am, I'm Marsh Anderson, this is my valley and it's safe to come out now."

Rachel couldn't help smiling, although she knew that she hadn't that day a quarter of a century ago, as she slowly began stepping down toward Marsh.

Marsh watched his wife approach and couldn't help his own smile from dominating his face. He let his eyes find hers and just as she had when he first saw her step out of those trees more than a quarter of a century ago, she took his breath away.

Rachel felt the same rush she had felt when his eyes looked into her soul and kept slowly stepping towards him.

When she finally drew near, she asked quietly, "Will you help me?"

Marsh whispered, "From now until the day I die, my beloved wife."

Rachel was so overcome, she just reached out to Marsh who hugged her closely. Neither could say anything as he kissed her softly.

After another minute, they slowly turned and began walking down the slope to the lush grass of their valley.

1	Rock Creek	12/26/2016
2	North of Denton	01/02/2017
3	Fort Selden	01/07/2017
4	Scotts Bluff	01/14/2017
5	South of Denver	01/22/2017
6	Miles City	01/28/2017
7	Hopewell	02/04/2017
8	Nueva Luz	02/12/2017
9	The Witch of Dakota	02/19/2017
10	Baker City	03/13/2017
11	The Gun Smith	03/21/2017
12	Gus	03/24/2017
13	Wilmore	04/06/2017
14	Mister Thor	04/20/2017
15	Nora	04/26/2017
16	Max	05/09/2017
17	Hunting Pearl	05/14/2017
18	Bessie	05/25/2017
19	The Last Four	05/29/2017
20	Zack	06/12/2017
21	Finding Bucky	06/21/2017
22	The Debt	06/30/2017
23	The Scalawags	07/11/2017
24	The Stampede	07/20/2017
25	The Wake of the Bertrand	07/31/2017
26	Cole	08/09/2017
27	Luke	09/05/2017
28	The Eclipse	09/21/2017
29	A.J. Smith	10/03/2017
30	Slow John	11/05/2017
31	The Second Star	11/15/2017
32	Tate	12/03/2017
33	Virgil's Herd	12/14/2017
34	Marsh's Valley	01/01/2018
35	Alex Paine	01/18/2018
36	Ben Gray	02/05/2018

Made in the USA
Middletown, DE
24 September 2019